NEVER STOP RUNNING

Dr. Melissa Caudle

Absolute Author
Publishing House

Never Stop Running
Copyright© 2019
Dr. Melissa Caudle

Publisher: Absolute Author Publishing House
Project Editor: Dr. Carol Michaels
Developmental Editor: Jamie Dwyer
Final Proof Editors: Kathy Rabb Kittok, Robby Cook Stroud and Helen V. Ray
Copy Editor: Monique Johnson and Thomas McCreith
Line Editor: Elisha Grace Dracoulis
Graphics, Cover and Back Page: Created by Rebecca @RebeccaCovers
Cover Model: Helen Virginia Ray (1954 Photo)
Author Photographer: Robby Cook Stroud

Library of Congress Cataloging-in-Publication Data
Caudle, Melissa.

      Never Stop Running / Dr. Melissa Caudle

        p. cm.

ISBN-13: 978-0-578-44782-7

   1. Thriller   2. Reincarnation and Afterlife

0 1 2 3 4 5 6 7 8 9
Printed in the United States of America

DEDICATION

For my mother, daughters, and granddaughter. We come from a strong lineage on both sides of our family, may it continue as we leave our individual mark and legacies.

ACKNOWLEDGEMENT

I am more thankful than words can describe for the assistance from the many people who helped me to learn about hypnotic regression and reincarnation.

I want to thank my mother, Helen Virginia Ray, who first introduced the subject and for her unconditional support and forever love. You are my inspiration. I love you from the depth of my soul. I will always cherish the beautiful photograph of you from 1954 that graces this cover. Thank you for allowing me to use it. After eighty-five years you can add a check onto your bucket list next to wanting to become a cover model. You are my hero.

Next, I must thank a brave woman who wishes to remain anonymous. She allowed me the privilege of listening to her regression sessions which inspired this novel on reincarnation and past lives. I couldn't have completed it without you and your hypnotherapist. May you find your peace and change your fate.

Also, to my three daughters Erin, Kelly and Jamie who are also my best friends for always believing in me, no matter what. Each of you brought a twist to this novel in your own individual way.

To Erin, for your guidance in Buddhism and Catholicism having earned a master's degree from Loyola University in World Religion your knowledge proved extremely beneficial.

To Kelly, for your touch in the historical timeline and double checking the historical accuracy.

To Jamie, for you adding a special flavor to the dialogue and you became the best developmental editor. Without your input and dedication, this novel wouldn't be the same as you added your individual touch to strengthen the characters and dialogue. Now please write Part Two; so, I can return the favor.

To Tina Rubin, my best friend, thank you for the wine and the time you spent reviewing the first, second, and final edition of this novel.

To my editing team from Absolute Author Kathy Rabb Kittok and Dr. Carol Michaels always I welcomed your edits, feedback and comments. To the rest of the editing team, Elisha Grace Dracoulis, Monique N. Johnson, Robby Cook Stroud, and Thomas McCreith, thank you for your eagle eyes. Each of you brought something different to this novel in the editing stages that made it what it is today. To Jamie Dwyer, although I mentioned you prior as my daughter, I would be remised not to include you in this section as you served as the developmental editor in the early stages of draft one and at the very last minute provided insight into changing the opening chapter with only four days to publication. Your insight and encouragement added a special flavor to this book. Last but not least, to my mother Helen V. Ray who received the final copy of this novel before I published it and caught three errors, we all seemed to miss. That's my mom, always to the rescue and has my back.

Additionally, I'd like to thank Rebecca of RebbecaCovers for her beautiful design of the front and back jacket of this book. It exceeded my expectation, and you showcased my beautiful mother as a cover model.

To my focus group members, I value your opinions and I'm grateful for your insight and your time and support. In no particular order, the focus group members included: Freida Johnson, Mary Whitworth, Timothy Mayeux, Sandra Belington, Sasha Standford-Smith, Helen V. Ray, James T. Bradford, Tina Rubin, George Flanderson, Diane Lang, and Dr. L.A. Davis.

Lastly, I am grateful to Dr. Brian Weiss, Regression Hypnotist and his book, *Many Lives, Many Masters*. It has been an inspiration.

BY THE AUTHOR OF

The Keystroke Killer: Transcendence Part I
A.D.A.M.
Secret Romances
MK-ULTRA

TABLE OF CONTENTS

1. OPEN THE DOOR

D r. Grayson sat in a Victorian chair; his eyes focused on Jackie who lay in a deep hypnotic state on a worn royal blue velvet chaise. The scar which ridged from her scalp to below her cheek covered by make-up embarrassed Jackie as she leaned her face against the pillow to hide it.

"From this point on, when I say sleep and snap my fingers, you will remember this state and go to it. Now breathe in and out." Dr. Grayson drew a deep breath.

Jackie responded to his suggestion with a huge-heaved sigh of relief.

"Jackie, I'm going to ask you a series of questions. You will not awaken but stay in this peaceful state. You will remain aware of your surroundings. Noises won't bother you. You will only respond to my voice. Do you understand?"

"Yes."

"Jackie search through your past and find a door and enter." Dr. Grayson observed Jackie's body language and eye movement beneath her eyelids giving her time to select a door. "Do you see the door?"

1

"I don't know which one to enter."

"The choice is yours. Think of a time in your past and open the door."

Her eyelids fluttered, her facial muscles flattened, and she looked more mannequin than human. Her right index finger lifted. "That one."

Dr. Grayson shook his head in approval. "That's great Jackie, open the door and step through. Where are you?"

"I'm in a scary place. I feel cold. It's really cold... dark... It's misty."

"Nothing can harm you, Jackie you're safe. What are you doing in this place?"

"I'm in a dark alley."

"Are you alone?"

She barely shook her head. "Someone else is here... He's calling a woman's name."

In his hypnotherapist mind, Dr. Grayson analyzed her statement. "What name?"

"Gertrude."

"What is Gertrude doing?"

∞

Gertrude, age twenty-three, dressed in an 1880s overcoat with a silver-fox fur collar and an 1880s hat ran down a dark alley lit only by the orange glow of the oil street lamps and the blood moon. Fog graced the area as a light mist sprinkled. She tried to catch her breath. Smoke from the heat of her breath clashed with the cold misty night air.

A large man who wore a black Gothic cape chased her. "Gertrude! Stop! You'll never get away with this."

Gertrude ran to escape him. She tripped and fell scrapping both knees; the ground ripped her silk stockings. With the man in close pursuit, she pushed herself up and ran. She lengthened her stride as she looked over her shoulder.

Within an arm's-length of her, the man gained ground; he swiftly closed in. He lifted a butcher knife, lunged at her and pierced her through her back.

Her body lurched forward as she fell in slow motion and landed in a mud puddle face down. The clammy chill of death gripped her.

He knelt, rolled her over and jerked her brass crystal domed watch pendant from around her neck. She heaved as she took her last breath.

∞

Jackie raised her hips, wiggled her shoulders and exhaled.

"Relax Jackie, he can't harm you, you're safe."

Jackie jolted. "He killed Gertrude, I saw him kill her." Jackie heavily breathed as her heart pounded against her ribcage.

"Jackie, what year did Gertrude die?"

"October eleventh, eighteen seventy-nine."

He pondered the date. "All right, Jackie let's move somewhere else. I want you to think of a calm peaceful place, a beautiful place."

Jackie bolted up with her eyes wide opened. She put her hand on her forehead and heaved. "I don't want to do this."

"Please know you made extreme progress."

"I'm finished for today; I want to go home."

"Jackie, remember your subconscious has a way to deal with your fears if you allow it."

Jackie's voice cracked as emotions flowed. "It's just overwhelming." Jackie cleared her throat and held back her tears.

"I understand. Sometimes when we witness past events, we can become confused and scared. This is a normal process."

"I don't understand what just happened." A tear rolled down her mascara-smeared-scarred face. "Who did I see die?"

2. WHITE PICKET FENCE

One Year Earlier

The digital alarm clock's repetitive buzz blared in the otherwise silent master bedroom.

David groaned as he rolled over and swatted bleary-eyed at the obnoxious intrusion. The silver-framed photograph of he and Jackie kissing on their honeymoon in front of the Golden Gate Bridge wobbled dangerously close to the nightstand's edge. He slapped the alarm clock again and accidentally collided his fingertips against the picture frame sending it crashing onto the floor. When it smashed against the hardwood floor, the glass across the frame cracked down the middle which divided the couple and flipped over onto a pair of fuzzy brown moose slippers.

Exasperated, David bashed the alarm clock, and at last silenced the annoying abrupt alert. "Just five more minutes." He buried his head into his pillow, groaned and pounded his fist onto the mattress. "Five forty-five is too early!"

Jackie pulled the taupe thick goose down comforter over her face with her right hand and nestled deeper into the rackmonster pillow top bed complete with sage green thick bamboo luxurious sheets. "Did you hit the snooze button?" Her words muffled by the comforter barely caught David's attention.

"Do you really need to ask?"

"Considering you forgot last week, I thought I should. I can't be late to work again."

"Go back to sleep while you can, unless you want a morning quickie."

"Five more minutes of sleep sounds good. I was up with the baby most of the night, he's cutting his back teeth. He was miserable."

He snuggled against her warm slim body as he gently pulled her waist closer to him; his eyes remained opened. *She must be exhausted.* "I'll take the shift tonight if he's still in pain. Now close your eyes and get five more minutes of shut-eye while you can."

"They're already closed, silly. Do you mind giving me a little space?" She scooched away from him and rolled over onto her stomach.

David rotated onto his other side accommodating her fatigued request. He found it challenging not to stare wide-eyed at the digital alarm clock which now blinked "5:47 a.m." *What good is a snooze button if I can't snooze?* He gazed at the intermittent red numbers as the intrusive seven changed into an invasive eight. His green eyes seemed to absorb the color. Even after he closed them, the obtrusive numbers seemed as if possessed by a neon emergency flashing light as they brightened through his eyelids, and in his mind the time clock's ticking annoyingly amplified. He tossed one way, then flipped to another. *Seriously! I just want five more minutes of sleep.*

Click. Click. Click.

"Can that clock get any more annoying?" As he sat up, he yawned, and then he wiped the crusted-sleep from his eye. After he stretched, he gently stroked Jackie's long thick brown wavy hair, gave her a gentle kiss on the back of her neck, and then eased out of bed almost stepping onto the favored honeymoon photograph conveniently cradled between one moose horn and the other moose slipper.

As he retrieved the silver-framed photograph, the cracked glass caught the morning sun. *She's going to kill me.* He rubbed his finger along the fracture that divided he and Jackie, and then shuddered as if a cool chill filled the air. *I'll buy her a new frame for our anniversary, she'll love that.* Gently, he returned the photograph to its rightful place onto the middle of the nightstand.

After David reset the snooze button for ten more minutes, he grabbed his brown terry cotton mid-calf robe from the valet to the right of the nightstand. As he wrapped his robe around his torso, he gazed at Jackie. A broad white-toothed smile beamed as he drew a deep breath. His feet slipped into his moose house shoes.

He tiptoed out of the room, eased toward the bedroom to the right at the end of the hall and checked on his oldest son, Tyler age four, who snuggly slept beneath his *Paw Patrol* fleece blanket. A grin crossed David's sleepy face. After he closed Tyler's door, he tiptoed to Sebastian's nursery and peeked inside. Sebastian's twelve-month-old foot protruded between the crib's slots as he slept cuddled on his stomach clutching his blue fleece *Thomas the Train* blanket. *They are so cute when they sleep.* He gently closed the door.

The cold wooden floor creaked below David's feet as he headed down the stairs for the kitchen.

∞

The aerial view of the upscale area of Metairie, Louisiana represented a revival after the devastation wrought by

Hurricane Katrina in 2005, but that was the last thing on Margarette Manafort's mind as she lifted her foot from her red Jeep's gas pedal and turned onto Transcontinental Street.

She looked younger than sixty as anyone who guessed her age never came close which always brought a sense of pride to her as it served as her testament to her skin cleansing routine. Her blue-green eyes framed by her medium brown Rachel haircut gave her a throwback look. She tapped to the rhythm of *Landslide* sung by Stevie Nicks which drifted from the console. Margarette's hippie style boho chic top and jeans reflected her laid-back demeanor, and they suited her retro-vibe.

Four blocks later the Jeep slowed and turned into Magnolia Place, a gated subdivision. The guard recognized her and waved her through as she proceeded her route. Midway her progression slowed as she turned right onto Heritage Street; the brakes squealed, and the Jeep stopped in front of 1942, the most elegant house on the block which belonged to her daughter and son-in-law. Conscientious of her parking Margarette pulled forward, then backward to parallel park as close to the curb as possible. Her skill to do so never fully blossomed. She held her breath as she pulled forward one last time, slid the gearshift into park, and flicked the key to power off the engine. *I'm glad that's over.* After exiting her car, she glanced at David's white SUV and Jackie's silver BMW.

Margarette gazed at the white plantation-style home appreciating the inlaid stained glass in the oversized door, and the profusion of spring flowers populating the equally oversized pottery urns which flanked the door. On the porch a pair of rockers swayed slightly in the spring breeze. The yard highlighted the white picket fence portrait. From the welcome banner painted with butterflies and spring flowers to the hanging ferns, this home earmarked the foundation for the

Hennessey family of four. The house made a statement to anyone who passed -- dreams do come true.

I'm so proud of them to have made this home for their boys.

The chirping birds who gathered in the blooming Magnolia tree welcomed her to the beautiful spring morning with their song. A bright green wild Quaker parrot with yellow tail feathers flew past and landed in a nest in the King Palm tree. She flashed a soft smile toward the bird. *Today will be a lucky day.* Another parrot flew over. *Yep, now twice as blessed.* She looked toward the sky. *Lord, thank you for this glorious day.*

She retrieved a small bouquet of spring flowers, a large aluminum spaghetti pot and a large blue recyclable Rouse's bag filled with groceries from the back of her vehicle. When she shut the hatchback, she recognized a couple who jogged toward her.

Margarette flashed a welcoming-gentle grin. "Good morning Kathy and Shane."

The couple jogged past. "Have a wonderful day!" Kathy waved and ramped up her jogging speed as Shane caught up to her.

Margarette stepped onto the manicured Saint Augustine lawn frosted with dew and glanced over her shoulder to inspect her curb parking skills. *Whew! I'm not on the grass.*

The honeysuckle aroma from the neighbor's side fence transported her parking stress away as the cool breeze rustled the blooms. She strode to the door and used her left elbow to push the doorbell. After a minute of waiting, her brow wrinkled.

She placed the items onto the porch, searched for a fake rock in the flowerpot, and then retrieved a house key.

David wore his brown terry cloth robe and moose slippers as he sleepily opened the door. "Good morning Grandma, the boys are excited you're coming today. They missed you over the weekend." He yawned quickly covering his mouth, and then

8

rubbed away the crusted sleep caught in the corner of his eye. Dazed and half asleep he stepped backward into the house as his eyes glazed over. He stood almost as if a trance held him in place.

"Me too, it's a lonely world since Charlie died." She placed the key back into the faux rock, then she retrieved the flowers, the aluminum pot and the bag of groceries.

David recognized her struggle and her full hands. "I'm sorry, let me get those for you Grandma."

"Stop calling me that, I'm your children's grandma, not yours."

He yawned again and rubbed his eyes. "I'm not quite awake." He retrieved the items from her. "You know I love you, right? It's a name in adoration to the mother of my wife and for the grandmother of my children."

"I love you too." She winked at him. "I was just teasing."

"I'll cherish the day when I don't have to get up and go into work."

She smiled broadly as she followed David into the house. "Be careful what you wish for, you just might get it."

"Okay then, I wish Jackie didn't have to work so she could enjoy those flowers."

"I thought I'd brighten things up with this spring bouquet considering it's y'alls anniversary week."

Both proceeded into the foyer. To the right the varnished wooden staircase glistened from the sunbeams which radiated like rainbows through the transom above the stained-glass door. A crystal chandelier hung from the eighteen-foot ceiling made a grand statement. Above the staircase hung several family photographs and Jackie's wedding portrait. Her porcelain skin against the backdrop of the blue ocean water glowed as if the sun kissed it and her large brown eyes seemed to follow Margarette with each step she took.

Margarette closed the door behind her. She touched the smooth cool glossy handrail and exhaled a sigh of relief. "You finally installed the railing and finished varnishing the stairs. Now I can quit worrying about falling, thank God."

"I spent all weekend on them just for you, Grandma."

"Right? You did it for me and only me. I guess it didn't have anything to do with Jackie's ultimatum or for the safety of the boys."

"You got me there. I don't think Jackie would've let me not do it especially since Tyler almost fell down them last week."

The two made their way into the front formal area. A three-piece sofa set by Lavelle Melange with cherry wood trim reflected a Victorian style and Jackie's taste for the finer details in life.

Margarette retreated to the door and locked it.

A scowl developed across David's forehead as he lifted one brow. "You realize you're safe in here, you didn't have to deadbolt us in."

"One can never be too safe." Margarette stepped onto a palm-size toy car which caused her to slip. "See what I mean?" She retrieved the toy and tucked it into her back pocket.

"I hear you, boys will be boys and they will always have their cars and toys." David yawned again. "Man, I didn't get enough sleep. Although Jackie stayed up with Sebastian all night, I couldn't rest hearing his painful cry. With that monitor you gave us, I hear everything that goes on in the nursery."

"I take it he's cutting his one-year molars."

"That's what Jackie says. I volunteered for teething duty tonight if he's still in pain. I plan on using the recipe my mother told me my father always used when he had teething duty."

"Pray tell, what would that be?"

"An old-fashioned remedy. Grab a bottle of whiskey and a shot glass. Pour the whiskey into the shot glass, soak your finger

10

in it and rub the whiskey onto the baby's gum where you think the tooth is trying to come through. Then, drink the whiskey and repeat. Before you know it, we both will be out."

"You will do no such a thing with my grandson."

"I was just kidding Grandma, I don't even like whiskey."

They strode to the open floor plan of the immaculate great room decorated as if it belonged in a *Better Homes and Garden's* ad. The golden granite 'L' shaped countertop separated the spotless kitchen, *dining* area and the living space. It smelled clean with a hint of lavender and the aroma of freshly baked blueberry muffins.

The elegant family room matched the style of the home with a three-piece beige Versa Cleopatra Traditional Style living room set. Next to the fireplace an antique wooden rocker served as Margarette's favorite chair. Several scattered toys left by the children in front of the sofa added to the comfort of the room which showed the room lived in and enjoyed rather than presenting as sterile and untouchable.

Over in the corner by the laundry room, a play area showcased the family's adoration for their children which included a child-size table with four chairs, a stackable case for toys and two wooden toy boxes with engraved names -- "Sebastian" and "Tyler."

The cherry wood dining table could easily sit eight which matched the kitchen cabinets and separated the formal area from the family great room. A small and elegant silk floral arrangement served as the table's centerpiece.

David unloaded the grocery bag and placed the items onto the countertop. "I can't wait for tonight, you make the best spaghetti ever."

Tyler wore his Chase character pajamas and slippers as he shuffled into the kitchen dragging his *Paw Patrol* fleece blanket over his shoulder.

"You don't think I'd disappoint my grandson, do you?" She gave Tyler a hug and a kiss, wrapped his blanket around his shoulders and tied it to make a hero's cape. "He asked for spaghetti, he gets spaghetti."

"Daddy, I'm hungry. Where's Mommy?"

"Mommy's getting dressed. I made blueberry muffins, her favorite."

"No, I don't want muffins. I want Mommy's eggs and chocolate milk."

"Maybe tomorrow Tyler. Mommy's running late, so blueberry muffins will have to do."

Tyler's lips formed a small pout of disappointment. "Grandma! Cartoons please, and eggs."

"Because you used your manners, what would you like to watch? Then I'll scramble you an egg."

"*Paw Patrol.* Chocolate milk, please."

She retrieved the remote and powered the television to Tyler's favorite show and handed him a pair of headphones. "Use these."

Her eyes darted at the crystal vase next to the Hennessey family portrait on the fireplace mantel. *That will be perfect.* She grabbed it and returned to the kitchen.

Tyler slipped the headphones onto his head and viewed his favorite cartoon. He belted the theme song off-key. "*Paw Patrol, Paw Patrol,* whenever there is trouble, we'll be there in a double." He mumbled the rest.

Margarette stared at the coffee pot and twisted her lips.

David noticed her reaction and set the bottle of orange juice next to the tomatoes. "Sorry Grandma, what was I thinking? I'll make it right away."

"I'll make it this time, you're running a tad late."

"No offense, you may make the best spaghetti in the world, but your coffee, let's say it's not at the top of my list."

12

"I'd have to agree, I don't like mine either." She filled the vase with water, arranged the flowers, and carried them to the living room. Before she placed the flower-filled vase onto the mantle, she sniffed them which brought a soft-tender smile to her lips.

Sebastian wailed from upstairs.

Margarette's eyes whizzed upward. "That's the baby, I think someone is wet and hungry."

"I'll get him."

"Let me, you stay and finish the coffee."

"Then I'll make Tyler his eggs. That's the least I can do."

"Deal." Margarette headed for the staircase.

Jackie in a pink, teal and gray polka dot bathrobe, and Garfield slippers passed at the top of the stairs. She stopped and wiggled her toes inside the slippers which made it look as if the cat's ears moved up and down from Margarette's vantage point. "Good morning Mom, I'll get him."

"I will honey. The way things are going this morning, you need extra hands. You seem to be running late again."

"Thanks Mom." Jackie flashed a more-than-grateful smile, turned and headed to her bedroom.

Margarette zoomed to the top of the staircase and rounded the corner. She entered Sebastian's nursery; her nose tilted upward. "I smell a poopy butt."

Surrounded by several small stuffed animals, Sebastian stood in his crib; his hands clutched onto the sidebar. As she approached the cutie pie, his hands went up into the air. "Up." He swatted the mobile attached to the end of the crib and grinned. His balance got the better of him as he plopped his butt onto the mattress.

"That won't help your situation." She smiled and delivered a kiss onto the top of his head. "I'll get you changed, bless your little heart."

13

Margarette redressed Sebastian, lifted him and carried him on her hip down the stairs. She stopped midway and gripped the new banister. She ran her fingertips across the smooth cool surface. *I feel safer already.* She descended the staircase as a thankful-approving smile graced her face and she glimpsed Jackie's wedding portrait.

Margarette entered the kitchen with Sebastian to the smell of brewed coffee.

David pulled the blueberry muffins from the oven and placed them onto the stove's front black coil.

"It smells wonderful in here. Jackie is lucky you love to cook. Charlie never lifted a finger, he'd starve before he would pick up a pot or pan."

"I made them to start our anniversary week off right for Jackie."

"If I was a betting woman, which I am, I'd bet you have cream cheese and raspberries too."

David kissed Sebastian's cheek. "You know it." He retrieved the cream cheese and fruit from the refrigerator and placed them onto the countertop next to the stove.

Margarette opened a cabinet door to retrieve a bottle for Sebastian's morning soy milk.

"You don't need that. I have your coffee and Sebastian's bottle ready and almost finished with Tyler's egg. Y'all just snuggle up in the rocker and I'll bring them over. Would you like a blueberry muffin too?"

"I'll wait on the muffin, I need my coffee first."

"Sometimes it's the simple pleasures in life that count."

Margarette made her way to the rocker. "A fresh cup of hot coffee and feeding a baby are two of mine. It doesn't get better than this." She sat and cradled Sebastian onto her lap. "Ouch!" Her back arched as her butt lifted. She whirled the toy car from her back pocket quickly tossing it toward the children's play area.

"Are you okay?"

"I sat on that car I put in my pocket. I forgot it was there."

"As long as you aren't hurt." David strode to Tyler and lifted the earphones. "Get to the table, your eggs are ready."

Tyler bolted to the table as he held his earphones in place. He quickly sat, readjusted the earphones as he stared at the cartoons and waited patiently.

David returned to the kitchen and served Tyler. He patted him on his back and gave him a gentle kiss. "Coffee is coming Grandma."

"I'm a patient woman."

David retrieved a mundane beige café style mug from the cabinet and filled it with the fresh brew.

Margarette adjusted her position to allow Sebastian more room. "There you go sweetheart. Grandma has everything under control." She kissed him on his head. In return, he hugged her and returned a cherubic grin.

David brought the coffee and Sebastian's bottle to Margarette. He placed the coffee cup onto the side table and handed Margarette the milk. Sebastian grabbed it at once and popped it into his mouth.

"Thank you, David." She smiled and nodded.

"Anything for the world's best grandma. Just don't burn yourself or the baby."

"Like I would." She glanced at the beige mundane coffee mug. "If I'm the best, why doesn't my coffee cup have Grandma on it?"

"I'll fix that right away."

"I'm just kidding." Margarette hugged Sebastian. "He's a growing boy."

"Yes, he is. He's growing up way too fast."

"They all do, trust me. Then one day you'll be a grandfather."

"I look forward to growing old and watching my boys become men."

"Just don't rush things, time goes by fast. My advice is to make every moment count as if it were your last."

"That's great advice coming from a very wise woman."

Upstairs the toilet flushed, and the water gushed through the pipes.

"Seeing you have everything under control, I'm heading upstairs to get dressed for my work day. Jackie and I have only minutes before we both have to leave."

3. HAPPY ANNIVERSARY WEEK

Jackie drove through the suburban neighborhood. She sipped her coffee and looked at the muffin. *I'll wait to eat that.*

Her cell phone rang through the car's speakers. She pressed the accept green button on the car's navigation system. "Geez, David. We haven't talked all day." She chuckled; a grin touched her lips.

"Happy anniversary week. I miss you already."

"It's only been ten minutes."

"I know. I can't help but think of you and how beautiful you looked this morning. What can I say?"

"Well, thanks. Now let me go so I can concentrate. You know how distracted I get trying to avoid wrecks like they're the plague. I love you, I'll see you when I get home." She pressed the end call button on the panel.

∞

After a quick fifteen-minute drive, Jackie pulled into a parking space at Stephen Hawking Elementary reserved for "Teacher of the Year." She exited the car as Beth Andreas, a biracial woman age thirty-two dressed casually in jeans, a T-shirt and tennis shoes exited her orange Mini Cooper.

Jackie frowned as she watched Beth approach.

"Good morning Jackie, you ready for today?"

"Ready for what?"

The two walked up the sidewalk toward the front entrance to the school.

"We have a field trip today."

"I completely forgot. That explains the way you're dressed. For a second, I thought it was casual Friday, and I missed an entire week of work." Jackie sighed and rolled her eyes. *Why does it have to be today?*

"How can you forget about a field trip to the World War Two museum? Andrew Higgins was a hero and somewhere in your bloodline you're related. If it wasn't for his PT boats, we might have lost the war."

"I know, believe me. My family doesn't let me live that down. I'm not even sure how we're related."

"There's nothing to live down. It's something to live up to."

Several giggling children who wore backpacks ran past them. Samantha Pennington, an adorable Caucasian girl, age eight, with long curly blonde hair waved to them. "Good morning, Mrs. Hennessey."

Jackie waved and then glanced at Beth sideways. "For you maybe, but when nobody lets you forget about the past, it seems to haunt you forever."

"The past isn't all that bad. Don't you ever wish you could time travel?"

"Nope, I'd rather stay right here; the present is perfect. I have a husband who adores me, two wonderful boys and I couldn't ask for a better grandmother for my children."

"You're not even a little curious?"

Jackie glared toward Beth not amused as more students ran past. "Not for all the money in the world. I'm staying right here in this time zone."

"Come on, if given a chance you wouldn't want to meet Andrew Higgins?"

"That would mean one of two things. I'd have to be a time traveler, or reincarnated. Neither are possible."

"You don't believe in reincarnation?"

"Reincarnation goes against my religious beliefs. I believe in John three sixteen. 'For God so loved the world that he gave his one and only Son, that whoever believes in Him shall not perish but have eternal life.' I'll just have to wait to meet Andrew Higgins in heaven."

"Well, you never know. There's a famous regression hypnotist holding a seminar at the Pontchartrain Center, do you want to go?"

"Not just no, but hell no!"

"Your loss." Beth shrugged. "I think you would want to know your past lives and how they affect you today."

"Keep on dreaming Alice and go down that rabbit hole. During your next life, come back and tell me about it."

"Very funny, Jackie."

Jackie opened the door. "After you."

∞

Higgins Shipyard on the Eastbank of the Mississippi River in Avondale, Louisiana, built and repaired large barges and cargo ships. Two ships under construction filled the docks and three others in various stages of restoration provided a busy and profitable workplace.

Higgins Manafort, age forty, Mr. Ty Ishita, a Japanese businessman, age seventy-two, and David strode the shipyard as they conversed.

"David, is this where your grandfather built the PT boats that defeated us?" Mr. Ishita's thick Japanese accent made it difficult for David to understand him.

"No Sir, my wife is related to Mr. Andrew Higgins. I took my first job in the shipyard at sixteen to help my parents with their bills. That's how I met my wife. I worked my way up through the ranks to Senior Vice President."

Higgins cleared his throat. "Sir, I'm the one related to him on my mother's side of the family. She honored Andrew Higgins by giving me his last name as my first to keep his legacy alive."

"I see. Yes, yes. Lots of family pride. Pride is good backbone for business, I respect that. I will sign the deal. My government is very anxious to move forward on this project."

"Yes Sir, this way." David escorted Mr. Ishita to the office as Higgins followed.

∞

Jackie's organized third grade classroom equipped with several learning centers provided a welcoming environment and plenty of areas to enhance the children's educational experience. The student's desks in seven rows provided a traditional classroom atmosphere.

Samantha decorated the front bulletin board's edges with artificial spring flowers and butterflies and posted student poetry glued to a variety of colored construction paper.

With her roll book in her hand, Jackie leaned against her desk. "Jonathan Smith, Melissa Thibodeaux, Roger Wallace, and Mitchell Zacharias. Good morning class."

"Good morning Mrs. Hennessey." The students responded in unison as rehearsed.

"Congratulations are in order. All twenty-one of you returned your field trip permission forms, so we're all going. We have five minutes until we go to the bus area and load up. Then it's off to the museum. You know the rules, stay with your buddy, behave, learn and have fun."

"Yes, Mrs. Hennessey."

Dr. Cunningham, age fifty-seven, the spunky Caucasian female principal, entered carrying a vase of flowers and set them onto Jackie's desk. "What's the occasion? Today's not your birthday, is it?"

The flowers surprised Jackie as a just-between-us smile filled her face. "Not my birthday, but my anniversary is Saturday. Thank you for bringing them. I'll be starting the seven-year itch."

"Nonsense, I'm going on thirty-five years. The seven-year itch is an old wives' tale. Happy anniversary." The principal turned to address the students who filled the air with idle chatter. "Have a great field trip." Then she made her leave.

Samantha returned the stapler to Jackie's desk and placed it by the vase. She smelled the flowers. "Who are they from Mrs. Hennessey?"

"Well, I don't know."

"There's a card, open it."

Jackie opened the card and previewed the sweet words from David. *To the love of my life, my queen. I will love you for all eternity. Hugs and Kisses. Love always, David.*

Jackie closed the card. "They're from my husband. We're celebrating being married for seven years this Saturday."

"Seven years Mrs. Hennessey? That's a really, really long time."

Three short bells rang.

"Class, you know what that means, it's field trip time. Please gather your things and line up next to your buddy. Don't forget your lunches."

The students gathered their things from their cubicles and lined up as they chattered. After Samantha grabbed her lunch, she approached Jackie. "Mrs. Hennessey, I don't have a buddy."

"I'll be your buddy. What could go wrong with that?"

Samantha leaned in and again sniffed the sweet aroma of the flowers as she closed her eyes. "They're beautiful Mrs. Hennessey. My dad used to give my mom flowers that smelled like this before she died. They remind me of her."

"You miss your mom, don't you?"

"I do, but sometimes she visits me in my room."

Jackie puzzled and concerned avoided the subject. "We better hurry. Go to the head of the line."

Samantha skipped to the front of the line. She looked as if she spoke to someone, but no one stood in front of her. "I will, Mom. I love you too."

Jackie retrieved her cell phone and dialed David's number. When he failed to answer, it forced her to leave a voicemail. "Hi, I got the beautiful flowers you sent today. I wanted to say thank you and to tell you I love you. Hugs and kisses." Jackie grabbed her purse, put her phone into it and strode toward the door.

Her heels clicked against the tile floor as she approached the front of the line. *I wish I'd worn my tennis shoes. This will be a painful day.*

Jackie took Samantha by the hand. "Everyone ready? Remember to stay with your buddy at all times. This means you have to sit with them on the bus too."

"Yes, Mrs. Hennessey."

∞

David, Higgins and Mr. Ishita signed the contract passing the documents one at a time to the next person for each signature. David signed his last signature, placed the pen down, took a sip of water and stood straightening his suit jacket. "The deal is secure. It's been a pleasure."

The other two men stood and exchanged handshakes.

With a slight bow, David respectfully nodded toward Mr. Ishita. "We look forward to a wonderful business relationship."

Mr. Ishita bowed. "We look forward to receiving news of your progress. This deal is a good for both our countries."

∞

Jackie and Beth stood on the side of the playground and supervised their students. A scowl formed across Jackie's brow as she glanced at her watch. "Why is our bus always the last one to arrive? They need to fire that bus driver and get one more reliable. He's got to go."

"Some things are out of our control. I try to get along and follow the rules. Look at the bright side, at least the children are getting rid of their excess energy before we go. In my book that's an advantage for a rambunctious group of third graders."

Samantha ran in front of Jackie as a boy chased her in a game of tag. "You can't catch me, I'll never stop running."

"Beth, you might have a point. Oh look, our bus just arrived."

"I told you it wouldn't be a problem."

Jackie took a deep breath as a scowl crossed her forehead. "I don't want to go today. I wish I had been the teacher chosen to stay back."

"It's too late for that, you're already here."

"Please God, let me be anywhere but at the museum today." Jackie's tone reeked of sarcasm although it reflected her true feelings.

"Come on, it's not going to be that bad."

The school bell rang.

Jackie stepped forward and clapped three times. "Children! Children! Line up. It's time to board the bus. Get with your buddy and line up behind me."

Beth cupped her hands around her mouth. "My class line up over here. Let's hurry, make it quick. Get in line with your buddy."

The air brakes hissed as the bus came to a stop. The bus driver, Leonard, an overweight middle-aged African American opened the bus door. His face flushed and sweat glistened on his brow. "Sorry for the delay. I wasn't feeling too great this morning and I couldn't find a substitute."

"Glad you made it in one piece. I hope you're not coming down with the flu." Jackie turned up her nose at the smell of the diesel fuel.

"I just don't have energy. I'm not sleeping very well these past couple of nights. Nothing to fill me with worry."

"Glad to hear it, let's do this."

Leonard nodded, took a deep breath, wiped the sweat from his brow and forced a complacent-ill smile.

The children formed one line behind Jackie and another behind Beth. Jackie nodded at Beth. "My class will take the back. Your class sat there, last time."

"That's not necessary, I don't mind."

"I insist." Jackie faced her students. "Listen up, as you board go all the way to the back and take a seat. Please do this calmly and as quickly as possible. There's plenty of room for everyone and remember to sit with your buddy."

The students boarded in an orderly manner as they chattered with excitement.

Samantha stepped onto the first step of the bus, stopped and glanced at Jackie. "I'll save your seat since you're my field trip buddy."

"Great thinking, now go claim our spot."

24

The rest of the students boarded followed by Beth and Jackie.

Beth sat in the seat behind the driver as Jackie stood midway down the aisle and addressed the students. "This will be a fun day of learning. As a reminder, you will need to complete your field trip worksheets."

The bus driver tapped his fingers onto the steering wheel and waited for the recitation of the rules to end. He looked at Jackie as his head wobbled; his vision blurred in and out of focus. He took a deep breath and exhaled.

Jackie walked to the back where Samantha waited. "When we arrive, I'll hand each of you a worksheet and a pencil. You're responsible for keeping up with both. Ms. Andreas and I will help you along the way and if you have questions, just ask one of us. This museum is one of the best in the nation. We're lucky and proud that it's right here in New Orleans. People visit it from all over the world. How many of you have been before?"

Only three hands raised.

"I see, it's a good thing we're going. Now buckle up."

Samantha rose from her seat. "Do you mind sitting by the window? I get nauseated if I'm not on the outside."

"Not a problem." Jackie slid into the seat next to the window and buckled her seatbelt.

Samantha sat and struggled to clasp hers. "Mrs. Hennessey, my seat belt won't buckle."

"Here let me help you with that."

Leonard pressed the accelerator as he clutched the silver metal knob closing the school bus bi-fold doors.

∞

David sat at his desk signing work orders, blueprints and various tedious paperwork. *There has to be a better way.* His fingers cramped as he placed the pen onto the stack of unsigned documents, rubbed his hands together and cracked his knuckles. He picked up his cell phone, checked his messages and listened to the one Jackie left earlier. His leg anxiously bounced as he pressed his intercom button. "Anita, can you come in here please?"

Anita, a fifty-year-old Cajun, small in stature, entered. "How can I assist you this morning?" Her Cajun bayou accent always pleased David. She reminded him of his family in Houma, Louisiana.

"Please make reservations for tonight at Commander's Palace for two between six and six-thirty. I want to celebrate the Japanese deal with my beautiful wife and start off our anniversary week making an impression she won't ever forget."

"Sir, are you sure you want to take her there tonight? You have reservations on Friday to celebrate your anniversary."

"You better make it Mr. B's then."

"Consider it done. Oh, the flower shop delivered the floral arrangement today as you requested. The singing telegram will be tomorrow, and the chocolate covered strawberries will arrive on Wednesday. On Thursday she will receive the edible bouquet and on Friday the limousine will pick her up from work and take her to the spa. So, don't worry about your anniversary week. You planned everything to perfection; nothing will go wrong."

"Thank you, Anita. What about her present?"

"I'm picking it up on Wednesday."

"I hope she likes it."

"Look, that diamond and sapphire tennis bracelet, ring and earrings are gorgeous. If she doesn't like them, you can give them to me for Christmas." She made her way to the door.

"I need everything perfect for her, she's my one and only. Thanks again Anita for sorting all of this out for me. It's not a part of your job description."

"It's my pleasure." Anita closed the office door behind her.

David glanced at Jackie's wedding photograph on the corner of his desk. *The one true love of my life.* He picked up the phone and dialed Jackie's number. When she didn't answer, he recorded his message. "Meet me at Mr. B's at five for cocktails and an early dinner around six. The Japanese deal went through. This calls for a celebration, I love you."

∞

Tyler sat beside Margarette while Sebastian sat on her lap. She read to them the book *A Land of Long Ago* by Elsa Beskow.

The phone rang. She stood with Sebastian in her arms, strode to the phone mounted on the kitchen wall and answered. "Hennessey residence."

"Good morning Mom." David's peppy tone brought a chipper smile to Margarette's face. "How're the boys?"

"Perfect as usual. We're just reading a story about a dragon, a tree and rescuing a princess in distress."

"Sounds like an adventure. I have a special favor to ask of my favorite mother-in-law."

"I'm your only mother-in-law."

"That doesn't mean you're not my favorite."

"What's the favor?"

"Do you mind babysitting the boys tonight? I want to take Jackie to an early dinner. My deal went through and I want to celebrate."

"So, you'll miss my spaghetti?"

"Not at all. It'll be better tomorrow night after it sits for twenty-four hours."

"You're right about that. Of course, I don't mind."

"You're a sweetheart, maybe you should move in. You know that's why I built the mother-in-law quarters outback."

"I like my private time, but thanks for the offer. At least I know I'll never be homeless."

∞

DR. MELISSA CAUDLE

The school bus headed eastbound on Interstate 10 toward New Orleans. The students chatted, laughed and exchanged stories they believed to be true.

Jackie stared out the window and watched the cars pass.

Samantha tapped her shoulder. "Mrs. Hennessey, do you believe in magic?"

"I believe in many things. Why did you ask?"

"Well, last night my mom told me she was planning on coming back to life. How is that possible?" Samantha waited in anticipation for the answer in the hope of ridding herself of her confusion.

Jackie caught off guard by Samantha's question silently searched for an answer as she took a deep breath. "Samantha, your mom will always be in your heart. She watches over you from heaven."

"I know that, I talk to her all the time."

The bus driver took a deep breath, shook his left arm, jerked and grabbed for his chest taking one hand off the steering wheel.

As the bus swerved out of control, everyone on board jolted to the right as Leonard's head collapsed onto the wheel.

Screams reverberated throughout the bus as did pleads for help. A car to the right of the bus pounded hard against the tail end. The bus spun as it swiped two more cars sending them into the morning commute traffic which caused a fifteen-car-pile-up behind the spinning bus. Crash! Bang! Crunch! Boom!

Beth leapt to grab the steering wheel as the bus continued to spin striking a pickup truck. The impact tossed Beth toward the bus's door where she landed onto her shoulder and arm against the bottom step; her head slammed against the glass doors.

Leonard's foot pressed heavily onto the gas pedal as the students panicked and screamed. Crash! Boom! Jolt!

Beth struggled to stand between the jolts as the end of the bus swung from the impact and collided into another car which caused the bus to roll onto its side. A scrambled egg toss of children ensued as the bus rolled.

Beth, airborne, thrashed between the windshield and the dash as the bus rolled. The children screamed terrified as the bus slammed against the twenty foot concrete sound barrier between the interstate and the homes on the right and came to a stop with its wheels on the ground.

A large semi-trailer truck smashed into the side of the bus as Jackie's head banged against the glass causing a head wound and blood to splatter.

Samantha horrified screamed as her life passed before her eyes.

The semi-trailer truck pushed the bus thirty more feet before it came to a complete stop.

Jackie lay static and bloody across Samantha's lap. Each unbelted student piled sandwich style onto one another and most lay motionless; fragments of window glass pierced their skin.

Beth's lip bled as she lay at the bottom of stairs against the glass doors. It took several seconds for Beth to open her eyes. Her body juddered as the world before her phased from clarity to fuzzy. She pushed herself up with both hands. Her left arm buckled, the radius bone protruded below her elbow and it profusely bled. She collapsed screaming in agony to a chorus of children's screams.

It took several minutes for her to focus and use her right hand to push herself up. Her left arm uselessly draggled as the blood flow dripped copiously down her arm as she climbed up the stairs. She frantically pulled her cell phone from her pocket and attempted to dial nine one, one. The pain took her breath away. She struggled to raise her broken left arm as she screamed in agony. She placed the phone onto the front seat, used her right hand to make the call, and then lifted the phone to her ear.

Beth conducted a visual scan of the children. "Everyone okay?" She waited for nine, one, one to answer as she located Jackie.

Samantha trapped by her seatbelt next to Jackie wiped the blood away from Jackie's swollen face with part of her school uniform. "Mrs. Hennessey wake up. You can't die, please wake up." Fear in her voice encapsulated the wreck. She shuddered and whimpered as she glanced at her classmates. "Mom are you still with me?" Her classmates couldn't hear her question muted by the screaming and crying.

Beth's body trembled as she spoke on the phone. "Yes, there's a wreck on the interstate just before Bonnabel Boulevard." Her voice quaked. "I'm on a school bus with forty-three children and one other teacher. The bus driver isn't moving. I think he had a heart attack... Some students are injured... The other teacher is unconscious and very bloody... More scared than anything... I think I broke my left arm... I don't know, I'll check."

Beth clutched her broken arm, stepped over tossed personal items, backpacks and notebooks to reach the bus driver who lay in a prone position against the steering wheel. As she moved, she grimaced in pain. "Leonard, can you hear me?"

She touched his back. "He's not breathing... I don't know if I can get to her, but I'll try."

Samantha struggled to stand but a part of the seat's frame pinned her. "Ms. Andreas, Mrs. Hennessey won't wake up. Her head is bleeding really bad. What should I do?"

"Are you hurt?"

"Yes, Ma'am. My arm hurts. Other than that, I'm stuck."

"Just stay still Samantha and keep talking to Mrs. Hennessey. Try to wake her."

"Yes, Ma'am. Mrs. Hennessey wake up, please wake up."

"Stay calm everyone, help is on the way. Raise your hand if you're not severely injured."

Mason, one of the boys on the opposite side of Samantha tried to raise his hand. "Ouch! My leg is broke. I just want to go home. I didn't want to come on this stupid field trip, anyway." He cried uncontrollably.

"Ms. Andreas is Mrs. Hennessey going to die like my mom and dad?" Samantha's heart sank as fear pinched her throat.

∞

News helicopters flew above and observed three fire trucks, ten ambulances and a dozen or more police cars progress through the heavy traffic.

Beth tried to help the terrified ambulatory students exit the bus. Her effort proved difficult because a car pressed against the exit side door. Now the escape route consisted exiting through the windows or through the emergency exit in the back. "Children, help is on the way, just stay calm."

A young boy screamed in agony. "I want my mommy." His field trip buddy hysterically cried like most of the children on the bus.

The screams of injured and panicked children rang with a poignancy in Beth's ears. The world seemed to move in slow motion to the sounds of sirens and ghastly hysteric screams.

Beth supported her left arm with her right hand as she tried to make sense of her surroundings. In shock, Beth didn't feel the pain, the adrenaline took care of that.

Several drivers and passengers involved in the crash exited their cars. Those who could assist Beth to evacuate the children through the windows did so in the confused chaos.

The Emergency Response teams arrived. Officer Jenkins, first on the scene bolted from his unit. "Listen up. Everyone must leave this area and let us do our jobs."

Other responders arrived and immediately secured the area and treated the injured.

Finally, the rescue crew used axes to break open the emergency exit door.

Officer Jenkins herded the crowd to allow the paramedics and fire teams space to perform their duties. "Please move to the side. A white canopy is being set up as the triage area for injury assessment."

The injured, both unaided and assisted moved toward the triage area.

Beth's heart raced as fear took control. Her throat pinched as she recognized her responsibility to the students and to Jackie. She approached Officer Jenkins. "These are my students, I'm helping."

"Ma'am, today you're a hero. We'll take over now. You need to have your injuries addressed." Officer Jenkins waved toward a paramedic. "Take this woman, now."

∞

Two excruciating hours passed since the bus wreck. Beth, with her arm in a sling, paced between the triage area and as close as the police allowed to the bus talking to Dr. Cunningham. "I know, it's difficult and chaotic. I'll keep you updated but as far as I know, Jackie is not doing well. Have you notified all the families?"

"We are working on it. Please keep me informed with the injury update."

"I'll call when I can." Beth stuffed her phone into her pocket.

Two paramedics pulled a stretcher past her with a body covered by a white sheet. "Is it one of the children?" Frantic and fear filled her voice as chills ran down her spine.

"No Ma'am, it's the driver."

"What about the other teacher?" Her eyes narrowed as her heart skipped a beat and pounded deep within her chest. She feared the worst outcome.

"They're working on her now. The child next to her will be fine. The firemen cut through the metal that trapped her. Looks like she broke her arm and she'll be brought out next."

Beth bolted toward the bus, but Officer Jenkins stopped her as he stepped in front of her. "Ma'am, please stay back and let us do our jobs."

"That's my friend Jackie." She forced herself to breathe. "I need to be there for her."

"I'm sorry, you must stay back."

Beth's heart thundered as her tears swelled.

A paramedic carried Samantha toward Beth. "Samantha, you okay?"

"Mrs. Hennessey stopped breathing, she died." Samantha buried her head into the shoulder of the paramedic and cried as he headed with her toward the triage area.

"Wait! Officer, I have to go see about my friend."

"Let the paramedics do their jobs. The biggest help you can be for your friend is to stay out of the way."

"Wait!" Beth's heart ramped as her skin prickled in fear.

The paramedic strode to the nearest ambulance and carefully placed Samantha onto a gurney.

Beth viewed the paramedic team transport Jackie from the bus on a rescue stretcher. They quickly lowered it onto the ground. A female paramedic secured Jackie's neck and head. "She's coding." To expose her patient's chest the paramedic cut through Jackie's blood-soaked shirt. "Hand me the defibrillator." A sense of urgency filled her voice.

The male paramedic handed the defibrillator paddles over.

"Stand back." The paramedic hovered the paddles over Jackie's chest. "Clear." She pressed the paddles onto the left and to the right of Jackie's sternum.

Jackie's body jolted. The paramedic lifted the paddles.

"Again, clear." She pressed the paddles firmly again onto Jackie.

Jackie's body jolted.

Beth clenched her fists and willed an outer calmness. "Come on Jackie."

"We have a heartbeat, get her head wrapped."

The paramedics wrapped Jackie's head injury and secured her onto the stretcher for airlift transport.

∞

Anita bolted into the office out of breath as David glanced up from his paperwork.

"You have an urgent call on line two from your wife's principal."

"That doesn't sound good, I hope everything's all right."

"Answer the call and find out."

∞

Tyler played with his monster trucks as Sebastian played with his own blocks in the play area.

Margarette used the remote and located her favorite talk show. "Let's see what they have to say today."

She strode to the kitchen. In a bowl on the granite countertop, a dozen large ripe tomatoes, two green bell peppers, two onions and two pods of fresh garlic for the spaghetti sauce awaited her sous chef skills. She retrieved a chopping board, a knife and diced the vegetables as she supervised the children.

A news bulletin's three loud beeps caught her attention. She continued her prep work as she focused on the broadcast.

∞

News reporter Tina Reynolds stood one hundred yards away from the crash site.

"We interrupt this programming for a breaking news story. I'm Tina Reynolds reporting live to bring you the latest details on the crash of a school bus with forty-three students, two teachers and the driver on board. One person has died on the scene, and first responders confirmed multiple injuries to the elementary students when the bus crashed into a twenty foot concrete sound barrier on Interstate Ten near the Bonnabel exit. The school bus was taking a group of students and two teachers from Stephen Hawking Elementary School in Metairie on a field trip when the crash occurred. Louisiana Law Enforcement Captain Jerry Hart said the agency is still investigating how the bus ended up crashing. Authorities believe the bus driver suffered from a heart attack. One severely injured teacher airlifted to East Angels Hospital remains in critical condition. The other teacher and several students received major to minor injuries with two students in critical condition. Paramedics assessed numerous children's injuries trapped inside the bus as rescue units work diligently to free those most at risk. Names of the deceased and injured are being withheld until authorities notify parents and next of kin. We will stay on top of this situation and bring you the latest developments."

4. TURN BACK THE TIME

D r. Evangelista, the emergency room neurological surgeon, and his team of six residents waited at the emergency room entrance. "Who knows the E.T.A.?"

"They're seconds away." Dr. Carol Viale, age thirty, a brash and beautiful surgical resident stepped forward. "Airlift transport landed several minutes ago."

"Everyone on point, this is not a rehearsal. As soon as they arrive, take your positions."

The paramedics pushed Jackie's stretcher through the airlift emergency entryway. Dr. Evangelista rushed toward them. "My team will take her now, update and vitals."

As the hospital team pushed the gurney down the hall, the senior female paramedic followed close behind Dr. Evangelista. "The patient is Jackie Hennessey. We've stabilized her as much as we can. She presents nonresponsive, coded twice and has a contusion on her forehead. When awake she was confused and bled from her nose. Her heart rate is ninety, blood pressure eighty over fifty-eight, respiration twenty breaths per minute and her skin is cool and clammy."

36

"Team, we're taking her to surgical bay three. Scrub up quickly. We don't have any time to waste or she'll die."

David rushed down the hall to catch the team. "That's my wife, where are you taking her?"

Dr. Evangelista turned toward David as the team continued to push Jackie. "Sir, she has to go to surgery now or we'll lose her. Wait in the emergency room waiting area and as soon as I know something, I'll meet you there."

Jackie and the team disappeared behind closed doors as Dr. Evangelista pursued them into the secured surgical wing.

David sobbed. "Son of a bitch. Dear God, don't let her die. I believe in Your mercy and divine healing power."

He leaned against the wall as tears swelled. He clenched his fists as he felt his life sucked from him. "God, please don't let her die. Our Father, who art in heaven, hallowed be your name. Thy kingdom come, thy will be done, here on earth and in heaven…"

A nurse hurriedly passed David.

"Please, could you find out what is going on with Jackie Hennessey, my wife? They just took her to surgical bay three."

"I'll try, but I can't guarantee anything."

"Son of a bitch! I'm sorry, I don't normally curse."

"Sir, the best thing you can do for your wife is to wait in the surgical emergency room waiting area. As soon as they know something, the doctor will find you. Excuse me, I need to get in there to help your wife."

"Thanks, I guess."

The nurse used her scan badge, the door opened; and she entered the surgical area.

David tried to peek inside, but the door automatically closed behind her. He leaned against the wall and prayed. "God, I know you are merciful. Please send your healing power to Jackie. You above anyone else holds this power. I believe in

your miracles, watch over her and guide the surgeon and his team. In Jesus' name, I pray. Amen."

∞

The waiting room area filled with dozens of frightened students from the crash painted the frantic-chaotic scene. Some injured students cried while others sat as if frozen and stared at the floor either in disbelief or shock.

Beth stood at the front to address the students; her left arm bound in a temporary cast. "Children, I know you're scared. Dr. Cunningham has contacted your parents and they're on the way."

Samantha covered by Jackie's blood sat with her right arm in a sling as she swung her legs; her feet didn't reach the floor. Samantha's eyes teared. "Is Mrs. Hennessey going to die?"

"I don't think so." Beth sat next to Samantha. "The doctors are very good at what they do."

"Then why did they let my mom and dad die?" Samantha took a deep breath as she averted her eyes from Beth's.

"Your parents' injuries were a lot worse; so, try not to worry about Mrs. Hennessey. Look, they already fixed me up by putting my arm in a cast. Are you in much pain?"

"I can handle it. I broke my leg in the car crash that killed my parents."

"That's very brave of you."

"Does your arm hurt?"

"Not that bad, it mostly throbs."

"Mine too, I guess we have one thing in common."

"I'd say more than one sweetie, we're both very brave."

"My mom told me I had to be brave for Mrs. Hennessey."

Beth shook her head and patted Samantha's leg. *She must have some really good karma.*

David burst into the emergency waiting area and proceeded straight to the receptionist. "Can you tell me how Jackie Hennessey is doing? I'm her husband."

The receptionist scanned her computer screen. "Sir, please have a seat, she's in surgery. A doctor will be with you shortly."

"How badly is she injured?"

"I'm sorry, I don't have that information. You'll have to wait on the surgeon's report."

Beth, who overheard David, strode to him. "Excuse me, I'm Beth Andreas. I was on the bus with your wife."

"How badly is she hurt?"

"I wish I had something positive to say, but I don't. She hit her head hard when the bus rolled. It was horrifying. She was conscious at first, then she closed her eyes. I saw the paramedics use a defibrillator, but she is alive. Thank Buddha for that. Let's sit down and I'll tell you what I know."

David nodded and followed Beth to the two empty seats next to Samantha. David sat with his head rested in his hands. "Please tell me this isn't happening."

"I'm sorry Mr. Hennessey, I can't."

Samantha rose and stood in front of David. "Are you Mrs. Hennessey's husband? I'm one of her students, Samantha."

"Nice to meet you Samantha. Yes, she's my wife."

"Is she going to be okay?"

"I sure hope so." *God, please don't let her die.*

"She loved the flowers you gave her this morning. She smiled really big when she smelled them."

"That's good to know, thank you for telling me."

"They made her happy, I could tell. Don't worry about Mrs. Hennessey, my mom is watching over her right now."

"Your mom is one of the doctors?"

Samantha frowned. "No, she's a lawyer."

"Where's your mom and dad? You shouldn't be in here alone."

"They died in a car crash, they're angels now."

David felt a knot of nerves in the pit of his stomach as his spine stiffened.

Beth glanced at Samantha. "Sweetie leave Mr. Hennessey alone and sit down."

"Yes, Ma'am." Samantha frowned as she returned to her seat.

Mrs. Forester, an African American, age sixty-five, rushed into the emergency waiting area. "Samantha! Samantha!"

Beth pointed to the woman. "Look, there's your foster mother now."

Samantha's lips formed a confused-little-girl smile as she rose.

"Wait here Samantha, let her come to you." Beth grimacing in pain stood and waved. "Mrs. Forester, she's over here."

Relieved, Mrs. Forester ambled to Samantha and hugged her. "Oh baby, I'm so glad you're okay."

"But I'm not okay, my arm hurts."

"Considering what you've been through, I'll take that. You had me worried." Mrs. Forester relieved took a deep breath and winked at Beth. "Thank you for watching her until I could get here."

"It's the least I could do."

A nurse entered the waiting area. She glanced at the chart she carried. "Samantha Pennington."

Beth flashed a grin toward Samantha. "They're calling for you. They'll fix you all up. Remember to be brave."

"I'm not worried."

Mrs. Forester placed her hand on Samantha's shoulder. "Come on sweetie, let's go get you fixed up so we can get you home and get you into bed to rest."

∞

The medical monitor to the right of the operating table rhythmically beeped as Dr. Evangelista and his team worked methodically to save Jackie's life.

Dr. Evangelista glanced at the MRI computerized results on the monitor to his left. "The MRI confirmed she has elevated intracranial pressure. Which resident wants to perform a ventriculostomy?"

Dr. Viale volunteered and stepped forward. "I'm confident, I want to perform the procedure." Her tone reflected the astuteness of a surgical scholar.

"You all could learn from Dr. Viale." Dr. Evangelista's tone reflected his superiority; his brow creased above his surgical mask. "When given an opportunity to perform surgery, take it." He glanced at the hotshot surgical resident. "What is your plan?"

"First, I'll shave the area and sterilize it. I'll use the bone drill to make a one-fourth inch hole in the frontal skull just above the contusion. Then, I'll insert the tube and drain the blood to relieve the cranial pressure."

"Very well spoken. Anyone who has any questions, ask now; during surgery isn't the time."

The surgical residents remained silent and poised.

"Dr. Viale, proceed."

The skilled young surgeon executed her plan textbook style. The monitor slowed as Jackie's blood pressure dropped. "We're losing her!"

∞

Tyler played in front of Margarette. She patted Sebastian on his butt as she rocked and sang to him. *"Hush little baby don't say a word, Grandma's gonna buy you a mockingbird. And if that mockingbird won't sing, Grandma's gonna buy you a diamond ring."*

∞

Five long hours passed since David arrived at the hospital. He paced the floor in the emergency waiting room in front of Beth. "Why haven't they told me anything?" A frown creased his forehead.

"They will when they know something. Have you called her mother?"

"I've been so worried I forgot, I better do it now. This isn't going to be an easy call to make."

"That's probably why you've been putting it off."

"Did you know a drunk driver killed Jackie's father? Her mother hasn't finished grieving for him. I'm not sure if I should tell her this over the phone or not. She might need my shoulder to cry on."

"She's stronger than you might think. You can't wait too long not knowing the outcome of Jackie's surgery."

"You talk as if you expect Jackie not to come through it."

"Not at all. I think she needs to know and not be kept in the dark. The way I understand things, Jackie's mom is a God-fearing woman; she'll want to pray."

"I've already put it in God's hands. Jackie's mom is the one who will think the worse. After her husband's wreck, they told her he would be fine. He never woke up from surgery, his heart couldn't take it."

"Remind her Jackie is young, healthy and strong. She'll make it. You must believe that."

"I saw her on that stretcher and I barely recognized her."

"Whatever you do, don't tell her mother that, stay calm and reassure her. That's what she needs to hear in your voice." Beth touched David's shoulder. "I'm going to go get us another cup of coffee and give you some privacy. Now call her." Beth took her leave.

David retrieved his phone and dialed. He bit his lower lip as sweat beaded across his upper lip. "Come on, answer." A sudden queasiness overtook him.

"Hennessey residence." Margarette, puzzled, glanced at her watch.

"Margarette." David's voice hard as iron relayed a serious unexpected tone.

"Do you plan on staying later for y'alls date to celebrate your big deal?"

"Margarette, please just listen and don't say a word until I'm finished."

"Such formality, everything all right?" She drew a deep audible breath.

"Jackie is in surgery." His knees weakened.

"What do you mean surgery?" Her voice trembled as she felt her heart thrum against her chest.

"She had a field trip with her students today. The bus driver had a heart attack, and the bus crashed."

"You mean the wreck I saw on the news?" Her words broken between her rapid breaths and tears upset David even more.

His body trembled as his hands shook. "The principal called me. I'm sorry I didn't call you sooner, but I've been dealing with all the paperwork and trying to figure out how to tell you. There was just no easy way to tell you this. I wish I had better news. As far as I know, she has a head injury. The good news is she's alive."

"What hospital?" Her laid-back demeanor audibly relinquished. "I'll pack up the boys, I'm on my way."

"There's nothing you can do here, and I don't want Tyler or Sebastian in this environment. They're too young and it will only upset them. Please, just take care of them and keep them safe. I'll keep you informed, I'm waiting on the surgeon now."

"How bad is her injury?"

"The other teacher on the bus told me she hit her head and flatlined."

Margarette rushed to the television. She cradled the phone receiver to her ear and frantically changed the stations until she found one that covered the wreck.

"Mom, she'll be fine; she's a fighter. You raised her that way. I'll let you know as soon as I hear from the surgeon. I love you."

"Don't worry about the boys, I got them. Take care of Jackie." She held back her tears as she lovingly stared at her grandsons.

David hung up the phone.

Samantha with a cast on her arm and Mrs. Forester entered the waiting area. Samantha shuffled straight to David. "Please tell Mrs. Hennessey I'll be praying for her. I'll send my mommy's angel to take care of her."

"I will, you take care of yourself."

Mrs. Forester grasped Samantha by the hand. "Honey leave the man alone. It's time for us to go home and get you in bed. You heard what the doctor told you. You need your rest."

"Bye." Samantha glanced over her shoulder toward David as she and her foster mother exited.

David shook his head.

Beth extended her kindness and brought David a cup of coffee. "Here, it looks like you could use the caffeine."

"Thank you, Beth. You don't have to stay."

"Oh yes I do. That should be me in surgery and not Jackie. She insisted her class sit at back of the bus."

"You can't blame this on that, it's not your fault."

"The cafeteria closes in ten minutes. Do you want me to get you a bite to eat?"

"No thanks, I'm not hungry. I only want to see my wife."

"How did Jackie's mom take the news?"

"About as well as could be expected."

Dr. Evangelista entered and approached David.

David immediately stood anxious for information; his stomach fluttered, and his heart pounded.

"Mr. Hennessey? I'm Dr. Evangelista, I supervised the team who operated on your wife."

"How is she?" He held his breath and then exhaled.

"She will be in ICU recovery overnight and transferred to a private room in the intensive care unit sometime tomorrow."

"How is she though?"

"Your wife suffered from an intracranial injury and severe trauma to her frontal lobe. We drained the hemorrhaging to relieve the pressure and swelling around the brain. We won't know the severity of her traumatic brain injury or how severe the effect it will have on her mental functioning until she wakes up. However, she will have some degree of disfunction. The question is how much? For now, we have her in an induced coma to prevent further swelling. I'll closely monitor the cerebral blood flow to make certain that pressure doesn't build again within the skull."

"That sounds serious. How will she be when she wakes up?"

"Like I said, we won't know until she awakens. I'll be blunt with you. Her prognosis could range from a host of physical, cognitive, social, emotional and behavioral deficits. Some patients recover from a traumatic brain injury with minimal effects while others die from secondary injuries. As in your wife's case, she has a subarachnoid hemorrhage. Due to the location and depth of her injury, you're looking at extensive rehabilitation for at least one year. Statistically, at the minimum she'll experience some form of amnesia and at the worst level may lose all mental capacity. I'm more concerned that she'll experience retrograde amnesia. Again, we won't know until she awakens, so don't jump to any conclusions."

"I don't understand, what's retro amnesia?"

"The diagnosis is retrograde amnesia; it's a condition where she can't remember anything or anyone. She'll have to form new memories."

"Just tell me she'll be all right."

"I can't at this moment. Do you and your wife a favor, go home, get some rest and eat. You won't be any good to her worn out. Recovery for her won't be easy, nor will it be easy for you. Until we move her tomorrow from the ICU recovery you can't see her."

Beth placed her hand onto David's shoulder. "I'll stay right here and call you the second her condition changes. You need to get some rest like the doctor advises."

"I can't leave her." David's hands trembled as he lost his breath. He glared at Dr. Evangelista. "If your wife was in the hospital, would you go home?"

"Mr. Hennessey, she's in capable hands and is under constant monitoring. There is nothing you can do for her here right now."

∞

At the Hennessey home, Tyler and Sebastian soundly slept upstairs in their rooms. Margarette sat alone downstairs in the rocking chair and stared out the window as the clock on the wall annoyingly ticked and taunted her the closer the hands moved to midnight.

The front door opened.

"David?" Margarette rose from the rocking chair.

"Don't get up." David gently closed the front door and locked it. He took a deep breath as he gazed at the family photographs hung over the stairs and Jackie's wedding portrait. *She has to be all right.*

Margarette met him in between the dining area and kitchen. She wrapped her loving arms around him. He sniffled and pushed her away. With a blank expression on his face and his mind spent from the horrid day, he gazed teary-eyed at her.

Margarette wiped her tears using a crumpled used Kleenex she held. "Any change in her condition?"

"None." David proceeded to the bar to pour himself a martini.

"I'd have had that ready if you'd called to let me know you were near."

"You do so much for us already; and now, I don't know what's going to happen. Things are looking pretty grim." His tone faltered as if he'd surrendered hope.

"You know I'll be here for her, you and the boys. You'll need my help when you bring her home."

"It could be weeks or months before we know how extensive her brain injury is and how it will affect her."

"Is your mother-in-law quarters still available?"

"It's always been available, but I never wanted you to move in like this."

"She'll be all right, won't she?"

"That's my daughter we're talking about. She's a fighter and has everything to live for. She adores you and the kids."

David took a deep breath and forced a tight-lipped grin. "Thanks Mom, I needed to hear that. All this time I thought I'd have to give you a pep talk. This can't be easy for you."

"Nothing is ever easy David, but us Higgins, we're fighters. We never give up or give in. Remember, a setback is a setup for a comeback. My Jackie, she's the comeback kid. Don't you ever forget that."

David sighed and finally sat on the couch. He glanced toward Margarette teary-eyed. "If I could turn back time, I'd never let her leave for work today."

5. THE HOMECOMING

One Year Later – Hennessey Home

David stared at the gurgling coffee maker as if he could hurry the process. He desperately needed the hot Columbian brew. His unshaven face and dark circles beneath his eyes reflected the difficulty of the last year. Even his fuzzy moose slippers showed wear and tear as one of the antlers dangled in need of repair.

Margarette snuggled in her robe shuffled into the kitchen.

"Good Morning." David nodded as a conquering-hero smile jetted across his face.

"Don't speak to me, I haven't had my coffee yet. Not even the aroma is helping me this morning."

"It's almost ready, I know the drill." David retrieved two personalized coffee mugs, one with yellow roses with the name "Grandma" and the other one black with "Dad" in white written across it. He placed them next to the coffee maker.

"Sebastian kept me up all night cutting his two-year molars. He's getting big too fast." Her eyes shut as she yawned.

48

"I know, it upsets me that Jackie is missing it." David poured the coffee and handed Margarette the cup with the yellow roses.

"She's not missing a thing. Thanks to modern technology we take her videos, photo albums and tell her everything happening on the home front."

"She doesn't remember a thing."

Margarette forced a grin as she constrained her tears. She walked to the rocking chair and sat. She inhaled the aroma of the coffee. "Let's be grateful that the only thing she lost was her memory. We've all come too far to lose hope now. She comes home today. I have it all planned out." Margarette blew across her steaming coffee and took a sip. She picked up a small photo album from the side table.

"She only comes home if the doctor clears her." David sighed frustrated.

"He will, now go get cleaned up and please shave. Jackie needs us to be at our absolute best." Margarette handed David the photo album. "Take this to her, please."

Sebastian's cry from upstairs alerted David. "I'll get him, it's my turn."

"You get dressed and go get Jackie. I want her home where she belongs."

∞

Jackie sat up in her hospital bed and rubbed her fingers across the scar which started at her forehead and extended down her left cheekbone. Her once shaved hair showed about six months growth since her last surgery. The nurse entered with a breakfast tray.

"Good morning Mrs. Hennessey, you feel like eating? You can't go home until you eat."

"I don't know where home is."

David grasped a dozen red roses and the photo album as he stood at the door and waited for the nurse to leave. "How's the patient?"

"She's ready to go home." The nurse headed out the door.

"Good morning my beloved." David placed the roses on the side table next to her bed and kissed her on the cheek. Jackie flinched, then stared at him with eyes of steel. He backed away to give her space.

"Are you sure you're my husband?" She scratched her scar again.

Upon hearing her words, his brow furrowed in disbelief. "We've been through this a thousand times, just ask your mother; she'll vouch for me."

"I know, that woman keeps telling me we're the perfect couple."

"Yes we are, and we're the perfect family too. You'll see for yourself today."

"I don't think I'm ready for this."

Dr. Evangelista entered with his team including the hotshot resident Dr. Viale. "Good news, everything on our end panned out. I'm discharging you today."

Jackie's eyes flushed as her heart raced; her breaths short. "I'm not ready. Can I stay a couple more days?"

"Jackie, there is never the perfect day. Remember to take things slow. Procrastinating here in the hospital won't help you recover. It's time to move forward with your life."

An apprehensive-here-we-go smile crossed David's lips as he nodded in agreement. "Look, we'll take things easy. I promise you'll be happy. The boys can't wait to meet their mommy."

"See!" She slammed her fist onto the food tray. "My kids, who I don't remember, don't even know their own mother."

"That's not what I meant Jackie." David's tone extremely apologetic failed to ease her tension. "They know who you are."

Dr. Viale stepped forward. "Mrs. Hennessey, the social worker and home health representative have arranged everything for home health care visits and occupational therapy. She can arrange for any other needs that might arise. We'll leave you two with a positive new beginning. Good luck Mrs. Hennessey." The team of doctors left.

David handed her the photo album. "Here's the latest update on Tyler and Sebastian."

Jackie flipped through the pages. "I'm scared, I don't remember my home... My children... You... My mom. I'm a stranger in a strange world I don't know anything about. Who am I?"

"Well, if you think I'm pulling an *Overboard* on you, I'm not."

"What does that mean?"

"The movie with Goldie Hawn and Kurt Russell."

"I have no idea what you're talking about."

∞

Four hours later David and Jackie pulled into the driveway of their home. A large banner, "Welcome Home Jackie" hung above the door. Weeds filled the once immaculate flower beds, and the neglected overgrown lawn needed serious attention.

David honked the horn twice to announce their arrival, exited the car and proceeded to the passenger door to assist Jackie.

Margarette opened the front door. Sebastian and Tyler ran toward their parents.

"Daddy! Daddy!" Tyler wrapped his arms around David's legs.

"Look who I brought home."

Jackie stepped from the car.

Tyler buried his head into David's thigh as Sebastian stopped and plopped onto his diapered butt. Neither son wanted anything to do with their mother as if they were in a stranger danger situation.

"Come on Tyler, give your mother a hug and a kiss."

"Grandma, Grandma, save me." Tyler ran to Margarette and clung to her leg.

Sebastian followed his older brother's behavior. When he reached his grandmother, he held up his hands. "Hold you, hold you."

"Don't you mean hold me please?" Margarette beamed at Jackie as she lifted Sebastian. "Welcome home Jackie, we're all excited to have you back."

"I can tell by the boy's reaction."

Tyler peeked around Margarette's legs. "What's wrong with Mommy's face? It's not Halloween."

Jackie quickly covered her scar with her hand and lowered her head.

"Jackie, don't let a little thing like that upset you." Margarette patted Tyler on his back. "You have bigger crawfish to boil."

"What in hell are crawfish?"

"I'll plan a crawfish boil for this weekend, and you can discover them for yourself if you're up to it."

"Sounds disgusting."

David slumped his shoulders. "They used to be your favorite, but that's a bridge we'll cross when we get to it."

Margarette took Tyler by the hand. "Let Mommy get into the house." She took the boys inside.

Jackie's expression of promised retaliation took precedent. She drew in a long-deep breath. "The boys are horrified by my face. They think I look like a monster and they're right. There's no amount of plastic surgery that can fix this."

"You're beautiful the way you are. They'll get used to seeing it."

"I'm not used to seeing it. This will never go away, I'm marked for life."

"I wouldn't say that. Like you, they need time to get adjusted."

"Were Tyler and I ever close? Did I love him?" Her voice quivered as she held back her tears.

"I never saw you without a loving smile on your face around the boys, you adored them. They were your life."

"Those two children are really mine?" She bit her quivering lower lip.

"Jackie, they are ours. We both wanted children, they weren't accidents."

Chills ran up Jackie's spine. "Accident! I think that word needs to be blocked from our vocabulary."

"Consider it done. That 'A' word is gone. Are you ready to go inside?"

"Not really; so, this is where you live?"

"Correction, this is where we live. Welcome home."

"I guess it's now or never." Jackie hesitated before she took her next step. "One step at a time, right?"

"Jackie, remember we all love you and want you home. There will be an adjustment period for all of us. It's been a year since your acci… since you've been home. Everything will be fine. This is the only home where you belong."

"I can't do this, I don't know this place."

"I'm positive you can. You have the best support system, you'll see." David grasped her hand; she at once jerked it away. "Follow me, this way."

David opened the front door for Jackie.

As she entered, she froze and stared at the photographs which hung above the stairs. "Well, I guess I do live here. That is definitely me. That is, a version of me before this ugly scar down my face."

"I take it you don't remember framing and hanging those."

"Do I need to answer that?" Her tone sharp as a blade that could shear metal pierced through David.

"Not in the least." He flashed a comforting thin-lipped grin to her icy reception.

They entered the living area. Jackie stopped and scanned the room to take it all in as if she stepped into it for the first time. She gazed at the corner wooden toy cases with the names of her children which she couldn't read; both boys played quietly in front of them. Frustration filled her soul. "It's not as small as I thought it would be by the pictures you showed me."

"Is that a good or bad thing?" David retrieved several toys and handed them to the boys.

"Don't know." She inhaled and sniffed the air. "What is that smell?"

After stirring the large pot, Margarette placed the spoon inside a mason jar filled with water and faced Jackie. "That's my famous homemade spaghetti meat sauce, it's your favorite."

"Are you sure about that? The smell is making me sick to my stomach."

Margarette took an exasperated breath. "I'll make anything you feel like eating. What would you like?"

"I just want to lie down." Jackie took two steps toward the kitchen and stopped. "Where's my room?"

Tyler bolted into the kitchen. "Grandma, juice please."

"Of course, honey." She wiped her hands onto her apron and retrieved a small red plastic glass and a blue sippy cup.

"Yea, red, my favorite color."

Jackie studied Margarette's and Tyler's interaction as David leaned against the granite countertop.

Margarette proceeded to the refrigerator, grabbed the juice, poured it into the cups and handed them to Tyler. "Take your brother his too."

"Thank you, Grandma." He retreated into the living room and continued to play with his brother.

Jackie gaped at her mother dismayed. "They both seem to love you very much."

"Yes, they do; and I love them and you very much. Your room is up the stairs to the right. I changed the sheets today and used Downy, your favorite fabric softener."

"I didn't know I had one."

David glanced perplexed toward Margarette as Jackie headed upstairs. "This isn't going to be easy, is it?"

"Whoever said life was easy got it all wrong."

The doorbell rang.

David wrinkled his brow. "We're not expecting anyone, are we?"

"Not that I'm aware of by any means."

The doorbell rang again.

"I'll get it." David proceeded to the front door and answered it.

Beth held a stack of cards and letters wrapped with a pink silk ribbon tied in a bow.

"Hello, Beth, what can I do for you?"

"I hope you don't mind me dropping by, but Jackie's former students asked if I could bring these to her on my way home. They miss her and want her back."

"Beth, thank you."

"May I come in and give them to her?"

"I think it's best for now that Jackie rests. She just got home, and it's been a bit overwhelming."

Jackie descended the stairs. "Is that the nurse?"

"It's your friend, Beth."

55

Jackie stood behind David. "I'm sorry, who are you?"

"I'm Beth." She handed Jackie the items. "Your former students wanted me to give these to you."

"I'm sorry, I don't remember that part of my life."

"It's okay, I'd better be going. It's good to see you Jackie. You look well." Beth turned to leave.

"Wait, please stay."

Confusion crippled Beth's face. "Maybe in a couple of days I'll come back for a visit. I only wanted to stop by to give you the student's get-well cards they made for you."

"Please tell them I said thank you."

"I will. Welcome home, *Amitābha*." Beth formed her hands into a prayer position over her chest and bowed. "May you be well and find peace." Beth took her leave and David gently shut the door.

Jackie's eyes smoldered as her muscles tensed throughout her body. "That was completely embarrassing."

Before Jackie could storm back up the stairs to her room, Margarette entered the formal area. "It won't be long until dinner is ready. Jackie, at least try the spaghetti."

David placed his hand onto Jackie's shoulder.

She jerked away from his touch. "Please, I want to be alone." She bolted upstairs and into her bedroom slamming the door shut.

David frustrated punched the wall. "I know, give her time."

∞

Jackie stared at her scarred-face reflection in the mirror above her dresser. "I don't know you." She traced her scar with her fingertip. Her eyes swelled with tears as she stroked her short hair rubbing the scar on her scalp. *I look like a monster.*

Jackie turned and scanned the bedroom. She noticed every detail and glided her hand across the damask jacquard blue and gold bedspread. The bed skirt featured a woven pleated texture which added a rich dimension. *Did I buy this and like it?* She slid her fingers across the lavish matching shams. *It's not mine, can't be.*

The silver-framed photograph on the nightstand caught her attention. She retrieved it and stared at her unfamiliar self on their honeymoon. *I have no memory of this.* Her cheeks lost their color at the site of her kissing David on the lips. She touched the cracked glass. *That's weird, it's broken. Just like me.* Overwhelmed, she placed the photo face down onto the nightstand and undressed.

She strode to the side-by-side closets with bi-fold doors. *Which closet is mine?* She opened the left door where she discovered David's clothes arranged by shirts, slacks, jeans and suits. His shoes aligned on the shoe rack below looked as if on display rather than stored in a personal closet. Unnerved, she closed the doors and glanced at the other.

The right closet seemed menacing. Her heart pounded against her ribcage. She cautiously opened the doors. *Is this how I left it or do these clothes belong to another woman?* A scowl developed across her brow as she held it up against her chest. *This is disgusting. What kind of woman would wear this?* She threw the dress onto the floor and noticed the polka dot fleece bathrobe and grabbed it. *I know I have to have house shoes.* She searched through the pile of shoes until she discovered her Garfield slippers. She at once tossed them back into the closet.

Barefoot, she went into the bathroom and hung the robe onto the hook. Her eyes darted between the shower and the bathtub. She sat on the side of the tub, started the water, and then tested the temperature by allowing the water to flow over her wrist. *I only had showers at the hospital. I wonder do I like a bath hot, cold or warm?*

David entered without knocking with a steaming cup of tea. Startled, Jackie jumped. "Thought you'd enjoy a cup of Earl Grey with your bath."

"Earl Grey?"

"Hot tea. You're favorite English tea. Remember high tea time in London or at Windsor Court every Christmas?"

"I didn't know I drank it. I never did in the hospital."

"Trust me, you love it." He sat the cup onto the side of the tub. "You even insisted on importing English tea because you wanted to drink it like a queen."

"I'm sick and tired of everyone telling me what I love." Her harsh tone lanced David's heart. "First, those crawfishy things, then the spaghetti. Now it's the tea. Oh, the children, you, my mother. It's an endless list. Can't I make up my own mind what I do or do not like without any reminders from you or my mother? That is if you're really my husband, and she's really my mother."

David, caught off guard by Jackie's tirade, stood and gaped at his wife. He knew he must walk on eggshells while Jackie adjusted to her environment. Dr. Evangelista warned him about times just like this. He held an expressionless gaze. "It's good to have you home."

"I'm sorry for that, you didn't deserve it." She regretted her choice of words. Tears formed as she took a deep breath and sighed.

"I'll leave you to your bath for you to figure out if you like it or not." David left and gently closed the door behind him. He glanced at the silver-framed photograph on the nightstand. "That's not good." He turned the frame upright and huffed. *I wish for those days again, everything was perfect back then.* He lifted his eyes toward the heavens. *God, please give me the strength and clarity to take care of my wife.*

Jackie sat on the toilet seat and placed her elbows onto her knees. She buried her face into her hands and cried as the tub filled.

Downstairs Margarette and Tyler worked together to set the table. She placed five sets of silverware and five placemats onto the rectangular dining table.

David slumped into the kitchen. "That didn't go well, she doesn't know if she likes tea or not." The sharpness in his voice surprised Margarette. "And, she turned our honeymoon picture face down."

"Give her time, just take a deep breath."

Margarette handed Tyler the placemats. "You know what to do."

Tyler placed one down at the head of the table. "One for Daddy." He made his way around the table and placed a placemat down as he counted. "One for Grandma. One for Sebastian and one for me." He handed the fifth placemat back to Margarette. "You gave me too many."

"No, honey, that one is for your mommy. Put it where she sits."

Jackie who wore her robe entered the room unnoticed and watched.

"Where's that Grandma?"

"Even he's confused." David's tone harsh hit a wrong nerve in both Jackie and Margarette.

Margarette scowled at David's comment. She tapped the table on the opposite side where David always sat. "Put it at the end, right here."

Tyler set it down as instructed. "Here Grandma?"

"That's perfect, great listening skills. Forks go on the right side of the plate."

"I remember Grandma."

"You're doing an excellent job. You're Grandma's little helper."

When Jackie heard the comment, she sniffled.

"Grandma look, I'm finished."

"The table looks great. Now run along and play with your brother."

Jackie made her presence known. "I decided I'd try to join the family for dinner before I take a bath, I'm starving." Her stomach growled.

"Great news, it's ready."

David strode to the play area, picked up Sebastian and returned placing the younger son onto his booster chair. He quickly buckled the strap around Sebastian's waist.

Margarette situated Tyler and proceeded to the kitchen for the final meal preparation. Jackie took a seat at her designated chair.

David's eyes met Jackie's. "You haven't forgotten everything, you remembered where you sit."

"No, I overheard Mom's instructions to Tyler."

Margarette retrieved five small oval platters which served as plates from the cabinets and handed them to David. "Please place these where they belong on the table."

"No problem, I'd be glad too. I can't wait for your famous spaghetti, I'm famished."

"Good to hear because I made enough to feed an army." Margarette placed a huge bowl of noodles and another bowl of sauce onto the table and sat to Jackie's right. "I forgot the freshly grated parmesan cheese. We can't eat spaghetti without it, you know that."

David pushed his chair back. "I'll get it, sit down, Mom." He strolled to the refrigerator.

"Oh, can you get the garlic bread out of the oven too?"

"Of course, I can."

For some odd reason a surge of jealousy overtook Jackie as she observed the interaction between David and Margarette. Her face flustered as a sprint of heat prickled her skin.

He grabbed an oven mitt, slid his right hand into it, retrieved the bread, snatched the parmesan cheese, and then briskly returned to the table. "Hot, hot." After he placed the bread on a trivet and set the grated parmesan in front of Margarette, he sat.

Margarette lifted her hands palms up. "Shall we pray? David, if you will." She clasped her hand onto Tyler's and held the other open toward Jackie as David, Tyler, and Sebastian joined hands.

Jackie struggled with the routine and placed her hands onto her lap. "Have we always held hands when we pray?"

"Well, of course." Margarette extended her hand to Jackie again.

Jackie acquiesced, grasped Margarette's hand and bowed her head.

"David, please pray." Margarette winked at him.

"Lord, thank you for this glorious day by bringing my wife and the mother of my children home to us. May you continue to bless this family and continue your healing hands upon Jackie. Bless this food and help it nourish our body. Amen."

"Amen." Margarette made the sign of the cross over her chest.

Jackie watched from the corner of her eye and mimicked the gesture.

Margarette looked at David. "Please pass me the noodles."

"With pleasure, Mom." He handed her the bowl.

Margarette used the spaghetti tongs and placed the noodles onto everyone's platter. In return, David covered them with the meat sauce.

Margarette sliced the noodles for Tyler as David cut Sebastian's into tiny pieces.

Jackie's face clouded with concern after she witnessed the fine-tuned routine to serve dinner to the boys. *They act married as I sit and do nothing.* "Tyler, blow on your food, it's hot."

"I don't have to listen to you, you're not my mommy."

Jackie remained speechless although she desired to scream and did on the inside.

David placed his hand onto Tyler's. "Son do not speak to your mother like that ever again. Do you understand me?"

"I understand." Tyler averted his eyes from his father's.

"Now eat your spaghetti."

Tyler reluctantly took a bite. "Yummy, it's good Grandma."

"Yum." Sebastian's adorable face grinned at Margarette.

David twirled the noodles onto his fork against a tablespoon and took a bite. "This is exactly how I remember it, the best in the world. You haven't made it since… in a while."

Jackie aimlessly stared at her food as a hint of nausea surfaced.

Margarette noticed her reaction. "Jackie, it's really good, try it."

"I'm sorry, I thought I could do this, but I can't. Nothing is right about any of this." Jackie in tears pushed her chair from the table and bolted up the stairs.

David dropped his fork onto his plate and shoved his chair back to follow.

"No David, give her time; don't force the issue. Enjoy your meal with the boys. They need you more than ever right now."

"I know you're right, but this is so difficult. I thought things would be better once she got home. What ever happened to happily ever after?"

"In my world I don't know of anyone who gets a happily ever after, but you have to believe she'll get better."

"I'm trying my best to stay strong."

"Good, it's important we do." She attempted to smile but pursed her lips instead. "Let's finish our dinner."

Tyler held up his empty cup. "Grandma, can I please have chocolate milk?"

"Sure, you're doing a fantastic job eating your spaghetti."

David shrugged in dismay with a forlorn frown. "You finish eating, I'll get it for him." David grabbed Tyler's glass and headed for the kitchen. "You mind if I take a ride after dinner? I need to clear my head. I won't be long."

"Not at all, I'll put the boys to bed. It might be better for Jackie that way. You know, to give her time and space to settle in."

David returned with Tyler's milk. "Who wants ice cream for dessert?"

"I do Daddy." Tyler grinned then sipped his milk.

"Me too."

Margarette heaved a sigh. "I'm sorry, with all the excitement of Jackie coming home I completely forgot to buy ice cream. Dishes first, then I'll go to the store." *I can't let anyone leave to go get ice cream ever again.* Her heart raced at the thought.

"You don't have to do that. I'll go and get stuff to make banana splits. Jackie loves banana splits, maybe she'll join us."

"Why don't you stay, and I'll get the stuff we need tomorrow?"

"I think it's important for us to start a happy memory and banana splits is the perfect opportunity. We have to start somewhere, don't we?"

"I'm all for that, but I'm not sure she'll be."

"Remember to stay strong; we have to keep trying."

∞

A light mist covered the windshield as David drove. Deep in thought, he pulled into Kelly's Irish Pub. His cell phone rang.

He pushed the green button on the navigation panel to accept the call.

"Margarette, everything okay?"

"Yes, yes. I noticed that we are almost out of milk. Can you pick that up too?"

"No problem, I just pulled up to the store now." His heart raced because he lied. "I won't be too long, anything else you can think of?"

"Just the milk."

Margarette placed the phone back into its cradle. "Okay boys, it's bath time." Margarette looked at the dishes. "They'll just have to wait."

"Can we take one with lots of bubbles?" Tyler hopped down from his chair. "Please, Grandma."

"Umm, let me think about it, yes." Margarette removed Sebastian from his booster chair and lowered him onto the floor.

"Yea, Bubba, we get to take a bubble bath." Tyler jumped again as Sebastian mimicked him.

The giggling boys ran up the stairs.

"Slow it down, be careful. Use the handrail so you don't fall." Margarette followed the boys although a little slower as pain took her breath for the moment. She stopped midway up the stairs, grasped the handrail and massaged her lower back.

The boys screamed once inside the bathroom which amplified down the hall.

Jackie exited her room. "What's going on out here?"

"It's the boy's bath time, would you like to help?"

"I guess, it is my job."

Once Jackie and Margarette entered the bathroom, Tyler threw a hissy fit stomping his feet. "No, I don't want her in here. She's not my mommy."

"Tyler Hennessey, she is your mother; watch your tongue."

"It's all right, Mom. He doesn't know me, I get it. Like Dr. Evangelista told me a thousand times, everything will take time to adjust. I can't expect children to welcome a stranger into their home. I'm sure I taught them about stranger danger."

"You remember that?"

"Not at all. It's what a parent does, right? I'm a stranger to them."

"You're not a stranger, you belong here."

"Let's face the facts; hell, I'm even a stranger to myself. It's better if you bathe them."

Jackie bolted down the stairs in tears. She stopped at the bottom, sat on the last stair and sobbed. The overwhelming pressure to become a person she no longer knew rested heavy on her heart. *I wish I would have died in that crash.* Every time she tried to gain composure, the laughter of the children in the upstairs bathroom brought another wave of emotion. *I can't do this, I want to run far away and never stop running.*

The front door opened which startled Jackie.

"I'm home with the ice cream."

Jackie wiped away her tears as she stood. Puzzlement creased her face. "Do I like ice cream?" A frown deepened in her brow.

"Well of course you do." David flashed a goofy grin. "Everybody likes ice cream and I'm making banana splits. So, let's eat ice cream and have fun. This family deserves it."

"I suppose you're right, it's now or never. I can't keep running away from my family, even if I don't remember them."

"Come on, let's make this happen." David headed for the kitchen.

Jackie took a deep long breath and ambled to the kitchen clearing her thoughts. *I can do this. I need to do this. He's right. Who doesn't like ice cream?*

Jackie observed David as he unpacked the small number of groceries. "So, you're making banana splits? What are those?"

"Bananas, three different ice cream flavors, whipped cream, and chocolate syrup. Oh, and sprinkles. Banana splits are your favorite.

Jackie's eyes darted; she clenched her fists. "Don't start with me on that. You don't know me anymore. Just like I don't know about this place or this family." Her eyes swelled with tears again.

"We'll just have to start all over and make new memories."

"This feels strange. Even over the last few months I've never felt any kind of connection with you or to my mom. I can't explain it."

"I can't imagine how you feel and wouldn't dare pretend that I do. That would be unfair to you. Just know that we love you."

"You've been kind, and I don't want to hurt your feelings, but…"

"…But what?"

"I can't do this, I don't belong here." She avoided his gaze and stared at the floor.

David placed his hand on Jackie's shoulder.

She recoiled. *Don't touch me.*

He crossed his arms over his chest, took a deep breath and stepped backward to give her the space she needed. "Jackie, you belong here. You're a part of this family and we've been together for almost ten years now. Last week was our eight-year anniversary. We've shared dozens of holidays, laughs and tender memories together. Look around, we've created a beautiful family and this home together. You and me, we did this; all of this."

She cringed as her skin prickled. *That means I had sex with that man.* The act of intertwining with a stranger brewed disgust in the pit of her stomach. Her jaw tensed; her eyes squinted. She shivered.

David noticed the awkward and bent expression on her face. "Jackie, did you hear what I said?"

"To be blunt and direct I'm concerned about the sleeping arrangements for tonight."

"No worries, we sleep in our bedroom."

Her eyes widened in fear. "Not tonight, it's too soon. I'll sleep on the couch as soon as the boys go to sleep."

"No, I'll sleep on the couch, I insist. We'll work our way up to sharing the same bed. I love you too much to lose you and I won't put any pressure on you. I promise you that."

Jackie sighed as if the weight of the world lifted from her shoulders.

∞

Sunrise didn't come soon enough for David as the couch had proven incredibly uncomfortable. He rejoiced at the sunbeams which peeped through the curtains as he yawned, rose and then stretched. He glanced at his wrinkled clothes and puckered his lips. After he tiptoed to the kitchen, he pulled a sticky notepad and an ink pen from the junk drawer, wrote a message, and then stuck it onto the coffee maker. *Where did I put my keys?* He picked up his keys from the dining table, tiptoed to the front and exited.

Just as he closed the door, Sebastian cried. Tyler stood at the top of the stairs. "Grandma, Daddy, Daddy, where are you?" Tyler ran down the stairs.

The back door opened.

"Grandma, Bubba is crying."

"I heard him on the baby monitor. You're such a good big brother."

The floor upstairs creaked as footsteps headed for the nursery. Sebastian screamed louder.

"I'd better go help your Daddy."

"Daddy isn't here."

"What do you mean Daddy isn't here?"

"He left."

That's strange, he didn't even make coffee. Margarette, saw the note stuck onto the coffee maker and read it to herself. *I've gone to work early. Call me if you need anything. Love David.*

"Grandma." Tyler hugged Margarette around her legs. She bent and kissed him on his cheek.

Sebastian cried louder.

"I better go help your mother."

"She's not my mommy, I don't want her here."

I haven't even had a drop of coffee. Margarette headed for the stairs.

∞

David sat at his desk signing documents.

Higgins entered with a concerned frown across his brow. "Shouldn't you be home with Jackie?"

"No, your mom is with her. I want our lives back to normal as quickly as possible. Dr. Evangelista said we needed to establish our routine, and the way I see it, me going to work is my routine."

"How was her first night home?"

"I'll leave it at this. Not so good and I don't want to discuss it; so, if you plan on asking me again, leave. Otherwise, let's discuss the progress on the Japanese cargo ship."

"Do you think things will ever be the same again?"

"Didn't I tell you I didn't want to talk about it?"

"Well, you did, but you have to believe things will return to some sort of normalcy."

"If I can't believe in that, what can I believe?"

"I don't know. I'm still having trouble trying to grasp the concept she can't remember any of us. It seems impossible. For

Pete's sake, she's my baby sister and I've known her all of her life. Hell, I changed her diapers and stood up for her when her classmates bullied her in school. When do you think she learned to love to run? She wouldn't even allow me to visit her in the hospital and I have a feeling she won't let me visit her at home either for an awfully long time."

"It's probably for the best. The boys are having a tough time. Basically, Tyler is rejecting her as his mother. Sebastian cries if she gets near him and she doesn't want to be there. She'd rather be back in the hospital rehabilitation center; that's where she considers home because that is where her memories are, her friends too and the staff she considers her family. Now, all of that is gone, and she feels like she has to start over in a strange home with strangers. Things seem impossible for any normalcy right now."

"The Higgin's philosophy is to dream the impossible for the possible. How do you think the PT Boat came into being and we won the war? It wasn't by the old man sitting on his ass and giving up. If he had, Germany might be in charge of America today. He set the example of finding an answer to solve the current situation. That's what this company is about and that's what the Higgins are about."

"You're right."

"I'll let you get back to work. I said my piece." Higgins closed the door behind him.

All right then, let's find a miracle. I'll do it the Higgins way. David began a search on the internet. He tapped onto the keyboard. "A... M... N... E... S... I... A."

He pressed the enter key, scrolled down through the search results and clicked on a website for the Health and Wellness Institute of America. He mumbled the findings. "Hypnosis. Regression hypnosis is used for a variety of reasons. Hypnotism can be a remarkably effective means to assist patients suffering from amnesia to regain memories with ease from the subconscious that have been forgotten." *I may have just found the possible for the impossible. Thank you, Andrew Higgins.*

He picked up the phone and dialed. The phone rang three times.

"You've reached the Health and Wellness Institute. I'm Jamie, how may I help you today?"

"Thank you for taking my call. I'm trying to locate a regression hypnotherapist in New Orleans, Louisiana and was wondering if you could refer me to one who is certified by your institute."

"Please hold as I locate a referral."

Elevator music played. He pressed the speakerphone and continued to work. "Really, this song?" The orchestration of the song *I Left my Heart in San Francisco* reminded him of his honeymoon. *Jackie loved the wine country.* His mind transgressed to a happier time.

∞

David drove the rental silver convertible Sebring along the winding roads in Napa Valley. A huge-honeymoon grin beamed from David as the wind blew his hair. "I can't wait to get to Cakebread Cellars."

"Me too, what a perfect-way to start our marriage. I love you, David."

"I had to plan it. Cakebread Chardonnay is our favorite wine. Do you remember when you first tasted it?"

"How could I ever forget that? You proposed while we shared a bottle at Commander's Palace. It became my favorite."

"Does this mean you're passing on Boons Farm Strawberry Wine?"

Jackie giggled with a broad-toothed smile. "I can't wait to see what our children will look like."

"Children?" He longingly glanced her way. "A boy for you and a girl for me, right?"

"We'll leave that up to the Lord."

"You're right, God's hands are in everything."

The song I Left my Heart in San Francisco *started. David bobbed his head to the music. "My heart will always be wherever you are."*

"For richer or poorer?"

"In sickness and in health."

"Until death do us part."

"Exactly, I take our marriage vows very seriously."

∞

"Sir, thank you for holding. I have a referral for you. His name is Dr. Michael Grayson."

The voice jolted David from his daydream. "Fantastic."

"Are you ready to take down his number?"

"Yes Ma'am, I have pen and paper in hand."

"Dr. Grayson's number is five zero four, five five five, nine three two, four."

"Thank you so much." David disconnected the call. Somewhat relieved, he hesitantly dialed the number.

"You've reached Dr. Grayson."

"Thank you for accepting my call. I'd like to discuss the benefits of hypnosis for an amnesia patient."

"Are you the patient?"

"I'm inquiring on the behalf of my wife, Jackie Hennessey."

"Jackie Hennessey, that name sounds familiar."

"She's the school teacher who was on a field trip last year when the bus crashed and killed the driver. She suffers from retrograde amnesia."

"I heard about her release on the news yesterday. It's been a difficult year for you both."

"That's an understatement." David heaved a sigh. "Do you think you can help her?"

"I've had immense success with patients with traumatic brain injury. I have an appointment available this Friday at eleven if you're interested."

"Definitely interested, that will give me time to break the news to her."

"So, this is your idea?"

"Yes, sir. Nothing the neurologist has done has worked. About the only thing she remembers is her name and I think that's because we call her that. She has no memory other than the last eight months after waking up from a four-month induced coma. Dr. Evangelista told me she may never recover her memories or could one day wake up and remember everything."

"The method I use is a gentle approach to retrieve memories from the subconscious. I'll guide her into her past allowing her to reveal locked away memories. The success rate I've seen has been positive with about only one in four not being able to recover past eighty percent recollection. I won't know more until I get her under hypnosis and discover how well she responds to the sessions."

"Well at this rate I'm willing to try just about anything."

"That's wonderful Mr. Hennessey. I'll see you both this Friday."

∞

Margarette fed Sebastian his dinner as Tyler played on the floor in front of Jackie who sat on the couch.

"Mom, thank you for being here for us."

"I wouldn't have it any other way."

"I don't know how David and the kids would have gotten through this last year without you."

"My concern sweetheart is for you, I'll be here as long as you and the boys need me."

"A part of me wants to run and never stop running."

"Where would you run to?"

"Away from my problems."

"There's no such thing as running from your problems. You must face them head-on. Once you start, you can never stop running."

"Any truth to that?"

"Absolutely there is, or I wouldn't have said it. You're a strong woman Jackie; a Higgins woman. Your memories will come back. I have faith in God and his power to heal. All things in divine order."

"I don't remember my wedding day, my honeymoon or the birth of my children. I don't even remember Daddy." A flash of a familiar man's face jetted across her mind. "Wait, I remembered I had a dad. Where is he?"

"He passed away years ago."

"What happened?"

"I'll explain it one day when you're ready. Dr. Evangelista said for now to talk about happy times until you get your memory back. Just know you were the love of his life." Margarette's heart-felt eyes flushed.

"Are you okay?"

"I'm fine, no pity parties here Jacqueline Adel Hennessey."

Margarette wiped Sebastian's face and removed him from his high chair. She brought him to the front of the couch and placed him beside Tyler. She opened the cabinet beneath the television and pulled out a DVD. "Let's get reacquainted, shall we? It's your wedding day; a joyful day for everyone. We'll watch it and keep watching until you remember everything. And, you'll make new memories for you and your family before you know it."

Jackie grinned. "I think I'd like that, at least it'll be a start."

Margarette began the DVD and sat down on the couch beside Jackie.

"You were the most beautiful bride, look how radiant you were."

"So that's how I looked without this hideous scar across my face?"

"Jackie, you're still beautiful and always will be."

"I'm not so sure about that. No matter what I do that scar is a constant reminder of someone I don't even know."

"Then let it remind you that you survived and allow it to stand for something. Consider it your Higgins war wound."

"How exactly are we related to Andrew Higgins?"

"Well, it's a long story, but to make it short, he's a distant cousin."

"The way you talk about him, I'd think you were his daughter or niece."

"Anyone who has Higgins blood running through their veins takes pride in the fact. Even President Eisenhower credited him for single-handedly winning the war."

"He single-handedly won a war? I find that difficult to believe."

"The PT boat was only one of his many patents and inventions. He was a brilliant man. Take pride that you're related."

"If you say so."

"Enough war talk, now watch your wedding."

Jackie stared at the television. "We had a beach wedding? Where?"

"Orange Beach, Alabama, just at sunset."

Jackie ogled the video. "Is that Daddy walking me to the altar?"

"No, that's your brother Higgins, remember? He came to the hospital a few times and you wouldn't see him, but that's not important right now. That's where Tyler gets his looks. They both look like your father."

"If you say so."

David entered the front door. "I'm home."

Both children hopped from the couch and ran to him. "Daddy."

"Hello, boys, did you have a good day with Mommy?" He crouched to embrace their hugs.

"No." Tyler stomped his foot and delivered a pouted lip.

By the expression on Jackie's face, clearly Tyler's behavior impacted her mood. "How was your day?"

"Very productive." David sat on one of the living room chairs as their wedding ceremony continued to play.

"I David, take thee Jacqueline Adel Manafort, to be my lawfully wedded wife. To love, honor, and cherish, for better or worse, in sickness and in health, until death do us part."

He gazed into Jackie's tormented eyes with pure adoration and love. "I mean it more right now than I did eight years ago. I love you with all of my heart."

"Okay, you two lovebirds." Margarette puckered her lips as she stood. "I think me, and the kids will go for a walk on that hint. Come on boys." She carried Sebastian on her hip, held Tyler's hand and escorted him out the side door.

"Alone at last."

Jackie cringed. *I don't want to be alone with him.* "Don't you love my mother?"

"I do, but I have something important to talk about." David grabbed the remote from the side table and powered off the television.

"This looks and sounds serious."

"It is, it's about you. Well, not about you, it's about Dr. Grayson and what he can do for you."

"I don't remember having a doctor by that name."

"You haven't, that is until today. Let me explain, Dr. Grayson is a hypnotherapist. I scheduled you an appointment for this Friday."

"A hypnotherapist?"

"Yes, he uses a technique that puts you into a state of mind that allows you to recover your memories. I've researched him and his work. He has had a high success rate with his patients recovering their memories after incidents like yours. I thought maybe we could try, it may help."

"Have you ever done it before?"

"No, I haven't. I just... I just want to help. I've missed us and who we used to be." He grasped her hand.

His hand felt awkward and unnatural against Jackie's. She jerked hers away as tears swelled; her heart ached from not being able to remember her life, much less his touch. The strangeness became unbearable. After a long moment of silence and time to reflect, she took a deep breath. "Okay, I'll do it. Will you go with me?"

"Are you kidding? You don't even need to ask, I've always been here for you."

A single tear trickled down Jackie's distraught face. She wiped it and hoped David didn't catch a glimpse of it.

"What's wrong now?"

"I wish I could remember the birth of my sons."

"You will, I promise."

Jackie stood and glared at David. "You can't promise me that, no one can. My memories are lost forever." She stormed from the room and stomped up the stairs.

A door slammed.

David scratched his head. *I can't win for losing. If I didn't have bad luck, I wouldn't have any luck at all.*

6. HIGHER GROUND

The white SUV turned onto Frenchman Street in the Marigny District of New Orleans. Just a few blocks down it stopped in front of a three-story historic home full of the architectural charm the area offered. The white paint exterior blistered by the sun peeled away which exposed the aged gray wood beneath it.

Jackie nervously blew air between her lips. "Interesting choice of colors, what color would you say that is?"

"Okay, next time you should work with Sebastian when he is learning colors."

Jackie didn't find his comment amusing by the frown that crossed her lips. "Like my therapist advised, I'm going to just let that bounce."

"Sorry, I didn't mean it that way; I meant it as a joke."

Her eyes darted toward his as she twisted her lips. "Now back to the color of the house."

"The house is antique white, and the shutters are lime green."

"Lime green, you don't say. At least the sign looks authentic from what I can tell." Jackie took a deep breath. "Are you sure about this?"

"Well, it can't hurt, it can only help."

"But does it work?"

"Everything I researched says hypnosis works in eighty percent of the amnesia patients to recover memories they have long forgotten, that sounds like you."

"I don't want false hope."

"You have nothing to lose and a lot of memories to gain, let's do this."

Jackie nodded in agreement. She nervously interlaced her fingers together.

"Stay put, let me open the car door for you like a proper gentleman."

"Whatever." Jackie rolled her eyes as David exited the car.

As he walked to the passenger's side his palms turned clammy and his heart rate increased. *This has got to work.* He opened the car door and Jackie stepped out.

David's eyes expressed hope. "Are you ready for this?"

"How am I supposed to know? I haven't been ready for anything since I woke up from that damn coma."

"I guess you got me there. Just for the record, you got this. Remember, you're a Higgins."

"Now that's something you and my mom won't let me forget."

"See what I'm talking about, you already remember things and Dr. Grayson hasn't even begun."

"Get real, David."

David and Jackie stepped onto the porch and David nervously pressed the doorbell button. The bell chimed a beautiful eight note ascending tune.

Within a minute, Dr. Grayson, a middle-aged African American man, answered. "Welcome, you must be David and Jackie Hennessey, I'm Dr. Grayson."

"Thank you for seeing my wife on such short notice."

"I'm glad I had a last-minute cancellation for you. Shall we?"

Dr. Grayson led the way through the foyer and into the parlor. The elegant room reflected the New Orleans culture. The two ceiling fans above whirled providing a cool breeze. Black-framed newspaper articles which covered him and his accomplishments on hypnosis regression plastered the north wall. A series of autographed official Mardi Gras posters and memorabilia from several Zula parades covered the south wall.

The velvet burgundy curtains hid the worn wallpaper which gave a peek at the red brick beneath it. The dingy floral velvet chaise lounge in the corner caused Jackie to shiver when she glanced at it. She quickly averted her eyes. *I bet Dr. Grayson identified lots of memories on that ugly thing.*

Next to it, an elegant Queen Victoria royal blue velvet chair awaited the master regression hypnotherapist. Two additional striped burgundy, hunter green and blue antique chairs separated the area from the dining room.

Dr. Grayson graciously extended his trembling hand toward the striped chairs. "Please, make yourselves comfortable. Let's get to know each other a little."

Mrs. Grayson, an older distinguished African American woman entered carrying a black lacquer tray with lemonade and finger sandwiches.

"This is my wife, Carla. Honey, this is David and Jackie Hennessey."

Mrs. Grayson placed the tray onto the coffee table. "It's a pleasure to have you both in our home." She nodded and creased her brow as she gazed at Jackie. "I've already dreamed about you Mrs. Hennessey. If you trust in yourself and free your thoughts of your fears, many memories are sure to resurface." She nodded a grinned at Jackie. "I'll leave you in the care of my husband."

Puzzlement overwhelmed Jackie as Mrs. Grayson exited.

After David recognized Jackie's discomfort, he at once changed the subject. "You have a beautiful wife Dr. Grayson."

Dr. Grayson ignored the compliment. "I'll address this to Mrs. Hennessey; may I call you Jackie?"

"Of course."

"Very well, Jackie. Do you know what I do here?"

"You're a hypnotist."

"I'm a certified hypnotherapist who specializes in regression. Have you ever undergone hypnosis before?"

Jackie shook her head to indicate her negative response. *How am I supposed to know?*

"It's not a magic eight ball; it requires your total trust and relaxation. You will be in control at all times."

David adjusted his sitting position. "You won't make her do crazy things on command or bark like a dog, will you?"

"I'm not a sideshow Mr. Hennessey. Everything I do is professional, beyond reproach and I videotape each session for my clients. Jackie will receive the tape before she leaves today."

"That's a comforting thought, I can't wait to watch what happens."

Apprehension filled Jackie as she tensed her body. "Only if I agree to it." Jackie's tone, uncompromising, indicated to the others she felt invaded and vulnerable.

"Mr. Hennessey, it's best for you not to be here to achieve the best results for your wife. Family members are a distraction."

David cleared his throat. "I'm not sure what to think about that."

"Can he be in the next room?" Jackie's spine tingled with nerves.

"You'll see that won't be necessary. You'll be aware of what is transpiring and have complete control at all times. It's perfectly safe and you have nothing to worry about."

"I'd feel better if he'd stay at least during the first one."

"Do you want progress or not?"

Jackie glanced at David with a discerning expression.

"Jackie, it'll be okay. He comes recommended and is a very well-known hypnotherapist." He didn't know if his words comforted her because they failed to provide comfort for himself. "Jackie, this is a chance for you to get your memory back which is why you agreed to this in the first place."

"If you think so."

An assuring grin tinted David's upper lip as he gave her a wink. "All right, I'll leave y'all to it. Just call me when you're finished, I won't be far." David exited the room, chock-filled with apprehension and uncertainty.

Dr. Grayson lifted his brow. "Jackie, are you ready to begin?"

"How long will it last?"

"Between two to three hours; it depends on you and where you want to go."

"I don't understand."

"I use a timeline guided approach. You have total freedom to go wherever your subconscious allows, I'm the guide."

"Like a tour guide?"

"In a sense, I suppose. Think of it as if you stood at the end of an exceptionally large hall with dozens of doors on each side. Behind each door there is a memory waiting to resurface. You enter the door of your choice." Dr. Grayson stood and tugged at his shirt in a dignified manner. "Please lay on the chaise and get comfortable. Feel free to remove your shoes if you like."

Jackie ambled unassured to the chaise and eased onto it as Dr. Grayson strode to the bookcase and started a CD. The song *Higher Ground* by Steven Halpern began. He adjusted the volume to a lower level, then sat in the royal blue velvet chair next to Jackie.

Mrs. Grayson entered carrying a camcorder attached to a tripod, placed it in a strategic spot to the side of her husband and directed the lens toward Jackie. She handed him the palm-size remote control.

"Anyone else going to see this tape?" Jackie's nerves flared as her throat pinched.

"Only if you allow them the opportunity to view them. I'll give you the original tape. You won't know the camera is there. So, just lay back and relax."

"I know it's there right now. It's kinda nerve racking." Jackie's stomach squeamishly churned as she swallowed. Her forehead knitted in confusion.

"Just relax Jackie. Most people find comfort to know each session is recorded, especially the husbands or wives who are sent away."

"I can understand that, this just seems unnatural."

"Again, please stretch and get comfortable. You can even sit if you feel more relaxed that way."

"I think I'd prefer to lay down." Jackie adjusted the pillow behind her head and settled herself into a horizontal position. She nervously took a deep breath. "What happens if I'm not able to be hypnotized?" A dreadful fear gripped her heart.

"That does happen on occasion, but I assure you more than ninety percent of my patients don't have a problem if they simply relax and listen to my voice. The idea is to allow yourself the opportunity and not to force the situation."

Jackie bit her lower lip and nodded.

"Are you ready?"

"I think so." Her voice quivered as she inhaled, then she forced air through her lips which created a puttered-rippled sound.

"Now just relax and breathe slowly." His tone melodious and steady calmed her nerves. "Stare at the ceiling and listen to the sound of my voice as the music carries you away. Breathe in and hold... And breathe out... And hold."

"Should I close my eyes?"

"Only when you feel ready, don't force anything. Allow yourself the freedom of relaxation. Clear your mind and listen to my voice."

"Okay, let's do this." She wiggled to gain maximum comfort and took a deep breath. Her heavy mascaraed eyelashes fluttered. She shook her hands and guided them onto her stomach. *I'm not so sure about this. This isn't going to work.*

"With each breath, feel the tension leave your body. We'll take our time. Just listen to the sound of my voice as you slowly breathe in through your nose... Hold... Breathe out even more slowly." With each word he lowered his volume and pitch.

Jackie nodded her head and gently pushed a long-extended exhale.

"Take a deep breath in, and as you let it out feel the tension start to leave your body... Breathe in... Hold. Breathe out... All tension is leaving you."

Jackie's chest rose with each breath inhaled and flattened upon exhale. She rubbed her neck and adjusted her position.

"You're doing great Jackie... I'm going to count backwards from ten to one, and with each count you will go deeper and deeper into a restful state of mind. You will be aware of everything around you. Any noise or sound won't disturb you. The sound of the ceiling fan calms you and the music allows you to float anywhere you want to go. Cars that pass, you won't care about them as they are a part of life and your environment. The birds singing, sing to you. Breathe in... And out."

Jackie's breath slowed as she sank into the chaise. She adjusted her position once again. She drew in a long deep breath.

"Ten. Focusing on your lower body, feel the tension leave your feet... Breathe in and out and release the tension in your calves... now your legs."

With each countdown, Jackie relaxed. Her eyes felt heavy and her breath became shallow.

"Nine, allow your tension to escape and now relax your hips."

Jackie inhaled again followed by a long exhale.

"Eight, you are now sinking heavier into the couch."

Jackie blinked, and her head fell forward. For the first time since waking up from the coma tension eluded her, and she wanted to close her heavy eyelids.

"Seven. Your belly becomes soft and supple. All tension in your lower body is gone. Feel how relaxed you are as if you are floating on a cloud with total freedom... Six, you are lighter than a feather... All your worries are gone as you listen to the sound of my voice... Concentrate on your upper body. Notice how relaxed you are... Five, all tension is gone from your chest. You're doing great. Four, release the tension in your shoulders. Pay particular attention to how good it feels to be free of tension and free of worry. Breathe in... Breathe out... Three, your jaw becomes heavy... your facial muscles relax... your eyes feel heavy as you sink deeper into the chaise; they can't stay open... Two, you want to close your eyes... One, sleep."

Jackie's eyes shut. A deep meditative trance encapsulated her.

"Where are you Jackie?"

"I'm not sure."

"Are you inside or outside?"

Beneath Jackie's eyelids her eyes darted as if she looked for something. "I'm inside."

"Where inside?"

"A house."

"Describe the house."

"It's an old house. Yes, an incredibly old house."

"Is it your house?"

"No, it's my parents."

"Are they there?"

"My dad is. We're in the living room. He's holding my present."

"That's wonderful, what does the present look like?"

"A small box with a pink bow."

"How old are you?"

"I think six."

"Who else is there? Describe what you see."

∞

The smell from baking lingered in the air as Margarette placed the fifth pink candle onto the top of the birthday cake. "Jackie!" She eased a two-inch pink number six candle strategically onto the center of the cake. "Charles, Higgins, let's get to the table. It's time to sing Happy Birthday to Jackie so we can cut the cake and open presents."

In the living room, Jackie, age six, jumped up and down with delight in front of her father who sat in his overstuffed recliner. An adorable-huge smile crossed her face as her dad rose, took her by the hand and led her into the dining room. "Come on sweetheart, I can't wait for you to see what I got you for your birthday."

"Daddy, I love you."

Higgins, age fifteen, bolted down the stairs into the dining room where he met Jackie and her dad and sat down. Margarette entered carrying the birthday cake with the lit candles and placed it onto the table in front of Jackie. Everyone in the room sang as Jackie's eyes sparkled in the candlelight. "*Happy birthday to you, happy birthday to you, happy birthday dear Jackie, happy birthday to you.*"

Margarette grinned as she clapped. "*Make a wish and blow out the candles.*"

Jackie closed her eyes. I wish I could have a thousand birthdays. *She took a deep breath and blew out the candles. The candle's smoke filled the air.*

"*I hate the way candles smell after being blown out.*" *Margarette's nose tilted upward.* "*It sucks the good smell from baking right out of the air.*"

Higgins glanced at his sister. "*What did you wish for?*"

Jackie's dad gave Higgins the evil eye. "*Higgins, she can't tell you that or her wish won't come true.*"

"*Daddy, Daddy, Mommy forgot the ice cream.*"

"*It's all okay sweetheart, I'll be back in a jiffy. We can't have you eat your birthday cake without ice cream, now can we?*"

∞

Jackie took a deep breath as a frown developed on her forehead and an uneasiness rifled throughout her body. "That was the last time I saw my father." She swallowed hard; her voice quivered.

"How does this make you feel?"

"Sad and depressed. I didn't get to tell him goodbye." A tear rolled down Jackie's cheek.

"You're doing fine Jackie, take a deep breath. Focus on the fact that you're not there. What you are seeing is an event you are remembering. Do you want to talk more about your father?"

"No, it's too painful." Jackie whimpered with deep-boned distraught. "It's my fault."

"What would you like to tell him if he were here right now?"

"That I love him and I'm sorry."

"Tell him now, tell him what you always wanted to say."

"Daddy, I'm sorry for being a brat. I wish I never wanted that ice cream. You wouldn't have died in that car wreck. It's all my fault." Jackie whimpered.

"Everything is fine Jackie, it wasn't your fault."

"That's not right, I was the one who insisted on the ice cream. He wouldn't have been in that car and the drunk driver wouldn't have crashed into him."

"Jackie, you can make atonement for this and forgive yourself. What can you do to make up for this?"

"Tell my brother and mother I'm sorry and ask for their forgiveness."

"That's wonderful Jackie, but you also must forgive yourself. Forgive yourself now."

"I do." She sighed.

"That's good Jackie. Let's go somewhere else. I want you to remember the morning of your bus accident. Where are you?"

Jackie's eyes darted. A slight pause incurred before she spoke. "I'm at home with David and the boys."

"What are you doing?"

"I'm in bed with him, we don't want to get up."

"Why don't you want to get up?"

"It's a workday. We would rather take the boys to the park. Anything, but go to work."

"Do you sleep in?"

"No, we get up. David wants to have sex, I didn't."

Jackie in a hypnotic trance inhaled.

"That's good Jackie. Relax. Embrace it. What happens next?"

"My mom came to the house to take care of the boys."

"Where are the children?"

"In bed."

"Tell me what you see and hear."

∞

David's suit, shirt, tie, and socks lay on the bed.

Jackie exited the master bedroom's bathroom and headed to her closet. She looked through her clothes and grabbed a floral dress and held it up to her chest. "No, not this one today. I wore it last week." After she returned the dress, she grabbed a pair of black slacks and a royal blue blouse.

David gleefully entered. "Your mother is special."

"I know, you tell me every day."

"You're pretty special too." David embraced Jackie from behind and gave her a soft kiss on her neck. "How late are you this morning?"

Jackie turned slowly wrapping her arms around his neck and looked him straight into the eye. "You know how much I love you, right?"

"Forever and a day." His warm breath fanned her skin. "Do we. . ."

". . . I'm late to work my dear. Your needs will just have to wait."

"Not even a quickie?"

"Let me see." She glanced at her wristwatch. "Nope, sorry love. I have twenty-one kids waiting for me at school." Jackie delivered a peck onto his cheek. She hurriedly dressed and slipped her feet into a pair of black pumps.

"Lucky kids." He gazed at her; a broad grin covered his face. "Let me know in a few seconds if you change your mind."

"It won't happen. Leave it alone and get dressed before you're late."

He gently grabbed her hand, twirled her, pulled her in close to him and planted a passionate kiss onto her lips. She tightly embraced him and seemed to melt in his arms. A warm tingle rose throughout her body.

"That was nice David. Now I wish we had time for a quickie."

"Oh, but your students await you." He chuckled.

"Don't rub it in, but tonight after the boys are tucked in and asleep, it's going to be a different story; and it won't be just a quickie."

"I like the way you think. You know I love you."

"I love you too and always will."

∞

"He really is my husband." Jackie's brow lifted, and she frowned.

Dr. Grayson nodded his head. "Relax Jackie. You are doing great. Take a deep breath. Now I want you to go somewhere else. Look around and focus on opening another door in your life."

Her head nodded as her eyes darted behind her eyelids.

"Do you see another door?"

"Yes."

"Okay, open the door and enter. What do you see?"

"Everyone is running. It is chaotic."

"Are you running too?"

"Yes, everyone is scared?"

"Why are they running Jackie?"

∞

The year 79 A.D., the fifth of August Mount Vesuvius spewed tons of molten ash, pumice and sulfuric gas creating a firestorm of poisonous vapors. Retina grasped Cornelius' hand as they bolted away from the volcano heading away from the center of Pompeii toward the harbor.

Retina eyes burned from the vapors and she gasped for air. "I can't run anymore. The ashes are suffocating me."

"We must gain passage on a boat to escape. Keep running." Cornelius pulled Retina as they pushed through the crowd; the ground rumbled beneath their feet.

The buildings shook violently as a black cloud of smoke engulfed the city.

Retina gazed back at the volcano and bewailed her fate. "Cornelius, I beg for you to take my life. I do not want to die this way."

∞

Jackie whimpered as her brow scowled. "Please, I don't want to die this way."

"It's all right Jackie. Breathe slowly."

7. BRIDGE OVER TROUBLED WATER

Margarette and Jackie wore vintage aprons while they chopped vegetables and prepared the family's evening meal.

"Jackie, your father's mother made the apron you have on."

"That would be my grandmother."

"The one I'm wearing belonged to my grandmother on my mother's side."

"Unbelievable things this old could last this long."

"They don't make things like they used to back then. That's why your Aunt Susie owns an antique store in Bay St. Louis, Mississippi."

"Our family came from Mississippi and not Louisiana?"

"Not at all. Aunt Susie married a man from Bay St. Louis and that's where they chose to live and raise their family."

"Makes perfect sense. Now tell me about this antique shop."

90

"The name is Family Tree Antiques and Treasures. She has a variety of items."

"What kind?"

"The usual. Furniture, tea sets, china from Occupied Japan, collectibles from a company called Ivory Dynasty, depression ware and marbles. Lots of antique marbles."

"Antique marbles? Well, unlike me, it doesn't sound like Aunt Susie has lost her marbles." She giggled. "Let's go visit. It might do me some good to get out and do something different other than rehab or therapy."

"Sounds wonderful, let's go tomorrow."

"I think that would make David mad. I'm supposed to see Dr. Grayson again. To tell you the truth, I don't want to go."

"I thought you remembered things from your past."

"That's an understatement." Jackie mumbled beneath her breath as she shivered.

"Before I die, are you ever going to tell me what you remembered?"

"It's not important, Mom."

"It is to me."

David entered from the side door and interrupted the conversation to Jackie's relief. "Well ladies, I have good news and bad news. Which one do you want first?"

Jackie shrugged; her eyes darted between the other two. "I'm tired of bad news, go for the good."

"The good news is the tomatoes are free of worms and look healthy."

"Okay." Margarette apprehensively nodded. "Give us the bad news."

"They're not ripe, yet."

"Now that's the kind of bad news I like to hear." A relieved-smile glimmered across Jackie's face.

Margarette waved her index finger upward. "Hold on. Ever heard of fried green tomatoes? They'd be wonderful with this meal."

"Not with my green tomatoes, I hate them fried."

A thud from upstairs and the wooden floor creaking caused all three to glance upward.

David headed for the stairs. "Sounds like Tyler is up from his nap. You both have your hands full, I'll get him."

Margarette wiped her hands on her apron. "You may as well wake up Sebastian or he won't sleep tonight."

"Mom, I was going to tell him that, I am their mother." A frown crossed Jackie's brow, and she tightened her jaw.

"I was only trying to help."

The doorbell rang which caused Margarette to glance toward Jackie; her brow tightened. "You want to get that, or should I? I wouldn't want to overstep my bounds again."

"I'm expecting Beth. She asked if she could drop by with more letters from my former students." Jackie left the kitchen in a huff as she wiped her hands on her apron.

By the time Jackie arrived at the door, David, who held Sebastian, already answered it. "Come on in, it's good to see you again."

"Thank you, David." Beth winked at Jackie. "How did church go?"

"We didn't go, he needed the rest." Jackie blamed David to avoid embarrassment. "Come on in, we'll go out back, sit by the pool and you can tell me about my life as a teacher."

They made their way into the living area as Margarette washed dishes. "Hello Beth, how have you been?"

"Fair to Midland."

Jackie took a quick breath as her mouth formed a complete 'O.' "Wait, I remember that; or, at least I think I do."

Margarette nodded relieved. "Like I said, your making progress with your regression therapy."

"Regression therapy?" Beth, surprised, shook her head and widened her eyes.

Jackie motioned her head toward the back door. She removed the apron and placed it onto the countertop as she passed. "Let's go talk outside."

∞

Attendees packed The Pontchartrain Convention Center and listened with bated-breath to the interview held by the Institute of Bjorn Hypnotherapy between Dr. Bryan Reiss, Caucasian late sixties, author of *One Man's Journey into the Past to Face the Future* and Opal Stedman, celebrity talk show host. "Dr. Reiss, how does a past experience help a present one?"

Dr. Grayson and his wife sat on the front row. He glanced sideways at Carla as he leaned toward her. "Now you know why I consider him the best in the field."

"I know, you've told me a hundred times."

"I have another surprise, we're meeting him after the lecture and going to dinner."

"How did you arrange that?"

"Remember, I trained under him?"

"Shhh, I'm trying to listen."

"How is it Dr. Reiss you could help this woman with her fear of bridges using regression hypnotherapy?"

"During one of her sessions, she recalled one of her past lives where she died after falling off a bridge."

"That almost seems impossible."

"Seems is the operative word. When someone experiences a past life during a regression session, they see it as if they were there or it plays in their mind as if watching a movie."

"That doesn't answer my question. How does a past experience help a present one?"

"In Erin's case, anytime she drives over a bridge, she has a panic attack; so, we worked on that. Sometimes knowing the cause of the fear from our past allows us to face our fear in the present."

"What did she say to make you believe it was something that happened in a past life?"

"First she told me her name was Estrild. While in a trance meditative state, she informed me she fell off a stone bridge called *Pons Fabricius* that was across the Tiber River. I asked how she got there, and she told me she walked."

The audience laughed.

Dr. Reiss smiled and then licked his lips. "Her answer may sound funny to everyone, but in this context, it isn't. I asked her before she walked over the bridge how she arrived to it; her reply astounded me. She proceeded to inform me she stood in a chariot pulled by a horse. Then she paused and told me cars hadn't been invented yet."

"A chariot?"

"According to her, she was on her way to the market when the chariot came up behind her and stopped. The driver offered her a ride, and she took him up on his offer as her legs ached from the distance she had already walked. When the road came to a split, he had to go the other way and dropped her off."

"Do you know if there is a *Pons Fabricius* bridge?"

"Indeed, I looked it up after our session and discovered that this bridge was built somewhere in sixty-two B.C. and is the oldest bridge in the world that still exists today."

"Couldn't she have learned about the bridge and made up the entire story?"

"I suppose she could have, but she also told me a strange fact that wasn't discovered until two thousand eighteen. And, remember, this regression session happened in nineteen eighty-nine before the internet was developed and we could sit and Google everything."

"What did she say?"

"She told me it was March fifth, twelve twenty-three, and she was watching the solar eclipse. She wanted a higher vantage point, so she could be closer to the marvel; so, she stood on top of the walled rock structure, slipped and fell into the Tiger River. Unable to swim, she drowned. Now this is where it gets interesting. In nineteen forty-eight, scientists discovered a tablet among the ruins of the ancient city of Ugarit in what is now Syria. It contained the description of a total solar eclipse that occurred on May third, thirteen seventy-five B.C. That's over one hundred, and fifty years difference between twelve twenty-three and thirteen seventy-five. That's substantial don't you think?"

"What does that have to do with her story?"

"It wasn't until after the twenty seventeen, August solar eclipse that scientists reanalyzed the Ugarit eclipse record. They made a significant discovery - a new historical dating of the tablet and when the eclipse had occurred. These scientists calculated that the visibility of the planet Mars during the twenty seventeen eclipse, and the month in which it occurred enabled them to determine that the recorded eclipse, in fact, occurred on March fifth, twelve twenty-three B.C. How could Erin, as Estrild, have known in nineteen eighty-nine that exact date when it was not discovered until twenty eighteen?"

"She was a time traveler?"

Laughter rippled throughout the auditorium.

"That is more truth than fiction. In regression sessions, my clients experience what I call mental time travel."

∞

The Hennessey backyard seemed more like a country club pool area than a backyard and offered the perfect respite for the family. Landscaped with Robeline palm trees, Birds of Paradise and yellow Azaleas gave it a tropical feel. Dozens of small signs such as "Welcome to Paradise" and "Bar Open" hung sporadically on the fence reflected the vacation style ambiance and vibe. From the covered pergola to the cabana bar the area invited all to escape.

Jackie and Beth sat in the two blue Adirondack chairs beneath a vibrantly striped umbrella and sipped iced tea.

"Why don't you want to talk about it?" Beth pursed her lips as she pressed her feet against the pool deck.

"It's way too early for that. I haven't processed any of the information I think I remember." Out of nervous energy Jackie crossed her legs and swung her top leg as her foot twitched.

"Tell me one thing you remember?" Beth sipped her tea.

"Let's change the subject." The softness of Jackie's body tensed as her leg swung faster. "I'm really trying to put everything behind me, but no one will let me; especially Dr. Grayson."

"Are you going to see him again?"

"I'm not sure, David wants me too."

"Forget what David wants, what do you want?"

"I feel uncertain about going and by me not being able to read prevents me from learning about regression hypnosis."

"Problem solved. I know last year you said you wouldn't get caught dead at a seminar on reincarnation, but Dr. Bryan Reiss is in town and is speaking today and tomorrow on past life regressions. He's a renowned regression hypnotherapist who has written tons of books on the subject matter. Actually, he's the most famous in the world who I asked you to go see about this same time a year ago. Do you want to go now? It'll be my treat."

"I'll pass. I don't want to put ideas in my mind that don't belong adding to my confusion. It's all too scary and complicated for me at this point in my life. My doctor says I need to take things slow and not to overload my brain. Besides, I have to think about whether I'm going to my next regression session in the morning."

"What's there to think about? Just go, relax and rediscover your memories. I think it's a great plan, that is, if my opinion counts."

The back door swung open and Tyler bolted out. When he spotted Jackie, he frowned and immediately stopped in his tracks.

"It's okay Tyler, you can come out and play."

He gazed at the pool as a huge kid-in-a-candy-store smile jetted across his lips. "Can I go swimming?"

Jackie's heart pounded. *Do I even know how to swim? Does he know how to swim?* "You better go ask your Grandma or Daddy that question."

"Daddy said for me to ask you." Tyler stomped his foot as his lips pouted.

Jackie's stomach turned to a ball of tight nerves as she glanced at Beth. "Do I know how to swim?"

"You don't remember that either?"

"Can I go, please can I go swimming." Tyler's brown-eager eyes pleadingly gazed at her.

"Only if your Daddy swims with you, go tell him that."

Tyler bolted back inside the house.

"Well, do I know how to swim or not?"

"There's only one way to find out, go put your swimsuit on and try it out. Take baby steps. It's your pool. I bet your muscle memory will kick in if you know how. Swimming isn't any different from riding a bike."

"I don't know if I know how to do that either." A forlorn look developed across Jackie's brow as she huffed. "The only thing I know I do athletically is to run. I think I'll stick to that."

∞

Margarette sat reading a romance novel in the rocking chair. David, who lay on the couch watched the NBA basketball game on the television between the Pelicans and the Golden State Warriors.

David leapt to a standing position. "Two points, score!"

Margarette jumped throwing her paperback book up into the air. "You scared the daylights out of me. Are you trying to give me a heart attack?" She retrieved her book.

"Sorry, Mom. We need to win this game to get into the playoffs."

"Next time warn me. I felt my heart skip a beat or two and you might wake up the kids so lower your voice."

"Hoop there it is, three points." David danced a victory jig pumping his fists. He turned to Margarette and held up his palm. "Give me five."

They victoriously slapped each other's hands.

"I haven't seen you this excited or this happy in a long time. It's good to see you this way again."

"The Pelicans haven't gone to the playoffs in a while. Yes, rebounded." He plopped back onto the couch.

Jackie, dressed in a black legging with hot pink stripes which perfectly accented her toned physique, a matching tank top and jogging shoes rifled down the stairs bolting into the living room. "I'm going for a run to clear my head."

David's eye's widened although they remained glued to the television. "At this time of night? It's nine-thirty. Maybe you ought to wait until the morning."

"I need to decide whether I'm going back to see Dr. Grayson and I can't do that standing still or lounging in bed thinking about it. All this excess frustration and energy is clogging my brain. The only way I'm going to get any sort of clarity is to run it off. I'm a ball of nerves."

David faced Jackie. "Then give me a minute and I'll go with you. It won't take me long to change and it's almost half-time."

She defiantly raised her delicate chin. "If I had wanted company, don't you think I would have asked you to join me? I just feel like running that's all. It's in my blood."

"I don't think that's a very wise thing to do at this time of night."

Margarette huffed, shook her head, and then cleared her throat. "All right you two, there's no need to fight over this. Our neighborhood is safe, and it is well lit. David, you never not once before Jackie's injury stopped her from running at night. She was a track star in high school and in college. The only reason she didn't go to the Olympics was to marry you. I don't see anything wrong with it because she has run most of her life. You need to get on board and support her. She's finally doing what she has always done since coming home from the hospital. She'll never stop running."

"Mom, thank you for the support." Jackie crossed her arms over her chest and leaned back on her left foot.

"It is what it is; I don't play favorites, I just see clarity."

"Fine, have it your way, please be safe." The undertone in David's voice left Jackie with a sense he didn't mean it.

"I will be David, thanks for the understanding." Her voice quipped at him with deep sarcasm. She averted her leer from him and stretched side to side.

David sat in silence with a sour-lemon-puckered expression which impacted the thick silence in the room.

"I'm going to check on the boys and leave you both to figure this one out." Margarette rose, placed her book onto the rocker and headed for the stairs.

Jackie not far behind Margarette bolted out the front door and slammed it shut.

Once outside, she looked to the left and to the right. *I'll go right, how can that be a wrong?*

Jackie began her jog. After she reached the levee, she sprinted as fast as she could. *I may never stop running.*

∞

Irene's, one of New Orleans best kept secret restaurants in the French Quarter bristled with business including patrons Dr. Grayson, his wife and Dr. Brian Reiss. The threesome sat in the far corner engaged in a private conversation as they enjoyed their gourmet meals and service which only Irene's offered.

"I'm so glad my husband brought me to your interview today Dr. Reiss. It was so interesting and captivating, I didn't want it to end. I've always believed in reincarnation as a Buddhist; and I'm aware of three of my own, but your wealth of knowledge and experience is beyond reproach."

"You're too kind Mrs. Grayson."

"Please, call me Carla."

"Carla it is. Would you mind sharing one of your past lives with me?"

"I'm not sure if you would find any of them interesting, especially after I heard you speak of the woman's story falling off the bridge. That was remarkable, wasn't Michael?"

"It was fascinating to hear you speak about her. I had only read of the incident in one of your books. Do you still have any contact with her?"

"I do and I'm happy to say she has overcome her fear of bridges over troubled water." A small proud grin creased his lips as if he accomplished a major hurdle.

Carla sipped her wine cautiously contemplating her next words. For her the importance of her past life she desired to share revealed her inner soul that until that moment no one comprehended. She swallowed deep as nerves shadowed her thoughts. Her temperature rose; she felt faint. *This is never easy.*

She recomposed to her accepting bubbly self. "I've chosen the one that haunts me the most. At least I understand my fear of large cats. By large cats, I don't mean a twenty-pound house cat, but lions and tigers. As a child I never understood why I hated to go to the circus or when I went to the zoo, I wouldn't go near the lion exhibit until I saw what happened during one of my regressions."

"Very interesting, I would like to hear it." Dr. Reiss flashed an encouraging grin.

"It was a terrible death not ideally suited for a dinner conversation."

"I believe I can handle it; I've listened to thousands of deaths over the years, some very brutal. Please share it with me. Before you do, also know I'm always on alert to hear if any of my other patients have reported the same death or being the same person. So far, there hasn't been, and I can honestly report without reservation that I've listened to hundreds of thousands of past lives. Suffice it to say, it's my way of verification of authenticity. No one shares the same past life; they can't. They may have been at the same place, but after thirty years in this field, I've never come across anyone who claimed to have been the same individual in the past. Go ahead, I'm extremely curious."

"Very well, since you insist, I was a lion tamer. Here's what happened."

∞

The year of our Lord, 1872, January the third and about half-past ten in the evening. A large crowd assembled for a Mander's Menagerie as part of Ilamder's Circus. Thomas MacCarte, a young man of thirty-four dressed in his signature gladiator attire which disguised his missing left arm he lost years ago in an accident while performing with a lion when he contracted with the Meyer's Circus in Liverpool. For this show, Massarati the Lion Tamer, his appellation billing name, commanded the center ring as a call-

back performer; his act billed as "The Lion Hunt" in a special cloistered appearance.

With his whip and falchion, a broad slightly curved sword with a cutting edge on the convex side in place, he prepared to strut proud as a peacock with feathers spanned into the lion's ring and face five male beasts with the thirst for blood. His never-fail-showman smile, radiance and jauntiness spread infectiously throughout the circus tent to wild applause as he grandstanded outside the center ring.

The Ringmaster stepped forward. "And now, the Ilamder's circus proudly presents, the one, the glorious, and the most magnificent lion tamer the world has ever seen, Massarati the Lion Tamer."

The audience of about five hundred responded with thunderous applause and cheers as the lions inside the cage readied for battle in defiance of their captivity as they sat on their assigned pedestals.

A roustabout stood in the shadows and faced the lion tamer. "You sure you can handle this tonight, I think you had a little bit too much to drink?"

"I only had a couple to calm my nerves, I know what I'm doing."

"You show any fear, make one mistake, it's over."

"I've faced many lions before, these five are no different."

"Then get in there. It's time to shine, just be careful."

"I plan on it. The bite to my hand last week by Asiatic is still fresh on my mind. I won't take my eyes off him. I've already lost one arm, I don't plan on losing another."

"Be warned, they appear unusually restless tonight, maybe we shouldn't have agreed on a call-back performance."

"Nonsense, you know the saying, the show must go on."

Massarati drew in a deep confident breath and puffed his gladiator chest as each sequin sparkled beneath the big top's multiple candle lit candelabras which hung from above and the lamp post style candelabras placed strategically throughout the circus tent to provide light. The master lion tamer could not portray a scent of fear before he entered the lion's performance circle as over five hundred spectators held their breath in anticipation.

He entered the caged ring, the five gorgeous lions, including Asiatic who bit the tamer the week before and Tyrant a black maneless lion leered at their tamer. The beasts' razor-sharp claws clicked against the platforms and their tails flicked as if each expected a raw bloody piece of steak thrown their way. Each lion trained and poised understood their captivity and the line of demarcation called "The Office." Part of each lion's training included not to cross the office line for the tamer's safety.

Massarati bowed, raised his one arm and waved to the crowd. He glared confidently at Asiatic as he pulled the falchion from his sheath. He tapped it once onto the ground, stood and threw his shoulders taunt. For Massarati, his decision to first command the lion who bit him last week demonstrated to the beast and to the others that no fear encapsulated him. "Asiatic come!" He guided the lion back and forth across the ring with no difficulty. Each trick performed to loud applause as Asiatic's roar brought delight as if the applause supplanted raw red bloody meat to the beast. "Asiatic return!" After the beast returned to his pedestal, Massarati led the other lions in their routine tricks with great zeal and to the pleasure of the crowd.

Massarati cracked his whip. "Tyrant, come!" Tyrant's steel-blue eyes met his as he showed his razor-sharp teeth, and then he roared to the delight of the crowd.

Crack, crack, went the whip. Tyrant flipping his tail jumped from his pedestal and stalked toward his tamer. His gaze fixed upon him.

Massarati pulled his falchion; Tyrant stood on his hind legs and hopped forward once. The crowd applauded, and Tyrant growled as if he took a bow.

As Massarati returned his falchion back into his sheath, he slipped and fell across the "Office." Tyrant pounced onto his tamer, clenched to his tamer's haunches and shook his master as if a kitten.

"Tyrant, stop! Return!"

Tyrant tossed Massarati five feet. The lion leapt onto his master and fastened his sharp teeth onto his armless shoulder as if it were a piece of raw meat and shook him.

Once the horrified crowd realized the attack didn't belong as a part of the show, they screamed panic-stricken bolting chaotically from their seats toward the exit.

In extreme pain, Massarati retrieved his falchion and stabbed Tyrant several times slicing the beast on his side, eye and shoulder only angering the lion further. Tyrant tore through the tamer's clothing ripping large chunks of meat from his thigh shredding the muscle away from the bone. Massarati's body full of gashes from the lion's sharp claws and fangs stung in sharp pain.

"Fire on Tyrant! He's going to kill me."

Outside the cage several roustabouts bolted to retrieve brooms, pitchforks and other items to use as weapons against Tyrant. Others scrambled to put iron rods onto the flame to heat them. They realized their error because they failed to follow protocol having not placing them onto the fire prior to the performance in case they were needed for the safety of the tamer. They grabbed their pistols, the only problem, blanks replaced real bullets – another protocol.

Tyrant frayed Massarati's gladiator garment as he sliced open his tamer's shoulder, rib cage and torso. The smell of Massarati's blood radiated throughout the den as the other lions' savage instincts awakened and they joined the attack as their feral fangs pelted like razors into the tamer as if to eat him alive.

Help from the others ensued as they entered the cage with their acquired brooms and pitchforks poking the lions to get back into their den. Another circus performer, a clown, dropped the caged iron bars from above to form a separation between three lions and formed a barrier which left Asiatic and Tyrant to feast on their tamer.

Tyrant chomped down onto Massarati's torso, tossed his bloody-torn body across the cage as the roustabouts now with the heated irons poked the lion burning his nose which angered him more. Asiatic retreated which left Tyrant to feast alone as he fastened onto Massarati and pulled him inside the den just as the clown dropped another bar.

Massarati now trapped in the den as Tyrant's prey realized his death fast approached. The other lions joined Tyrant's feast on their master tamer.

Pistols and guns fired which hit and wounded several of the lions, but not soon enough for Massarati.

Tyrant bit his tamer's head and almost scalped him; the tamer's flesh hung from his face and neck. The bloody attack and mutilation continued. In the end Tyrant tore his master to pieces, his face, arms, torso, and legs all gouged and lacerated; and his muscles detached from the bone presented a bloody site.

Tyrant took one last chomp to feast on his master. Satisfied, he returned to his corner as the roustabouts who came to Massarati's aid entered some fifteen minutes later in time to hear the faint whispers of the tamer's last words.

"Don't kill him, I'm done for."

∞

"I can hear my male voice in my head right now as I asked them not to kill Tyrant. I even remember taking my last breath." Carla's eyes flushed as chills trickled up her spine. "Now you've heard about me as Massarati, The Lion Tamer, have you heard my story before?"

"Not even close. I've listened to numerous clients about their days as circus performers, but not about Massarati."

Dr. Grayson cleared his throat. "Now that's over with, I'd like to get your opinion on a client I am working with to help her recover from retrograde amnesia. She's quite a remarkable woman."

"I'm surprised Michael, you're a very accomplished hypnotherapist, I trained you myself. You've never asked me for a second opinion before."

"I've never had a client like Jackie Hennessey."

"Tell me about her."

"Before I do that, have you ever regressed a client with retrograde amnesia?"

"Several, is that your client's diagnosis?"

Dr. Grayson nodded in affirmation. "Like your client, Estrild, Jackie has recalled numerous details about her past lives with historical accuracy. She hasn't recovered her ability to read, so I know she's not looking them up?"

"Do you have doubts as to the authenticity of her past lives?"

"Not doubts, like your client she has a fear she must face. So far, I haven't been able to identify it. That's why I'm asking you. I care what happens to her. Have you ever not been able to identify an underlying phobia?"

"Relax Michael, with enough sessions I have full faith you will make the discovery, then you'll be able to guide her in the right direction. When do you see her next?"

"Tomorrow, if she doesn't cancel. She had a shocking experience last time which frightened her because she doesn't understand what she's seeing."

"You asked for my opinion, so here it is. Start with self-disclosing one of your past lives. Help her understand what she is seeing and how she can use it to help her in the present. If she believes she's alone in her feelings, she's likely to clam up. Inform her it is normal to experience what she is seeing and how she feels is a normal reaction when seeing a past life for the first time. Tap into how you felt after the first time."

8. TOHONO

"That's correct, Jackie. In one of my past lives, although I was her older brother, I married Cleopatra. My name was Ptolemy the Fourteenth."

"Dr. Grayson, how do you know?"

"I saw my life with her. Sadly, she had me killed so her son could take her place on the throne upon her death and not me."

"That's awful."

"I don't see it that way, it's what makes me who I am today."

"Tell me something less gruesome."

"I've remembered many things about Cleopatra over the years not recorded in textbooks."

"Give me an example."

"The reason she wore the thick black eyeliner around her eyes wasn't to lure men into her trap. The eyeliner had a pharmaceutical purpose as it warded off eye infections."

"You know this, how?"

"Cleopatra was very skilled in medicine. She wasn't the seductress portrayed in films. I think you'll find this interesting. She told everyone she was the reincarnation of the goddess Isis."

"Was she?"

"I don't know, and I'm not sure if she did either, but it provided her with a solid following. She got what she wanted."

"How did you discover your past life with her?"

"From my mentor Dr. Reiss. It wasn't until after I had experienced my first past life in one of my regression sessions with him that I studied under him. It proved beneficial for my sanity. I was raised Southern Baptist, not exactly the doctrine that believes in reincarnation. I had a lot of growing to do because it went against everything I was taught to believe."

"Were you in shock like me?"

"More confused than shocked; I had tons of questions and did my due diligence in research. It was important for me to form my own opinion. You shouldn't care what others believe, believe in yourself. In one way your retrograde amnesia should prove beneficial in your journey for the truth."

"Not by my standards."

"Look on the bright side, you don't remember your past; so, you don't have a religious doctrine preached to you your entire life. You have the freedom to discover what you believe on your own without outside influence."

"Try telling David and my mother that, but I suppose you're right. Thank you for sharing with me your Majesty and for the words of wisdom. It's not every day you meet someone who knows Cleopatra, I don't feel so crazy."

He nodded and flashed a comforting-closed-mouthed grin. "You ready Jackie? Let's find out where you take yourself today."

"As ready as I ever will be."

"You know the drill. Each time you're hypnotized, you're able to go into a trance easier. You're a pro now."

"Let's do it."

Dr. Grayson pressed the record button on the camera's remote. "Remember, you can return to your safe place any time you feel scared or need a break. Now, breathe slowly in and out."

Jackie adjusted her position and sank deeper onto the chaise as her breaths slowed.

Dr. Grayson allowed several minutes for Jackie to find her safe place. He watched her eye movements and her body language. "Breathe Jackie, think about your personal safe place... And sleep." He snapped his fingers twice. "Tell me where you are." His voice adagio brought warmth and comfort for Jackie.

"It's a beautiful place, I'm at the beach. The waves are rushing in. Seagulls are flying overhead. I'm sitting in the sand."

"Sitting in the sand?"

"Yes, looking at the water. It's a peaceful place."

"I want you to look up into the sky, find a cloud and sit on it. Tell me when you get there."

"...It's like sitting on a pillow."

"It's very comfortable, isn't it?"

"Yes."

"Anytime you become scared, I want you to remember this moment. You are safe, comfortable and secure."

Jackie took a deep breath and any stress, if it remained, vanished.

"I want you to travel along this cloud. It has many doors that await you. Do you see the doors?"

"I see hundreds. It's like a hall of mirrors."

"That's great Jackie. Choose a door you want to enter. Go to the door that you are drawn to enter."

Jackie's closed eyes darted back and forth as if she searched for something. "I'm choosing the seventh door on the right."

"Open the door and enter. Look around. Tell me the first thing you see."

"I see a woman and a man."

"What are they doing?"

∞

The white puffy clouds opened to a meadow of flowers with a babbling stream below. The spring breeze transported the fragrance from the thousands of colorful wildflowers in the field which provided a sweet aroma.

Tohono, twenty-six, a Navajo American Indian squaw with long raven silk hair filled a black kettle with water from the stream. Her dress, made from animal hide, told her story in more ways than one. Embellished with elk eyeteeth, the dress symbolized that the men in her tribe were great hunters. An animal's tail adorned the neckline as did the beadwork on her headband.

Tohono carried the kettle toward an early 1800s style log cabin where Jonathan Longfellow, late twenties, repaired the roof with mud, leaves and twigs between the logs on the roof. His brown suede pants looked worn and his white-collared shirt a tint of dingy-gray. He wiped the sweat from his brow and blew her a kiss.

She approached a cooking fire pit and hung the kettle by its handle over the flame. On the wooden table next to the fire, lay washed red new potatoes, corn, green beans and onions. She diced the vegetables.

Jonathan stepped down each ladder's rung as he eased himself from the roof of the log cabin. He made his way to Tohono as the water in the kettle boiled. He gave her a kiss on the top of her raven silk hair which blew in the wind.

A warm loving tingle transferred from the top of her head to her toes. "It won't be long before our meal is ready."

"Let me help you." *He tossed the diced potatoes into the pot.* "This meal will be hearty." *He grabbed the carrots and tossed them in.*

"How's the roof?" *She put the rest of the vegetables into the pot.*

"Patched, we shouldn't have any more rainwater dripping through."

"That will make the harsh winter easier to survive."

Movement in the meadow across the stream attracted her attention as her tracker instincts awakened. It almost seemed as if she smelled danger. "Jonathan, get your gun."

110

"I don't understand, what is it Tohono?"

"We must hurry, Bidzil is here." Tohono directed her large brown eyes toward the movement across the stream. *"The day I feared has come, he's coming for me. I'm to be his bride."* She felt her rapid heartbeat pulse within her wrists.

Bidzil, also named Snow Hunter, recognized Tohono unveiled his presence as if she whiffed his essence. He rose and proudly stood with his bow and arrow readied. *"Tohono, I'm taking you back to our tribe. You belong with me and not with this white man."* His abusive voice roared from across the stream.

"She made her choice to be my bride, it's over injun."

Bidzil slogged through the stream with his arrow pointed at his enemy. Jonathan grabbed Tohono's hand, and they ran toward the cabin.

Bidzill released the arrow as Tohono looked over her shoulder. She jumped into the arrow's path.

"No!" Jonathan bolted toward his love.

The arrow pierced Tohono through her heart. Her body jerked. She stumbled three steps and collapsed.

Jonathan knelt over her. *"Are you happy now injun? You're a murderer!"* He lifted her head. *"Tohono, everything will be fine. I love you."*

Bidzil fell to his knees, extended his arms and looked toward the heavens. His stomach churned with remorse at what his action cost him — his beloved. He screamed as if he delivered a war chant which echoed in the valley as the cry in his heart filled the air.

Tohono struggled to glance toward the log cabin.

Micha, a half-bred boy, age two, stood in the doorway. *"Mommy!"* His tears fell as he ran toward his mother.

"Micha, stop!" Jonathan's screech amplified over Bidzil's war chant. He encased Micha in his arms and gazed at Tohono.

"Save him." Tohono's muttered voice tore into Jonathan's heart. She gasped her last breath.

9. BEHOLD THE KNIGHTS

David and Higgins strolled the boatyard. "I have to admit it's been a difficult adjustment for Jackie. Home has had its ups and downs." David declared to Higgins his feelings almost as if he talked about himself instead of his wife.

"I understand, after Rae's stroke, we had a challenging time adjusting. I'm not sure if we ever did. Nothing has been the same since. Basically, I have a shell of a wife I fell in love with. You on the other hand have a functioning person."

"Any advice?"

"Fall in love all over again."

"I never stopped loving her."

"Does she know that?"

"I tell her every day."

"But, do you show her?"

"If you're asking if we have sex, the answer is no. She pulls away from my touch, we're strangers."

"That's my point. She fell in love with you before the accident, date her again. Take her out and romance her. Show her the David she fell in love with during high school and she's bound to fall in love with you again. You two are meant for each other."

"You're serious, I need to date my wife?" David's bewilderment jetted across his brow.

"Only if you want her to stay that way."

"I wouldn't know where to start." David rubbed his eyes.

"What was y'alls first date?"

"It was after the first football game when we were in the eleventh grade. You were off in New York at the time avoiding the family business. I caught a Hail Mary pass and ran it into the end zone to win the game. She was a cheerleader. Everyone ran to congratulate me on my awesome catch. She put her arms around my neck and kissed me on the lips. I took her out for pizza, followed by a walk in the park."

"There you have it. Your new first date all wrapped up in a tight package."

"You're forgetting two things. We aren't in high school and it isn't football season."

"No, but it is basketball season and the Pelicans play at the Smoothie King Center tonight. Take her, order a beer or two and eat pizza. Just have an enjoyable time. Hell, I'll even give you my two tickets."

"I don't know if she even likes basketball."

"She doesn't, or at least she didn't. You'll never know unless you take her."

"I get it, take her out and just have fun."

"Exactly, act like teenagers again. Hell, you both need it."

∞

"Just breathe Jackie, go to your point of observation; find your safe zone. Remember how you felt sitting on the beach? Now breathe. I'm going to count to three, when I do, find another door, and enter. One... Two... Three... Are you inside or outside?"

Jackie took a long deep breath. "I'm in a tavern."

"Are you alone?"

"No, I'm surrounded by lots of men and women."

"What is everyone doing?"

"Waiting on our meat to finish cooking and we're drinking ale."

"What else? Describe what you see, hear and smell."

∞

In the year of 1337, fourteen Knights of the Templar all dressed in long white tunics and mid-calf capes which boldly displayed a large red cross on each garment gathered at an eighteen-foot rectangular table inside a medieval patron-filled tavern in the outskirts of England's countryside to feast and to celebrate. They guzzled ale in unrestrained absolution as they recapitulated their version of the foe in which they conquered the day before in His holy name.

Surrounded by whores and maidens, the knights' body odor permeated the tavern as it dissipated into the aroma of the slaughtered pig which roasted in the open-flamed pit near the north wall.

Talen Clowser, age fourteen, dressed in a dull brown peasant-style tunic cinched by a tattered brown leather belt at his waist, dried muddy woolen tan trousers a size too big and a pair of scuffled over-sized knee-high boots stood at the table's end as he recited poetry written by Dante to kiss the hare's foot for his growling belly. His face replete with smeared ash and dirt.

At his thighs, the young peasant's hands trembled as he held his urge to urinate from the fear of stage fright which encased him. "The day was falling, and the darkening air released earth's creatures from their toils, while I, I only, face the bitter road and bare my Master led."

"Begone!" The gruff and brutal voice of Sir Oriholt interrupted Talen's recitation. He flipped his hufty-tufty hand into the air toward the peasant.

114

"No more Dante Inferno. Bring to this celebration something unheard by our keen ears if thy hunger for our scraps from thy knight's table."

Riotous merriment belted from the other knights meant for the hoodwink who stood aghast and famished.

Grecia Moder, a beauteous maiden positioned behind Sir Oriholt rubbed her hands over the large crimson cross on his tunic as her plump bosoms pressed against his back which enhanced her cleavage to the delight of the other knights. She positioned her rosy moist lips next to his wax-filled right ear. *"Prithee, how about a little of me instead of tolerating what clearly defines a buffoon?"*

Sir Oriholt ruminated her smitten request for a mere moment. *"Knights of the Templar, we perchance have a battle to be won. Shall it be thy fair maiden or thy hoodwink for tonight's unabashed delight? Which of thy two do thy knights show favor?"* He guzzled his ale as he awaited the pronouncement.

Sir Moysant chortled and slammed his fist onto the table. *"I declare neither and eradicate both for such a nuisance to thy presence. Fetch the glutton and provide bellytimber for our bellies with swine to rid our voracious appetites."*

"Dilly, dilly!" Sir Oriholt smashed his ale stein onto the table and spewed spit onto the soil floor.

Talen took another step backward. *"Mayhap I sing for thy knight's ears glory?"*

Unimpressed by Talen or the maiden and with something to prove to the other knights, Sir Oriholt abruptly rose as he shoved the maiden to the floor; her bubble-bow contents scattered onto the dirt floor at the knight's feet. He towered thirteen inches above the young peasant as he glowered toward him.

Talen shook in his tattered boots as he gasped and stepped backward as if he faced a fairytale giant of mammoth proportion. Nerves got the best of him as he surrendered an alternative entertainment mode for Sir Oriholt's pig scraps and danced.

"Are you a jester? This is woodness. Begone you fool!" Sir Oriholt's menacing tone belittled Talen.

Ashamed, Talen cowered into a damp dim corner in the shadows afraid to show his face.

Sir Moysant lifted his stein mug. "To King Edward."

The other knights followed forthwith. "To King Edward."

The carved wooden door flew open as a harsh cold breeze blew inside which sent each knight to their feet as they pulled their swords ready for battle.

Scolace, a silver haired wizard with a long silver beard dressed in a gray flannel cloak flashed a handful of gun powder before his grand entrance to make it seem as if he magically appeared into the tavern.

Everyone scattered except for the knights who remained poised for battle unafraid of whatever or whoever the breeze transported to them.

Sir Oriholt's chair took flight unaided by man and crashed against a nearby table.

"Who dare trespasses these walls?" Sir Oriholt's eyes lit full of wrath and targeted Scolace.

Scolace waved his hand toward Talen who shamefully shivered dishonored in the corner. "Come hither and make thy claim."

Behind Scolace, a hunchback man who wore a mask of evil proportions which resembled a raven with a large beak slinked into the tavern and pounded his staff onto the soil. "Behold, what worth do thee as knights of the King have if thee defy justice and deliver mockery?" He pointed his long staff toward Talen. "Has this peasant wronged thy King or any of thee which caused thy hatred? I declare if not your protection of our land is not worth a grain of salt in thy King's cellar."

Red-faced, Sir Oriholt lunged violently toward the old wizard and the masked man. "Charge!"

"Talen run." The masked man bolted from the tavern.

Scolace flashed another handful of gun powder and disappeared along with Talen.

The knights engulfed in rage bolted in pursuit of the vagrant three.

Through the dirt streets and across the back alleys the chase heightened in intensity and concluded inside a blacksmith's shop.

Talen and the masked man hid in the shadows as Scolace bravely stepped forward. "Will thy be a coward and murder an unarmed man?"

Sir Oriholt raised his razor-sharp sword, charged toward Scolace and with one precise slice to the wizard's throat decapitated him. The wizard's head spewed crimson blood as it trundled toward the fire and left a trail from Solace's torso. "No, I take a wizard's last breath as thee must be from the devil."

"The boy and the raven shall fall to the same fate." Sir Moysant darted his eyes into the shadows. "Show thy face young peasant."

Talen and the masked man slipped through the broken boards and disappeared into the darkness of night. Their escape heard by the Knights.

Sir Oriholt kicked Scolace's head into the burning fire. "Leave them! Save this battle for another day."

Sir Moysant bowed his head in respect. "I shall see thee anon."

∞

Pelican fans filled The Smoothie King Center to capacity for the playoff game between the New Orleans Pelicans and Houston Rockets. David and Jackie each with a draft beer in their hand made their way down the aisle in section one hundred and twenty-four.

"This looks exciting." Jackie's eyes darted at the jumbotron and back to the players on the floor warming up for tonight's game.

"It should be. If the Pels win tonight, they advance to the finals."

"Then, I'll cheer for them like I cheered for you in high school."

"You remember that?"

"I looked at my high school yearbook. There was a picture of you on the field and me in a cheerleader uniform. I put one and one together."

"That's progress. Your sessions with Dr. Grayson must be working." David glanced at the seat numbers on his ticket. "We're right here on the aisle center court."

They eased into their seats as Jackie gawked in amazement over the pre-game activities.

"It was nice of my brother to give us these tickets."

"He, like the rest of us, loves you very much."

"I've been told."

The lights dimmed, spotlights circled the arena, and the crowd ignited into a thunderous roar.

"Get ready Jackie, the fun is about to begin."

"Ladies and Gentlemen, get on your feet and welcome your New Orleans Pelicans." Pierre the Pelican, the team's mascot, bolted from the tunnel followed by the dance team. They formed two lines. "Here come the Pels." The entire team ran onto center court.

"This is so exciting." Jackie grinned from ear to ear. "I can see why people would get into this. When do they kick off?"

"It's called a tip-off in basketball."

"Did I like basketball before my accident?"

"If you're asking if we ever went to a basketball game, the answer is no. We have season tickets to the Saints and have had them for eight years. You love NFL football."

"I do?"

"You're a superfan."

"I give, what the hell is a superfan?"

"You'd dress up, paint your face and coach the team from your seat."

"Wow, I don't remember."

"Give it time and you'll be a superfan again."

The crowd chanted. "Kiss. Kiss. Kiss." Jackie glanced at the jumbotron featuring her and David. Animated hearts blinked around their faces. Jackie's stomach felt as if it dropped to center court as she gazed upon her scarred face now larger than ever.

David leaned over and kissed Jackie's cheek to her disgust.

The crowd booed her reaction.

"It's okay Jackie, it's only the kiss cam. They'll pick out different couples all night."

"Sorry about that, I'm just not comfortable kissing you right now. Besides, now everyone saw my ugly scar up close and personal."

"No harm, no foul. Let's focus on the game and have fun. Tell me when you're ready for some pizza."

Jackie nodded and forced a grin as she ran her index finger across her scar.

He gazed into her eyes. "By the way, you're the most beautiful woman in the arena."

10. DEJA VU

The sun rose over the Hennessey home as the morning dew shimmered on the grass. Inside, Jackie slumbered peacefully while David tiptoed into the bedroom. He opened his closet, removed his shirt, his pants and grabbed his shoes.

Jackie exhausted from attending the basketball game the night before moaned and rolled over covering her face with the pillow. "I'm awake, you can turn on the light."

"You were sleeping, I didn't want to bother you."

"Thank you for that, but the boys will wake up soon and want breakfast. The life of a housewife isn't for me."

"Now how do you remember that?"

"I don't. It doesn't seem like I was. I only know I hate waking up early."

"You used to tell me you'd never get up early when you retired. You hated it."

"Nothing has changed then, has it?"

Tyler stumbled into their bedroom. "Daddy, I'm hungry."

"Okay, I'll get you some cereal."

"No, I want Grandma to cook me eggs."

Jackie glanced at Tyler. "I'll be glad to make you scrambled eggs and toast."

"No, you don't cook them right. They taste funny."

Visibly upset, Jackie's eyes teared. She clutched her arms to her chest, clenched her hands into a fist as her expression turned pitiful.

"Tyler, you hurt Mommy's feelings. Tell her you're sorry."

"I'm not sorry. Her eggs are yucky, really yucky."

"It's all right David. My mom can do it. She cooks everything else around here. I'm pretty much useless to everyone."

"Daddy, why don't you sleep with Mommy?"

Jackie and David concerned, glared at each other.

"My friend at school says it's cause y'all are getting a divorce."

David digested Tyler's words as he knelt. He gazed into his son's eyes and placed his hands onto his shoulders. "Mommy and Daddy love each other very much and we are not getting a divorce. I don't sleep with Mommy because of her accident. She needs her rest without me in her bed that's all."

"Okay, now will you get me cereal?"

"I'll meet you downstairs, go ahead."

Tyler bounced from the room.

Jackie shook her head. "We have some kind of marriage, don't we?"

"We're in an adjustment period, I'm in no rush. The rest of our lives awaits us, but it would help if you'd talk about things."

"Don't you mean if I'd tell you what happens with Dr. Grayson? If you are, you'll be waiting a long time."

"You could let me watch the tapes. He records your sessions, doesn't he?"

"Those are for my eyes and ears only; so, quit asking before I get pissed."

"At least that's an emotion rather than bawling your eyes out every night in our locked bedroom I'm not allowed to enter." He instantly regretted his choice of admonishment.

"Your bad side is finally coming out. You're human after all. I always thought you were too perfect. Just get out and leave me alone."

"Daddy, cereal!"

"We'll talk about this later. I can't drive you to see Dr. Grayson today."

"I'll drive myself."

"The doctor revoked your driver's license. Before you get it back, you must be seizure free for one year. You're not even close."

"I haven't had a seizure in three months."

"Like I said, you're not close."

"I'll take an Uber, or I'll hitchhike. I won't be a prisoner in my home."

David stormed from the bedroom slamming the door behind him.

Margarette poured milk over a bowl of cereal and placed it onto the table in front of Tyler.

David stomped into the kitchen.

"Good morning David, is everything all right?"

"I guess you heard us from down here."

"It wasn't hard to miss. Don't let it get you down, I'll talk to her. Can you take Tyler to school this morning?"

"He doesn't have school today, it's record's day."

"Then, you'd better go before you're late."

"You're right, have a great day."

"Bye Daddy."

∞

Margarette cleaned the kitchen as Jackie used a dust broom to sweep the wooden floors.

"Who had the brilliant idea to have these floors installed, me or David?"

"The way I remember it, it was both of you. You agreed on everything when you renovated this home."

"I won't do that again, I think I prefer carpet."

"You wouldn't like it. Carpet is nothing but a dirt trap. Your home stays cleaner with tile or wooden floors."

"Mom, can I ask you a very serious question?"

"What is it?"

"Do you believe in life after death?"

"What kind of question is that? Of course, I do."

"What happens?"

"Just like the word of God promises, we are guaranteed to have everlasting life."

Jackie indulged in a hopeless exhale. "I'm not in the Bible recitation mode, Mother. There must be other answers. What do you believe?"

"I believe in the Father, the Son and the Holy Ghost. Like it is written, I believe Jesus died for us, so we would have eternal life. He promises us this."

"Mom, stop quoting scripture; tell me from your heart."

Margarette dried her hands using her apron and grasped Jackie by the hand. "I know God exists. He is a merciful God, and He answers our prayers. You're still here to see your children grow, aren't you? How else can you account for that? You were on your deathbed. If it weren't for God answering our prayers, you wouldn't be here asking these questions right now; you'd be six feet under."

"What does the Bible say about reincarnation?"

"Reincarnation? What kind of question is that?"

"I need to know, is reincarnation possible?"

"Is that what happened yesterday with Dr. Grayson? He put it into your mind you were reincarnated?"

"It's just a question."

Sebastian wailed from his upstairs bedroom.

"I'll get him." Jackie headed toward the stairs.

Margarette grabbed her Bible from the coffee table and flipped through it. "I know I can find a verse or two that reincarnation doesn't exist."

The phone rang. "I got it, Jackie. Hennessey residence… She's with the baby, but I will have her call you as soon as possible… Oh, you have to reschedule her appointment… I'm sure she can come tomorrow Dr. Grayson. I'll tell her. Have a blessed day." Margarette hung up the phone.

Jackie held Sebastian as she strode into the kitchen. "Who called?"

"Dr. Grayson, he had to cancel your appointment. He rescheduled it for tomorrow."

"I was looking forward to it. I need to get out of this house, I'm going stir crazy."

"You know what we should do?"

"Get a new life."

"Silly, let's take a drive to Bay St. Louis and visit Aunt Susie's antique store. We'll make a day trip out of it, it'll be great for all of us to get out of here and do something different."

Jackie took a long deep breath and contemplated the suggestion. "That sounds like a wonderful change of pace, let's do it."

"You get dressed and I'll pack the diaper bag. This will be fun."

Jackie headed for the stairs, stopped and turned to Margarette as her frown faded into a slight grin. "Thanks, this is the distraction I need."

"Well, what are you waiting on? Go get dressed. Chop, chop." Margarette brushed her hands together.

∞

The hour and fifteen-minute drive from Metairie, Louisiana to Bay St. Louis, Mississippi went smoothly. The boys slept safely secured in their car seats as Jackie listened to her mom recant stories about her summers with Aunt Susie and their adventures.

"I'm excited, Aunt Susie sounds amazing. I can't wait to meet her."

"Honey, you know Aunt Susie. What I think you're trying to say is to get to know her again."

"Sad, but true. She does know I don't remember anything, right?"

"Honey, I think everybody in the southern half of the United States knows that. You made the news every day for a while."

"Oh, yea, I keep forgetting that too."

"We're here." Margarette drove into the parking lot of a two-story warehouse and office building.

"Okay, not what I was expecting. You told me it was an antique mall. I guess I expected it to be a large mall with forty stores."

"In the world of antiquing, a mall represents vintage items from several collectors. As in this mall, the items represent generations of collections and fine art. It's a family affair. I even have my little corner in the store."

"You do? What do you sell?"

"Well, you know we come from the Higgins family. Most of the men during World War Two in our family served overseas and sent home lots of items from Japan. Then, during the years following the war, items marked 'Occupied Japan' became collectible. I collected different pieces like it was an addiction. I never needed that stuff; so, Aunt Susie convinced me to offer my collection for sale here on consignment."

"You make any money from it?"

"I'm not getting rich, but I know the people buying my items will take care of them and treasure them. Are you ready to go in?"

"Do you think you could help with the stroller? I'm not sure how it works."

"You wake up the boys and I'll get the stroller."

It took several minutes for Margarette to retrieve the stroller from the vehicle and for Jackie to activate the boys. With patience and teamwork, the four made their path toward the entrance. Jackie held the door open as Margarette pushed Sebastian's stroller through. Tyler clung tightly to Margarette's shirt.

After Jackie entered, her jaw dropped as she glanced around the store. "It's a time warp in here."

"How do you know since you can't remember?"

"Not sure, must be *Déjà vu.*"

Everywhere Jackie glanced, antiques and collectibles just like Margarette warned filled the shelves. She sniffed the stale air as she listened to the soft music which filled the room from an old-fashioned CD player on a shelf. "I love that painting behind the register."

"That's Aunt Susie's portrait. She was thirty-six when she posed for that. The antique buffet table she uses as the check-out counter came from your dad's side of the family. It used to be in his great-grandfather's house."

"Wow, now I get why they named it The Family Tree."

"Margarette." Aunt Susie, the spunky eighty-four-year-old and great-great-aunt to Jackie ambled toward them. "I didn't know you two were coming."

"Neither did we until about two hours ago. Aunt Susie, do you remember Jackie?"

"I do, it's great to see you. You look healthy."

Jackie darted her eyes from one area of the store to another.

"I should've said look at these four." Aunt Susie pinched Tyler's cheek. "I could just eat them up. They're precious." She bent and kissed both boys on top of their head.

Tyler clung tightly to Margarette's leg with his head buried into her boho jeans. "It's okay Tyler, this is your great-great-great-aunt Susie."

"What makes her so great?" Tyler still clinging to his grandmother's jeans peeked around her toward Aunt Susie.

The three women giggled.

"Well, since you asked, it's because Aunt Susie is a Godly woman." Margarette nodded proudly.

Aunt Susie flashed a denture-white grin with Godly modesty and nodded in appreciation. Her light blue eyes gazed at Jackie. "Now honey, if you see anything you want, it's on the house. Just one item though. Anything else, I'll give you a twenty percent discount."

"You don't have to do that."

"Who said anything about having to do anything but live, breathe and die? Just let an item speak to you. You'll know it when you see it. It happens around here a lot. People from all over the world find a treasure they know they must have and can't live without. Take advantage of the opportunity in front of you, I insist."

"Okay, I'll make my choice wisely. Thank you in advance."

"My pleasure dear. I suggest you start to the right and make your way around and window shop until you find the item meant to be yours."

Tyler stomped his foot. "I'm bored."

"You know what Tyler?" Aunt Susie grinned at the children. "I have the perfect idea for you and your brother." She pointed to the right corner. "Do you see that? It's a play area. That rocker is for me so I can read stories to the children who visit. Do you want to go play and read stories?"

"Grandma, can I?"

Margarette took a deep breath and glanced at Jackie for permission.

Jackie nodded in approval.

Margarette patted Tyler's back. "Go ahead, I think Aunt Susie has this all wrapped up."

"Trust me, over the years it's safer this way. Little fingers get very touchy touchy." Aunt Susie took Tyler's hand. "Will you help me push your brother to the play area? We can all read together." Aunt Susie and Tyler pushed Sebastian's stroller together. "I'm so glad you're here to play with me Tyler."

"Mom, do we go right, or do we go left?"

"I say we take Aunt Susie's advice and go to the right. She can't be wrong, it's her store."

"Good point."

Jackie and Margarette strolled into the first consignment shop -- Rockyn Round Table. Round lit glass display cases or round tables showcased the largest collection of Moon and Stars glassware in the south under one roof.

Jackie's eyes widened. "Look at those canisters, I've never seen anything like them. So many colors."

"That is what you call Moon and Stars."

Without picking up the glassware, Jackie examined the pattern on an eight-inch cobalt blue cannister and rubbed her index finger along it taking in the indented moons and the texture of each star. "It is beautiful, do you know the history behind these?"

"I don't, but you can bet your britches your Aunt Susie does. Better yet, in the middle of the table is a brief history waiting to be read by those who seek knowledge."

Jackie frowned as she retrieved the eight by ten inch frame which contained a zoomed image of the unique pattern and to her a document with a foreign language she couldn't read. "Mom, you'll have to read it." She handed it over to her mother.

"Sorry, I forgot." Margarette read from the document. "According to the Official Moon and Stars Glass Club, I didn't even know there was such a thing, this glassware has a varied history with at least eight different manufacturers. The pattern was first developed in eighteen seventy-four by Adams and Company who introduced a new pattern of pressed glass they called 'Palace.' Then, U.S. Glass circa in the eighteen nineties."

"Mom, I don't need verbatim, just the lowdown."

"Gotcha, let me suffice it to say the pattern is still reproduced today, but the beginnings came in eighteen seventy-four. You see anything you want?"

"Nothing that is calling my name, let's keep moving."

Jackie and Margarette strolled to the next consignment area -- Caylen's Collectibles.

"Look at all these, these... I don't know what these are called." Jackie's blank expression showed her frustration as did her long exasperated sigh.

"They're Limoges boxes."

"I can't believe this, they're all so small and unique."

"That they are. Just wait until you look at the price tags if you want the real shocker. How much do you think they're worth?"

"By the size, I'd guess forty dollars at most."

Margarette giggled and scratched her nose. "They start at around two-hundred and fifty dollars and go up into the thousands."

"No way."

"Yes, way."

Jackie carefully retrieved a small box with three hand painted monkeys that represented 'See no evil, hear no evil and speak no evil.' Jackie gawked at it amazed as she turned the box every way for a closer examination. "What makes them so unique and expensive?"

"Well they come from Limoges, France. They are all handmade, hand painted and have brass fittings made popular during the eighteenth century. Some people collect them as if they were gold coins."

"I didn't realize you were such a history buff." Jackie set the box back onto the shelf and picked up a small flask with the original stopper.

"I'm not, I'm reading about them."

Jackie examined the flask which featured a gallant landscape and young lovers dressed in eighteenth century clothing. "This is like going to a museum where everything is on sale. Coming here was a great idea."

"Glad you're enjoying it."

"Holy cow, this has to be a mistake."

"What are you talking about?"

"The price tag is four thousand and eight hundred dollars."

"Jackie, you read that?"

"I guess I did. Somehow the numbers popped into my head."

"The doctor said memories would pop up."

"I guess, but did I read that price tag correctly? That one is four thousand and eight hundred dollars."

"I told you these boxes were expensive."

Jackie placed the flask carefully back onto the countertop. "I can't wait to see what is around the corner."

"Let's get to it then."

They strolled to the next area -- Mel's Marbles.

A large enthusiastic smile radiated Jackie's face. "I guess I found Aunt Susie's marbles, but why isn't it called Susie's Marbles?"

"It didn't match the naming theme. Also, Mel is Aunt Susie's great-grandfather and most of the marbles were inherited from him. She has marbles in here from the Civil War. Who knows, she may have some from an earlier time period."

"I get it. Wow! Look at this one." Jackie picked up a half-inch glass marble. "I recognize this."

"What do you mean, you recognize it?"

"I don't know, I just do. You know anything about it?" Jackie placed the marble in her palm and twirled it.

"Nothing at all, but I think I can find out." Margarette retrieved the book *The Collector's Encyclopedia of Antique Marbles* by Clara Ingram and flipped through the pages until she came to a photo of the marble Jackie held. "Okay, listen to this. This is an antique German handmade marble called a Latticino. Look at the center, they call that swirly thing a cage. The one you're holding has two shades of blue. The more cages in the swirl, the more expensive the marble depending on the condition."

"Well, nothing rings a bell." Jackie placed the marble back onto its holder. "But it is beautiful and fascinating. At least, if I lose my marbles, I'll know where they are."

"Cute, Jackie. Next area?"

They strolled to the next booth, Denny's Downtown Derby. "I love this." Margarette's eyes widened. "Nothing but vintage hats. We have to try them on."

"Seriously, I'm not so sure how safe that is. You know germs or lice. It grosses me out just thinking about it. It also reminds me of Jack the Ripper."

"Good grief Jackie, like you know who Jack the Ripper is. Besides, I'm sure Aunt Susie had them all dry cleaned before putting them up for sale."

"If you say so, you go ahead. I want nothing to do with those hats. They give me the heebie-jeebies." Jackie shuttered.

A couple dressed in Steampunk cosplay outfits entered the hat area. "See, I told you she had hats in here." The spunky petite twenty-something woman grabbed the brown derby. "These are perfect for you, try it on."

"I like that gray one." The twenty-something man grabbed the gray hat and twirled it around his index finger before plopping it onto his head.

"Never mind, let's see what's around the corner." Margarette tilted her head toward the next consignment area -- Livia's Lineage. "I think you'll find this next one intriguing."

They strolled into Livia's Lineage consignment area.

Jackie gazed at the items. "Now we're talking. I feel it, the item I'm going to ask Aunt Susie for is in this area."

"You sure?"

"I've never felt more certain, I feel it deep within my soul."

"Then, where do you want to start?"

"I love those pocket watches, I'm drawn to them exactly how Aunt Susie described."

"You know, both your father and grandfather carried pocket watches."

"I didn't, but that's a good piece of family history to learn. Mom look at this, oh my God." Jackie picked up a brass necklace pendant pocket watch, with Roman numerals cradled in a crystal glass dome with skeleton dial black hands. "Look at this, there are working mechanical brass gears in the center of the watch face." Chills tingled down Jackie's spine as she shivered.

"I like the brass tassel dangling from the bottom."

"How long is this chain?"

Margarette exhaled and pondered her answer. "I'd say it's about sixteen inches. You can easily put it on and pull it off without having to unclasp it."

Anxiety jutted down Jackie's spine as goosebumps prickled her skin. "This is it, this necklace is calling me to have it. I want it."

Margarette took an interest in Jackie's reaction to the pocket watch pendant necklace. "Any particular reason?"

"It's the *déjà vu* thing." Jackie grabbed her chest.

"What is it?"

Jackie drew a deep breath. *This necklace was once mine. It's the one Gertrude had on.* Frightened, she stared at Margarette as she clutched the pendent against her chest. "Mom, either by fate or destiny I was supposed to find this today. It's mine."

Margarette's brow furrowed. "Then, it looks like you found your free item."

"Looks that way, doesn't it?" Jackie dropped the chain over her head and adjusted the pendant watch. She looked into the mirror and admired her acquisition. "I'm never taking it off. Well, only to bathe. I love it." *This necklace belongs around my neck.*

Margarette reached for the pendant as Jackie flinched and jerked backward. She blinked and shook her head as a flashback glitched of Gertrude to the moment the sinister man jerked the necklace from her neck. She gasped for air.

"Jackie! Are you, all right?"

Jackie's eyes glazed; a frown crossed her brow.

"Jackie? Jackie honey." Margarette touched Jackie's shoulder.

Jackie snapped from her faded memory. "I'm just tired, I need to go home."

∞

The Hennessey family gathered at the dining table for a meatloaf, mashed potatoes, corn, and peas dinner.

"So, ladies. How was Aunt Susie and antique shopping?" David took a bite of his meatloaf.

"Full of piss and vinegar as usual." Margarette wiped her mouth with her napkin. "Aunt Susie is quite a character."

Jackie remained silent, deep in thought as she poked her mashed potatoes. She wore the pocket watch necklace and held the pendant in her hand.

David stared at Jackie. "I bet she was glad to see you."

"She played with us Daddy." Tyler sipped his milk.

"She played with you?"

"Yes, she read us stories and we colored. She put my drawing on the front door."

"That's special."

"She took to the boys quickly." Margarette took a bite of peas.

David noticed Jackie's thoughts were somewhere in outer space as she failed to take one bite of her meal. "Well Jackie, did Aunt Susie show you her spaceship?"

"Yep." Jackie mumbled beneath her breath as her focus remained deep in her own thoughts.

"I didn't see a spaceship." Tyler threw his fork onto his plate.

Jackie's eyes widened. "What spaceship?"

"You didn't know Aunt Susie had a spaceship?" Margarette patted Tyler and handed him his fork. "You need to eat your vegetables."

"I guess I deserved that, I was in my own world."

"Well, welcome back to this one." David winked at Jackie. "What were you so deep in thought about?"

"Trust me, you don't want to know."

"Yes, I do."

"Okay, I don't want to talk about it." Jackie's sharp tone filled the area. "So, don't ask me again or I'll go to my room."

"Here you go again, can we ever enjoy a meal without fighting?"

"If you shut up and quit asking me what is on my mind."

"Okay, parental units." Margarette's eyes scolded the adults. "Let's all change the subject and talk about our plans for tomorrow which will be a brand-new day."

"I got school." Tyler sipped his milk. "We're learning to write our names."

"That's a great skill." David nodded in approval.

"I'm going to clean out the refrigerator and do laundry." Margarette sipped her iced tea.

"I'm going to go see Dr. Grayson." Jackie took a bite of meatloaf.

A cold stare between Jackie and David ensued.

"David, will you take me?" She covered her mouth to hide the food she chewed.

"If that's what you want."

Tyler using his fork shoved his meatloaf around on his plate. David glared at Tyler. "Eat your meatloaf."

"It's yucky, I want peanut butter and jelly."

Jackie dropped her fork. "This isn't a drive-thru, just eat your dinner or go to bed." She slammed her fist onto the table.

Tyler pouted and swallowed hard; his eyes swelled. "I hate you. I wish you never got better." He elbowed his plate onto the floor.

Sebastian bawled. Margarette patted his back and offered him his sippy cup.

"Tyler Andrew Hennessey!" David scooted his chair away from the table scraping it against the floor. "Tell your mother you're sorry."

"I'm not sorry, I hate her." Tyler bolted from the chair and headed quickly up the stairs.

Margarette, David, and Jackie stared at each other as Sebastian continued to cry.

Jackie scooted her chair back and stormed out of the room, up the stairs and slammed her bedroom door.

"Son of a bitch." David kicked his chair. "Do something with Sebastian. Don't just sit there and let him cry."

Margarette threw her napkin onto the plate, rose and scooped up Sebastian. "Are you happy? Because I'm not." Margarette and Sebastian stormed out the back door.

David slammed his fist onto the table and shoved it. He punched the wall. "God, why are you doing this to us?"

11. THE QUARRYMAN'S MISTAKE

Jackie paced in the foyer by the front door. "If you don't get down here, I'll drive myself to see Dr. Grayson. I don't have all morning."

David's voice bolstered from upstairs. "I'm coming, just give me one more minute."

"I don't want to be late, this is important."

"You won't be late, please just show me some respect."

"I was thinking the same thing."

David jogged down the stairs gripping the keys in his hand. "See, I'm ready. Sometimes you can't help it when nature calls. You can't rush a good poop."

"Oh God, I didn't need to hear that."

"Then don't rush me next time. Are you ready?" He opened the door.

"I've been ready for twenty minutes."

Margarette strode into the formal area. "You two try to get along and stay safe."

"Bye Mom, I love you." David closed the door behind him and Jackie.

∞

Jackie in a hypnotic trance on the chaise clutched the pocket watch pendant with one hand; she sighed. Although in a somnambulistic state, she smelled the burning incense, heard the tranquil music and focused on Dr. Grayson's voice aware of her surroundings.

"Tell me what you see." Dr. Grayson adjusted his position in his royal blue velvet chair and scratched his chin academically.

"A graveyard?"

"Are you there for a funeral?"

"I think so."

"Tell me what you see."

∞

The year of our Lord, 1728 proved to be desperate times for the Moggs as the scarcity of money and food compelled Samuel to perform an irredeemable act to feed his family.

Molly, age fifty-four, and Elijah Mogg, age twenty-one, strolled side-by-side in a graveyard; both dressed in black. Molly carried a red fresh cut yard rose. Elijah carried a Bible against his chest. They stopped in front of a tombstone marked:

"Here lies Samuel Henderson Mogg, a faithful husband and father. September 25, 1672 – June 19, 1728."

Molly gingerly placed the rose onto the gravestone. "Your father was a good man. I'm lonely without him."

"Then why did you kill him?"

"Have you lost control of your senses? I never hurt your father, I loved him."

"No, Mother. It was you who encouraged him to become a shoe peg maker and made us leave our family home. He wasn't any good at it. It was torture and he couldn't feed us."

"We had no choice. He didn't make enough money as a quarryman. He did a dreadful thing."

"I don't believe you, Mother. You will become nothing more than a spinster, and rightfully so. I'm not here to help you pick up the pieces. I'm here to honor my father's life."

"When he stole those stones, the quarrymen hunted him. That's who killed him, not me."

A group of six men within earshot emerged from the bushes. They each carried guns.

Fear gripped Molly as she recognized the leader. "Son, those men aren't here to say goodbye to your father. They're from the quarry. We must take our leave now without hesitation."

"I don't understand."

"They came to the house looking for their gems your father stole. Who do you think beat your father to a pulp? They believe I have the stones. They'll stop at nothing to get them back."

"That's why you sent me away to stay with Uncle Thomas?"

The men stomped through the overgrown grass as they approached the Moggs.

"Yes, Son, we must leave quickly."

"Why did father not tell me the truth?"

"He was too ashamed, Elijah. We must leave. We can't stand our ground. They want the gems and they'll kill us to get them."

"Where are they Mother?"

"Long gone in exchange for a milk cow, three chickens and food for our table. It was a harsh winter."

The leader aimed his shotgun toward them. "Mrs. Mogg."

Molly's heart raced. "Run." She grabbed Elijah's hand, and they bolted toward the wooded area.

The men pursued firing their weapons.

139

As Molly and Elijah crossed into the woods, Molly glanced back.

The leader fired his shotgun.

The bullet penetrated her back. Thud. Her knees buckled; she collapsed as she pulled Elijah with her onto the ground. "Elijah run, never stop running."

"No Mother, I can't leave you."

The leader grunted. "Where are the stones? If you don't tell me, I'll kill your son."

"Mother, I beg you to tell him what you and Father did with them. They're not worth dying over."

The men stood over Molly and Elijah. "Listen to your son, where are the stones?"

"We… traded… them for food." She gasped and jerked as her eyes rolled into the back of her head.

Gunshot fired directly into Elijah's temple. He collapsed onto Molly as they took their last breaths.

∞

Jackie shivered and whimpered. A frown furrowed deep across her brow. "Never stop running." Her breath quickened as she mumbled her words. "Never stop running. It is what it is, and it always will be."

"Jackie, take a slow deep breath. Remember you're in a safe place; no one can harm you here."

Jackie exhaled and moaned almost as if she experienced pain.

"That's it, Jackie, breathe. Do you know how Samuel died?"

"He's been dead for one year." A tear rolled down Jackie's face.

Dr. Grayson's face hardened in confusion. "How did Samuel die Jackie?"

She whimpered and sniffled. Her facial muscles tensed as her grip tightened around the pendant. From the pressure of her hold, her knuckles whitened. "I don't want to tell you, I'm upset." Tears flowed from Jackie. "I keep hearing the same message over and over. It is what it was, and it will be what it will be. I want to stop."

"All right Jackie, take a deep breath and relax. I'm going to count to five, when I reach five, your eyes will open. One. Two. Three. Four. On five, you will awake and feel refreshed. Five, you're awake."

Dr. Grayson stopped the video camera using the remote.

Jackie opened her red, watery puffy eyes, and stretched.

"Jackie, how do you feel?"

"Like a freak in a roadside circus. How am I supposed to feel? Please call David and have him pick me up."

∞

David and Jackie drove home in silence. Jackie stared out the car window and avoided David's glare.

"Are you going to tell me what happened?" David tapped his fingers against the steering wheel.

Jackie remained silent and continued to stare at the scenery. When she glanced at St. Mary's Immaculate Assumption Catholic Church, she felt an unexplained wanting desire. "Please stop, I need to speak to a priest."

"It has been a while since your last confession."

"That's not it, I need answers about doctrine."

"If my dad was still alive, he could answer anything you wanted or needed to know. Why don't you ask Uncle Paul? He's a preacher."

"I'll pass, I want an unbiased opinion from someone who doesn't know me."

"Okay, I hope you find what you're looking for. I'll pull over."

"Thanks, it's extremely important."

David parked the car, exited and assisted Jackie with her door. She stepped from the car and put her hand in the air.

"Please, can you wait here? I won't be long. I need to do this on my own."

"If you insist. I won't pretend I like it, but I will honor your request."

∞

Jackie sat next to Father McFadden on a church pew midway from the front altar. She glanced in awe toward the beautiful stained glass windows. "This is a beautiful church."

"Yes, Mrs. Hennessey it is. I'm almost certain you didn't come here to talk about the architectural details of God's house. What can I help you with today?"

"What is the Catholic Church's position on reincarnation?"

"Is there a particular reason for your inquiry?"

"I have a friend who went to see a regression hypnotist. She told me about the lives she had in the past."

"A friend, Mrs. Hennessey?"

"Please call me Jackie; and yes, a friend."

He nodded as he gazed into her eyes for truth in her words. "Do you understand the concept of reincarnation?"

"I believe I do, but feel free to give me the Catholic definition."

"The word reincarnation comes from Latin and means 'Entering the flesh again.' In other world religions their leaders teach that once someone perishes on earth and their body decomposes that the consciousness of the soul is reborn into another body."

"Is there any truth to that?"

"Depends on the religion you hold to believe is true. For example, some religions preach that a person is born multiple times, even as much as a thousand times, before they achieve perfection. Once you achieve perfection, your soul will no longer be born into another vessel. They believe reincarnation can be in the form of an animal, plant or even an insect."

"Now, that sounds crazy."

"Well, other religions teach how you lead your current life determines your next reincarnation. They believe the wrongs you do in the here and now will occur to you in the next life or lives."

"You've got to be kidding me. It sounds as if you believe in reincarnation."

"Not at all. I'm making sure you understand the concept of reincarnation. I turn to the Bible for guidance and for the truth in defining my answer."

"So, does the Bible say reincarnation is possible like other religions claim?"

"On the contrary, the Bible clearly states that reincarnation isn't a possibility. Allow me to explain using scripture." He retrieved a Bible from the pew next to him and opened it. "I'll start with Luke, chapter twenty-three verse twenty-four at the point when Jesus was dying on the Cross as he was being crucified for his sins. I'm sure you know the story?"

"Yes, go on." Her face flushed from the lie she told as she only had a vague recollection of Jesus' crucifixion.

"Jesus looked over to the thief being crucified next to him and said, 'I tell you the truth, today you will be with me in paradise.' Jesus never said or alluded to the thief he would come back into another body, now did he?"

"I'll take your word on that."

"Not my word, but the word of Jesus Christ. Now, let me continue with chapter nine, verses twenty-seven and twenty-eight from the book of Hebrews." He thumbed through the Bible until he found the verses and handed it to Jackie. "The doctrine is clear. Follow along as I read." He pointed to the first verse. "This is what I know to be true in Hebrews. 'Just as people are destined to die once, and after that to face judgment, so Christ was sacrificed once to take away the sins of many.'

This passage has two important attributes in His words. First, with destiny on our side, we only die once. Secondly, the moment of Christ's sacrifice, he took our sins with him. I'll ask you this, was Jesus sacrificed a thousand times for each reincarnation?"

"Not to my knowledge, but then again my memory isn't all that great."

"Well, he wasn't. Jesus' sacrifice only occurred once. There was no second life on earth in another body or form. He wasn't reincarnated, he was resurrected."

"Now I'm more confused, he was resurrected. That indicates to me a second life on earth."

"Not at all. Jesus wasn't born into another person or as an animal. He was resurrected meaning brought back to life. I hope this helps you Jackie. I suggest you dig deeper into the Bible for your own answers."

"Thank you, Father McFadden, you've been a lot of help."

∞

Margarette placed the clear-glass lid onto the pan covering the jambalaya as Tyler played with Sebastian in the living room play area.

"It won't be long now boys, Mommy and Daddy should be back soon."

"I only want Daddy." Tyler threw one of his toy cars at Sebastian which caused his brother to scream. "Mommy isn't my mom."

Margarette strode to Tyler and knelt beside him. "Your Mommy is your mother, don't ever say that again."

"I hate her, and she hates me."

"She loves you and your brother very much."

"Then why doesn't she play with us or read to us?"

Margarette hugged Tyler and kissed his cheek. "She will as soon as she can."

David and Jackie entered the house. "See, I told you they'd be home soon, and dinner is ready. Perfect timing." Margarette stood as they entered the living room. "How did it go?" She sat on the rocking chair.

David shrugged his shoulders. His chest expanded as he took in some much-needed oxygen.

Jackie gave David a cold stare, bolted up the stairs and slammed the door.

Frustration filled David's voice. "She won't talk about it."

"Did you ask the doctor?"

"He's not talking either, a matter of patient-doctor confidentiality."

"Give her time, she's been through a lot."

"Like none of us haven't." David strode over and kissed Tyler on top of the head. "Hey little buddy."

"Hi Daddy, you want to play with my trucks?"

"Not now, maybe after dinner." David picked up Sebastian and swung him in the air to Sebastian's giggling delight.

"Don't worry David, it's only a matter of time before she gets her memory back. You can't give up now."

"Who said anything about giving up? I'm frustrated and tired of dealing with this crap. I want our old lives back when everything was perfect."

Tyler covered his mouth with his hand. "Oooo, Daddy said crap."

Upstairs in the master bedroom, Jackie sat in the corner; her knees up with her arms wrapped around them as she stared straight ahead. The sun beamed through the window blinds and soon faded into darkness as it melted into the horizon.

The doorknob jiggled. "Go away, it's locked for a reason."

"Dinner is ready." David's soft tone aggravated her more than it did to entice her to join the family for dinner.

"I'm not eating, go away."

145

"Whatever happened today with Dr. Grayson, we can work through it."

"I said go away!"

David slammed his fist onto the wall and kicked the door. He leaned his back onto it, slid down and sat on the floor. He grabbed his hair and tugged it.

The stairs creaked.

Margarette stood over David. "You have to just give her time, she's been through a lot."

"So, have I."

"Look at me."

David glanced upward at Margarette as his jaw clenched.

Margarette exhaled. "We all have, none of us have gone untouched." Margarette reached for David's hand. "Come on, let's go eat. You need to be with your children."

David shook his head. "She does too, don't you think?"

"Go ahead downstairs, I'll try to talk some sense into her."

He stood and strode down the stairs.

Margarette knocked on the bedroom door.

"Damn it, David! I said to go away."

"Jackie, I want you to know I love you. We won't give up on you." Margarette waited for a response. "Dinner is ready. Please consider joining us. Did you hear me?"

"What part of go away don't you two understand?"

Margarette gestured the Cross. "Dear Lord, please put your healing touch on Jackie and this family." Her eyes flushed as she turned to go downstairs.

Inside the bedroom, Jackie's position hadn't moved as she stared straight ahead; her eyes glazed over. "Dear God, if there really is a God, please listen. I don't know who I am. I don't know my family. Hell, I don't even know if you're real. If you are real, please help me and give me patience to cope with all of this mess." She sobbed and couldn't catch her breath.

12. THE CROWN JEWELS

The next morning Jackie trudged downstairs and glanced out the front door. "Where could he have gone?"

She strolled through the formal area, picked up a wooden toy block and entered the kitchen.

Margarette closed the refrigerator.

"Mom, where's David?"

"I'm not sure, he left before I got up. Coffee is ready, do you want a cup?"

"Can we talk?"

"You've always been able to tell me anything without judgment, don't you remember?"

"Frankly, no. I'll just have to take your word on that."

∞

David sat on the front porch of Dr. Grayson's home office. The front door opened. Dr. Grayson stepped out and retrieved the morning paper. "Mr. Hennessey, I wasn't expecting you. Where's Jackie?"

"She's at home locked up inside her bedroom and won't talk or eat."

"That's out of my area, but how may I help you?"

"Tell me what happened with my wife during her sessions with you."

"I can't, that information is strictly forbidden by our doctor-patient confidentiality."

"Screw that, this is my wife we're talking about."

"David, I know you and Jackie have gone through the ringer, but I cannot and will not divulge any information from our sessions. I can tell you she has made significant strides in recalling her memories."

"I don't believe you, you're a fraud and a scam artist. If you ever come near my wife again, I'll have you arrested." David stormed off.

∞

The school bell rang as children bolted down the hall and into classrooms. Beth stood at her classroom door and greeted her students as they filed in.

"Good morning Kelly, glad to see you're feeling better."

"Thank you, Ms. Andreas."

"Good morning, Ms. Andreas." Bobby ran past his teacher.

"Slow it down Bobby, you have plenty of time." She waved at Samantha who walked toward her.

"Well, good morning Samantha."

Samantha handed Beth a homemade card. "Will you get this to Mrs. Hennessey for me?"

"I sure will honey, it looks like you put a lot of work into this card."

"I made it special like the ones I make for my mom and dad. They can read them."

"You better run along before you're late for class."

"Oh, Ms. Andreas, please tell Mrs. Hennessey my mom said everything works out for the best."

"Run along Samantha before you're late to class."

"You don't believe me, do you?"

"I do, now run along."

Samantha skipped down the hall.

Poor girl. She can't let go of her mother. Beth closed the classroom door behind her.

∞

An Uber car stopped in front of Dr. Grayson's home office. Jackie took a deep-nervous breath. "Thank you for the safe transportation."

"That's what I do, have a wonderful day."

"Wait, can you stay for a few minutes? It won't take me long and I'll need a ride back home?"

"That goes against the rules. Just use the Uber app and request another ride. It shouldn't take long for one to arrive in this area of the city."

"Thanks anyway." Jackie exited the car, walked up to the porch, and knocked onto the door.

It didn't take long for Mrs. Grayson to answer. "Mrs. Hennessey, I didn't know you had an appointment today."

"Do you have a minute?"

Mrs. Grayson nodded and gestured for Jackie to enter.

Jackie followed Mrs. Grayson into the parlor.

"Please sit, Mrs. Hennessey. I'll get us some tea."

"That won't be necessary, I don't want to put you to any trouble."

"Nonsense, it's no trouble at all. I'll be right back." She jetted a slight grin toward Jackie and exited.

Jackie surveyed the room. *Dr. Grayson has a lot of books.*

She strolled to the bookshelf and touched a two-inch crystal pyramid. *Do I dare pick it up?* When she retrieved the pyramid, the sunbeam which came through the window refracted a rainbow. *Such beauty in a tiny object.* She returned it to the shelf next to nine other crystals and the book *Crystal Power, Crystal*

Healing by Michael Gienger. *Note to self. When I can read, get this book.*

She touched the spine of *The Diagnostic and Statistical Analysis of Mental Disorders* book by the American Psychiatric Association. A coldness swept through the room. She turned as if she expected to see someone. When she turned back toward the book, she recognized three of the words in the title. "The... I don't know... and... blah, blah of blah, blah. What is this book about? It's next to a statue of Sigmund Freud." *Wait, how do I know that?*

Jackie slid her finger across several more books. "Okay, he's a medical kind of man." *I think.* She grabbed the book, *One Man's Journey into the Past to Face the Future* by Dr. Bryan Reiss. From the kitchen, the tea kettle whistle jolted Jackie. She opened the book and tried to read the autographed inscription. Her fingers slid across the handwritten words although they were unidentifiable to her. "To one of my best clients, your soul lives forever." *He must have friends in high places.*

Mrs. Grayson returned carrying a tray filled by a tea pot, two tea cups and scones. "I see you found one of Dr. Grayson's favorite books. It's an interesting read if you'd like to borrow it." She put the tray onto the table between the two Victorian chairs.

Jackie returned the book into its designated slot. "It seems like it would be, but I haven't gotten that part of my memory back. Reading proves to be exceedingly difficult since my accident."

"I'm sure you'll get that back with patience and therapy."

"That's what I'm hoping for."

"Please, sit and join me." Mrs. Grayson poured the tea into the cups as Jackie took her seat.

"My dear, what brings you here today?"

"I needed someone to talk to."

"What about sharing with your husband? Can't you confide in him?"

"Not about this, he wouldn't understand."

"How do you know if you're not willing to share?"

"His dad was a Wesleyan Methodist pastor. He wouldn't understand."

"He must be steadfast in his religious beliefs."

"That's the understatement of the century. He is extremely hardheaded."

"So, what do you want to discuss with me?"

"When we first met, you suggested that I must free myself of my fears. What did you mean by that?"

"Often, my child, we're afraid to face the unknown because we're scared by it. If it is new to us or different from what we hold to be true, we often dismiss it and shy away from it rather than to face it. For my husband's gift to blossom within you, you must not question the outcome because of your fear of discovering the truth."

"I saw myself in a different life, I'm living in the *Twilight Zone*."

"Was it a different life or a continuation of the life you now live?"

"I don't know, I have a brain injury. It's probably my mind playing tricks on me."

"Could it not be that you have known all the time, but refuse to see?"

"I'm just confused, it feels so real."

"Because what you are seeing and remembering is real. All of what you remember in your past lives happened just like you saw them."

"It's crazy, it's like I'm watching a movie or something."

"That is a common explanation, nothing to be concerned about."

Dr. Grayson entered the room; a frown burrowed deep. "I wasn't expecting you, I'm quite surprised to see you again."

"Dr. Grayson, please excuse my intrusion. I'm just looking for some answers."

"You are in control of your answers, not me or my wife."

"How do I know what is real?"

"Your subconscious doesn't lie. It is there where the truth lives. I have time if you'd like another session?"

"Yes, I'll take you up on that. I need to learn more about myself."

"Carla, will you set up the camera? Jackie, why don't you go relax and get comfortable on the chaise."

"With pleasure." Carla exited the room.

After Jackie ensconced on the couch, she took a deep breath as Mrs. Grayson returned and set up the camcorder.

Dr. Grayson powered the soft music and adjusted the volume.

"I like your choice in music, it makes me relax."

"That's the idea for using it." Dr. Grayson sat in his chair. "It won't take you as long to get into a trance state, you've taken to hypnotherapy."

"Glad to hear it, I think."

"Okay, now just relax and breathe in slowly. Listen to my voice and my voice only."

"I will, I know the drill."

"Relax." Dr. Grayson waited a moment. "I'm going to give you a minute or two to settle before we begin. I want you to take a slow deep breath and hold it. Good, now release."

Jackie inhaled slowly again and exhaled.

"That's great Jackie. Breathe in… and out… Focus on the white puffy clouds, or the beach as the waves gently roll toward you. Listen to the ocean's waves and relax. Feel your tension slowly leave your body." Dr. Grayson watched for signs that indicated her relaxed and tranced state. "Great, Jackie. You're doing great. When I count backward from five, you will completely relax. Five… Four… Three… Two… One. Find a door and enter."

Jackie's breath slowed and deepened. With her eyes closed, they darted with rapid eye movement.

"Jackie, where are you?"

"I'm in a grand palace. Richmond Palace, I remember living here in fifteen fifty-eight."

"What do you see?"

∞

The Richmond Palace overlooked the Themes River and considered by all the favored of Queen Elizabeth the First who spent most of her time there in residence. It lay upstream nine miles and across the banks from the Palace of Westminster.

Inside, the Palace held a majestic ambiance with stone walls, mammoth candle chandeliers and expensive furniture. Every hall represented the throne – the Queen's throne. The grandeur unmatched by any other palace owned by royalty or nobility.

Queen Elizabeth, a beautiful woman with light brown eyes imposingly sat at the head of the thirty-foot dining table. Her red updo wig accentuated her porcelain skin. She wore a magnificent black and white gown hand embroidered with colored thread and embellished with rubies, pearls, diamonds and sapphires. Jewels also formed a crown in her elaborate wig.

Beneath her gown, a corset stiffened with wood, a farthingale and stockings, although uncomfortable, it elevated the Queen in status from the other women in the room. Neck and wrist ruffs just as elegant as her gown complimented her attire. None could match the gown she chose for the gala.

Her makeup, strange from modern times, painted her face with white lead and vinegar to cover her smallpox scars. A blush color rouge made from red dye and egg white highlighted her lips and cheeks.

The Queen fanned herself with a pomander in full control of her audience seated at the table. The jeweled rings on her fingers glistened beneath the candlelight chandeliers.

Robert Dudley, Earl of Leicester, sat to the right of the Queen. On her left sat Kate Ashley and Blanche Parry, her favorite Ladies-in-waiting. Several other important Dukes and Earls occupied the other seats.

On the outskirt of the massive dining hall, several guardsmen who wore royal red velvet cloaks stood sentry as the state banquet took place. Everything regarding this evening equated to the formality of pomp and circumstance of the Queen which represented her authority as head of the church. Every pageantry detail from setting the table to serving the meal signified her religious ceremony and presentation.

Kate leaned toward Blanche and whispered into her ear which caught the Queen's attention from the corner of her eye.

The Queen in conversation with Robert glared at her Ladies-in-waiting. "Do not tell secrets to those whose faith and silence you have not already tested."

"Yes, my Queen." Kate nodded apologetically. "That advice I shall take to thy grave. I express thy deepest regret if thy have offended thee."

The Queen nodded her head in forgiveness. "I pray to God that each of you shall have safe passage back to your homeland. Our alliance shall be fruitful for all." The Queen stood as one ruby fell from her royal dress which landed at her maidservant's feet.

The maidservant knelt, retrieved it and nonchalantly stuffed the crown jewel into her pocket.

"Your Majesty." Robert Dudley stood and bowed his head two inches. "Prior to your departure, I have a gift to bestow to thee. Shall I present it to thee, my Queen?"

"Proceed with your presentation, Earl of Leicester."

The Earl retrieved a ruby and diamond ring which portrayed a miniature enameled portrait of the Queen's mother, Anne Boleyn, along with a portrait of herself. He handed it to the Queen who shone a dignified *smile. "It gives thy sincere pleasure to be on the receiving end of thee smile. It is not often that I am graced by it."*

"Though the sex to which I belong is considered weak, you will nevertheless find me a rock that bends to no wind." The Queen's tone strong and fierce filled the room with an authority no one could question. "However, I accept your gracious gift and shall cherish this ring throughout eternity. Farewell to you all and shall you go in peace." The Queen glowered toward the maidservant as she extended her hand. Her eyes burned with anger upon her. Silence prevailed. "Young maidservant, return what thy have stolen and I will spare thee your life."

The maidservant froze in fear as her heart thundered. "My Queen, I have stolen nothing." Her voice quivered. "I gathered the ruby only to keep it safe until I could return it to thee."

"You have offered an explanation which thy cannot swallow. The punishment for stealing from thy Queen is death. Guards, search her."

The frightened maidservant bolted from the dining room, pushed through the heavy wood five-inch double door and ran down the stairwell to hide. Several royal Guardsmen pursued. She tripped on the third step, rolled to the bottom and landed in a prone position. A pool of blood formed around her as she tightly gripped the ruby.

The Queen stood regal at the top of the stairs and glared downward at the maidservant. "I pray to God that thy shall not live one hour after thy have thought of using deception."

"Shall the maiden be hanged or disemboweled?" The guard who stood by the maiden bowed. "My Queen, what is thy decree?"

The young maidservant lifted her head and struggled to speak. "I beg thee for thy forgiveness, my Queen. Please have mercy upon my soul as I protest my guilt thee has placed upon thy actions."

"Let this be a lesson to all thieves throughout the land. She professed her guilt and must now pay her penitence and suffer thy consequences."

"I beg you my Queen, let me be and I'll serve thee through eternity." She clutched the ruby in her palm.

The Queen took four steps as she descended the stairs. "I command thee to hand over thy crown jewel."

The maidservant lifted her right hand and opened it. The ruby rested on her palm.

"Guardsman, retrieve thy jewel and disembowel her now for thy maidservant is nothing but a thief."

The guard kicked the maidservant over onto her back and shoved his foot onto her chest. He pressed down to hold her in place, drew his sword and slashed it across her stomach, and again.

The maidservant screamed in agony until her body fell limp as the Queen watched satisfied the punishment fit the crime for all to proclaim throughout the lands.

The guardsman knelt by the maidservant and retrieved the ruby. "May God have mercy on your soul."

The maidservant gasped her last breath.

∞

David sat behind his desk. He stared at Jackie's wedding portrait. *Life was perfect then. Now I don't know what the future holds.* He picked up the phone and dialed his home number.

At home, Margarette prepared a roast as she watched her favorite daytime talk show. The children napped on the couch.

The phone rang, and she quickly answered.

"This is the Hennessey residence."

"Hey, Mom, will you get Jackie to the phone?"

"Hold on, she's still sleeping. You want me to just have her call you back?"

"I'll wait, I have something important to tell her."

Margarette placed the receiver onto the countertop and headed up the stairs.

Jackie's bedroom door cracked open, surprised Margarette. She peered inside. "Jackie! David's on the phone for you."

She waited for a response.

"Jackie! Pick up the phone." She looked into the bathroom. "Jackie, I'm worried about you. Answer me, answer me now."

Margarette stormed from room to room upstairs frantically searching for Jackie. "Jackie! Where are you?" Her heart felt like it sank to her stomach.

Margarette rushed back downstairs. "Jackie. Do you hear me?" Now frightened, Margarette picked up the receiver, her voice filled with panic. "David, she's nowhere. I've looked everywhere."

"You sure?"

"I'm positive, there's no sign of her."

"What about her car?"

"It's still in the driveway."

"I'm on my way home."

Margarette hung up the phone just as the doorbell rang. "Now what?"

She raced to the door and opened it. "Beth, nice to see you." Margarette, out of breath, wiped the small bead of sweat from her upper lip.

"You too, Margarette. I have another special delivery from the students for Jackie, can I come in?"

"Beth, she's not here."

"Oh, she told me yesterday she didn't have plans and to drop by."

"That's what has me worried, we don't know where she is."

"She's not with David?"

"No, we're both worried sick. Something upset her yesterday during her session with Dr. Grayson. She wouldn't talk to us about it."

"Margarette, we need to talk, may I come in?"

"I could use the company while I wait on her to come home from wherever she is."

Beth entered the house.

Margarette picked up the newspaper from the porch and shut the door. "Would you care for a cup of tea?"

"Not today, I have something important to tell you."

They proceeded into the living room.

Margarette sat in the rocking chair and stared at Beth. "Have a seat. What is it we need to talk about?"

"I'll stand. Has Jackie told you anything about her sessions with Dr. Grayson?"

"Not at all, she clams up and won't tell us anything. Has she said something to you?"

"Indirectly, yes."

"Spill the beans, what has she said?"

"It's not what she said, it's the questions she asked about reincarnation."

"Reincarnation?"

"Yes, Ma'am, in my religion we believe in reincarnation."

"What religion is that?"

"Buddhism. After I graduated from college, I lived in China for three years and taught English. One day, I visited a Buddhist temple and had a life-changing event during the meditation service. After that, I became a Buddhist."

"I won't judge you on your choice of religion, but reincarnation goes against our Catholic beliefs. Jackie is Catholic."

"I know, Jackie and I talked about that. That's why she won't tell you and David about her regression sessions."

"What does her sessions have to do with you being a Buddhist?"

"I'll try to explain this as delicately as possible. I'm walking a very thin line by even telling you this, but I think you need to know."

"Go on, please."

"The core concepts for Buddhism are reincarnation and karma. To simplify things, both concepts deal with how we as humans go forward throughout our life; or, with reincarnation, how we go forward to multiple lives."

"You're serious about this?"

"Yes, Ma'am, please let me finish. Karma has a lot to do with what we are or what life we will live once reincarnated. There is a moral compass we adhere too. If you hurt someone, you are likely to get that back in your next life. It's like this. I see a rock and pick it up. Nothing wrong with that, right?"

"I think not."

"But, if I took that rock, hit someone over the head and busted their skull, karma would come back on me negatively. If I used that rock to fill a crack in a leaking levee and prevented flood waters entering the neighborhood, then I would receive something positive my next time around."

"I guess that's why they say, karma is a bitch."

"Exactly."

"I'm still confused, what does this have to do with Jackie?"

"During her sessions, she's remembering her past lives."

"Excuse me." Margarette gulped and tensed her body. "She'll go to Hell for that."

Beth pursed her lips. "Now you know why she's not telling you and David anything."

"This is ridiculous, she doesn't know what she thinks. She doesn't need a hypnotherapist, she needs a shrink."

"Pardon me, being in the state that Jackie is, having judgment about what she is experiencing will only be a detriment to her process of healing."

"The only detriment I see here is she's being brainwashed into believing something that isn't true, and you're encouraging it. None of this is true."

159

"Nobody has the right to tell someone what is and is not true. Jackie is trying to figure out her life. Both you and David keep telling her you love her and that she has a happy life. Does that make it true?"

"Well, yes, because we do."

"Just because you believe it to be true, doesn't mean she believes it to be true. For her, the truth is only what she has known for the past eight months. Put yourself in her shoes. She can't read, she became a stay at home mom whose sons don't recognize her, her husband and her own mother are wrapped in their egos of religion so she can't be honest and truthful. If she does, she fears judgment and ridicule. That is her truth. That's why she shuts herself inside her room."

"Ridiculous accusations."

"Nothing you tell her will ever be the truth. What she witnesses and feels and breathes will be the tipping point of her awareness into who she is now. Who will you be when she reaches her destiny?"

The front door creaked and slammed shut.

"That must be David, I think it's time for you to leave."

David bolted into the living room. "Have you heard from her? Oh, Beth, I didn't realize you were here. Have you heard from Jackie?"

"No, I haven't, and I was just leaving. Good luck David, I hope you find peace in this life and the one after." Beth left the Hennessey home in a hurry.

"That was awkward." David frowned puzzled. "She didn't need to leave."

"David, I think you need to sit down and listen to what Beth just told me."

13. FRAULEIN

Three hours elapsed since Jackie revealed to Dr. Grayson the maidservant's fate. As her past lives flashed before her, it seemed as if she watched a movie. Jackie's hunger for the truth huddled between the recess of her subconscious to vivid lives once lived as she continued in a trance opening and closing doors representative of her past.

"That's good Jackie, where are you?"

"I'm at a formal dance in Nazi Germany. I think nineteen forty-three."

"How do you know?"

∞

The Clärchens Ballhaus *dance hall, in Berlin, filled to capacity by German soldiers, top Nazi brass officers and women ready to dance. The hall, magnificent in grandeur with twenty-foot ceilings, massive wood wainscot and large wooden doors provided the perfect place to dance during time of war. Almost every wall bolstered by a mirror; the largest at least twenty by ten feet framed in ornate gold stood as the dance hall's centerpiece.*

A beautiful woman dressed in a 1940s style dress stood on the side of the dance floor and observed Erwin Rommel, a German Field Marshall dressed in uniform, as he strode toward her. His steps, slow and confident sent unwelcomed chills down her spine. She ogled his hand as he twirled a small item in his palm. When he reached her, he nodded, clicked his heels and bowed with his arms to his side still clutching the small object.

She batted her eyelashes toward him, and a soft sensual curl of her lip formed. "Good evening Field Marshall Rommell." *Her voice rang of a German accent.* "May I be so bold as to inquire what you possess in your hand?"

He twirled the small object again. "I'm surprised that you took notice, most women don't."

"I always notice everything about a man and anything he may hold." *Her raspy tone flirtatiously lured him into her grasp as she continued to gaze into his eyes.*

A slight grin crossed the Field Marshall's lips. He held up the object between his thumb and index finger. "It's a marble I recently acquired from Hitler. It reminds me there is still beauty in life amidst war. Open your hand." *He cupped her hand beneath his and gently placed the marble onto her palm.*

She lifted the marble and examined the round glass piece. "It certainly is beautiful, I've never seen a marble like this."

"It's made here in the homeland, it's called a Latticino."

"Fascinating." *She returned the marble to its rightful owner.*

He stowed the marble into his uniform's pocket and extended his hand. "Fräulein, may I have the honor of dancing with you?"

"I would be delighted."

He grasped her hand and guided her to the dance floor just as a waltz began. The two glided around the floor in perfect unison as if they danced together their entire lives.

"Fräulein, what is your name?"

She hesitated before answering. "I am Adelsia Coltidel, but you may call me Adel." *Her voice soft, delicate and pure pleased her dancing partner.*

"You're a graceful dancer."

"Thank you, dancing with my father never hurt either."

"Your father sounds refined as to have taught his daughter of such beauty to dance with such elegance and grace."

She fluttered her lashes once again as she accepted the German leader's compliment.

He twirled her as the song ended.

She lifted her gaze as her feathery eyelashes fluttered teasingly to maintain her hold of him in which she recently secured. "Thank you for the dance." She departed sashaying across the dance floor.

His eyes riveted on his former dance partner as he retrieved the marble from his pocket and twirled it in his fingers.

Before she reached her original spot below the showcased mirror, another uniformed Nazi Officer stepped forward and bumped right into her.

Field Marshall Rommel's brow deepened; a scowl of discernment filled his eyes as he gazed upon the chance encounter of his last dance partner. He honed his focus onto their lips as his astute lip-reading skill allowed him to eavesdrop on most conversations from a distance. A fruitful skill during a time of war or potential romance.

Adel tilted her delicate chin as her eyes met the new German officer's deep blue eyes filled with eagerness. "I sincerely apologize for my clumsiness, it is such unbecoming of a lady's behavior."

"Pardon me, Fräulein. How's the weather in Berlin tonight?"

"No chance of rain."

"It won't snow either."

"I don't foresee the sun to rise in the morning."

"Will tomorrow bring sleet?"

"No, General it won't." She retrieved a piece of paper from her small delicate purse and handed it to him. She leaned close to his ear. "Allied troops must move, they know your location." She quickly took her leave.

Field Commander Rommel's body stiffened as he clenched his jaw. "Arrest that man and woman, they're Allied spies."

Chaos erupted inside the dance hall as the General and Adel bolted through the large wooden door.

Several Nazi soldiers and the Field Commander pursued them into the heavily Nazi guarded streets of Berlin. One Nazi soldier who stood at attention to guard Field Commander Rommel's black Mercedes Benz 320 Cabriolet paid particular interest to the chase. "Halt!"

The spies ran as the soldier continued his deadly demand.

The Field Commander raised his hand. "Stop oder ich schieße."

The pair ran.

"Feuer!"

Two shots fired; one thudded into the General's back and the other into Adel. They stumbled forward together.

As their knees buckled, two more shots fired.

The spies collapsed.

Field Marshall Rommel approached Adel and her counterpart. As he passed each Nazi soldier, they saluted him.

He stood over Adel and twirled the marble. "Fräulein, it never pays to be an Allied spy. This is war. Germany's war and we will win for Hitler."

Adel gravely gazed up at Field Marshall Rommel. "May God have mercy on us all." She gasped her last breath as her body fell limp.

∞

Margarette who held a glass of iced tea and David who held a bottle of beer sat in the backyard while the boys played in the sandbox.

David's brow furrowed as his cheeks flushed red. "Beth had no right, no right to say that to you. Who does she think she is accusing us of not loving her? It's a good thing she left because I swear, I would have had that woman arrested or hurt her."

"David, please calm down. The children don't need to hear you or to see you this way." She sipped her tea. "It's been hours and we still haven't heard from Jackie."

"My point exactly! I bet you anything that son of a bitch knows where she is. I'm calling Dr. Grayson, we need to know."

"You can't be certain of that."

"Let me put it to you this way. I went to his house this morning and issued him a warning for him to stay away from Jackie. If she's there, I'm going to send him a stronger message with my fists." He rose as he chunked his empty beer bottle into the nearby trash can.

"David, you don't fight fire with fire. Please sit down and take a breather for a minute. For once, focus on Jackie and her safety."

David sat, took a few minutes to recollect his thoughts and calmed his temper.

"How about I make you a cocktail? You sit here, relax and do your best to stay calm; enjoy the boys."

David nodded defeated.

Tyler ran to David. "Daddy, Daddy, can we go swimming?"

Margarette entered the kitchen, grabbed the phone and dialed Beth's number.

"This is Beth."

"Hi Beth, it's Margarette. I know we ended our talk on a bad note, but the fact is, Jackie is still missing. Do you have any idea where she may be?"

"No Margarette, I honestly don't. I'll drive around and look for her though. I'll bring her home if I find her."

"Thank you, we'd appreciate that. Goodbye." Margarette placed the phone back into the cradle, strode to the bar and made David his cocktail. Tears swelled. Overwhelmed with grief and sorrow, her awareness of her daughter's family falling apart sent a powerless emotion throughout her soul. *Why God did you let this happen? Please bring her home safely.*

14. THE PHAROAH'S DAUGHTER

Jackie, lay in a trance and burrowed deeper into the chaise. She readjusted her position and sighed as her eyes darted beneath her eyelids.

"Jackie, do you want to stop?"

"No, I want to visit somewhere else."

"All right move to another door. Remember you are in control of which door to open and to enter. Breathe in and float on your cloud to another place. Do you feel the energy?"

"I do, it's calming."

"Good, take your time and let me know when you arrive somewhere."

Jackie's eyes darted beneath her eyelids. "No, not there, I don't want to go through that door." Her words mumbled as she sought her next destination.

"Jackie, take a deep breath. You don't have to open any door you don't want to enter. It will always be there when you're ready. As a reminder, you are in complete control where you go next."

Jackie slightly nodded her head. "I want that one." She lifted her index finger and pointed it toward the ceiling.

"Good Jackie, open the door and enter. Tell me what you see."

"I'm looking at a pyramid just on the outside of Thebes."

"What are you doing?"

"I'm in a caravan. There are lots of people. Some are walking, some on camels and several well-dressed men and women are being carried in a chair of some sort."

"Do you know where the caravan is going?"

"I believe so. I've been there before, many times."

"Where Jackie? Tell me what you see, hear and what you remember."

"It's... Seven-hundred and fifty, B.C."

"Before Christ?"

"That's right, before Christ."

"How do you know?"

"The Pharaoh told me before we left the palace how important this date was for his kingdom. It's a special day."

"Tell me what you see."

∞

A small caravan of men and women traversed toward the ancient city of Thebes; a sand dust storm quickly approached from the west. In the front of the caravan, three chair carts each carried by six slaves and three guards on each side took precedence in a royal procession.

Pharaoh Kashta and Queen Pebatjma, both dressed in elaborate ceremonial attire with beautiful Egyptian neme headdresses of lapis blue and gold with a matching striped head cloth which covered the entire back of their heads and necks sat regal in the first chair cart.

Amenirdis I rode in the second cart chair alongside Painki, her brother. Like their parents, both dressed in an embellished jewel gown of royal blue with a matching neme with the same royal blue alternated by a gold cloth and accented with jewels. In the third chair cart, the rest of the royal family rode; their garb as pompous.

The caravan of men and women who accompanied the processional either wore a belted or unbelted sheath dress and woven sandals as they walked behind the chair carts until they reached the Karnak Temple.

Upon the arrival to the temple, Egnatius, the Pharaoh's servant stepped forward. "Lower the royal family." His decree heard by all.

The slaves lowered each chair cart and three royal guards assisted the King and Queen. Their sandaled feet soon planted heavy onto the sand.

Egnatius stood beside Amenirdis' chair cart. Once the cart lowered, he assisted her exit and escorted the royal family into the temple's entrance.

Inside the temple, torches illuminated the area in the Hypostyle Hall, an area of fifty thousand square-feet with one hundred and thirty-four massive columns adorned with hieroglyphics and arranged in sixteen rows. Standing over thirty-three feet apart, one hundred and twenty-two columns made a pompous impression of wealth and importance as did the other twelve columns which stood almost forty feet tall.

The altar, majestic and impressive presented an awe-inspiring place for worship. To reach the ceremonial altar required those who sought it to climb twenty-eight marble steps. The height of the altar in relation to the vantage point from the floor gave it reverence for only the Holy of Holies included in a royal ceremony.

To the left of the altar, three musicians played their instruments - a harp, a lyre, and a flute. The original angelic song provided the perfect background for the royal procession.

Devotees stood shoulder to shoulder on each side of the grand hall and formed an aisle down the center. The royal guardsman posted at each column kept a keen watchful eye on the crowd.

The Divine Adoratrice of Amun, Shepenwepet I, waited at the raised front altar for the royal family's arrival in silent prayer as she overlooked the assembled crowd. Today's gathering assembled to witness the announcement of her proclamation to adopt Amenirdis as her replacement - the new Wife of Amun. A tradition long held by wives or daughters of the royal family which granted them a leadership position to represent the family in political affairs for the country. As the new high priestess, Amenirdis, the Pharaoh's daughter would hold prestige and considerable power over Upper Egypt, the southern territories, and serve as the Voice of Amun to dictate the edicts of the Pharaoh's policies. She would also preside over the harem of Amun's devotees and followers.

Shepenwepet kept a close eye for the royal family's processional entrance.

The three royal guards led the way as the Pharaoh and Queen's procession pompously strode through the aisle amidst a silent crowd. Their devotees dropped to their knees and bowed before the Pharaoh and his family as they approached the elevated altar. They slowly ascended the twenty-eight stairs.

The elders who engaged in the processional held their own weight with carved walking sticks as they formed two lines behind Amenirdis in respect for her and for the kingdom. Painki stood to his sister's left as they ascended the stairs. Her sisters followed behind them.

After Amenirdis and her brother reached the top of the altar, he left her side and stood with the Pharaoh and his Queen; his rightful position as the Pharaoh's son.

The reigning Wife of Amun, Shepenwepet, turned her back to the crowd and lifted her arms to the heavens. "I give unto you your servant. Who here shall transfer Amenirdis the First to Amun for eternity?"

"I have given to Him my daughter to be God's wife and have endowed her better than those who were before her." Pharaoh Kashta's declaration heard clearly throughout the hall of believers. "Surely, He will be gratified with her worship and protect the land who gave her to Him."

Shepenwepet faced the assembly and stood in front of Amenirdis, the chosen, as she held a long-decorated shaft fit for kings and queens. As her eyes fixated onto Amenirdis, Shepenwepet nodded once in slow satisfied approval expressionless. "Amenirdis the First, please avail yourself as God's servant and may your land and wealth grow with your power. May *you govern wisely. Bow before me and take your place in your Father's kingdom."*

Amenirdis knelt as the reigning high priestess touched each shoulder with the tip of the ceremonial decorated jeweled shaft. "How firm you are in your seat of eternity."

Shepenwepet removed her gaze from upon Amenirdis and relentlessly lifted her shaft toward the heavens. "Amenirdis the First, your reign to be everlasting. Your virginity always intact as you succumb to Amun's desires. May your property fill with offerings of food because it contains everything of good. Your life force is with you now and through eternity. Your ka does not leave. May the north wind blow as does your sweet breath and may your lands be fruitful because you serve Amun."

Egnatius pushed through the crowd and ran from the back of the great hall. "Amenirdis! Te amo."

The believers gawked at the king's servant who ran toward Amenirdis. "Te amo. Deny this vow and follow your heart."

Amenirdis stood steadfast and refrained from acknowledging Egnatius, once a faithful royal servant now nothing more than a peasant intruder. She accepted her vow as the new Divine Adoratrice of Amun as more important in the royal tradition than her love which resided in her heart.

The Pharaoh commanded his guards with his eyes. He stepped forward in authority. "Kill him, no one dare approach the Wife of Amun with such disregard, indignity and disgrace. The appointment of my daughter Amenirdis as the new Divine Adoratrice of Amun is to be honored and respected. No man shall defile her cleanliness or virtue."

As Egnatius ran toward Amenirdis, the royal guard who protected Amenirdis hurled his spear through the back of Divine Adoratrice Amun's former lover. Determined to reach Amenirdis, Egnatius struggled to remain upright as he stumbled forward. He grasped his chest and heaved as his knees buckled trying to reach his true love in his final steps before he collapsed at the base of the stairs. He heaved his last breath as he gazed upon the woman he loved since his childhood.

∞

Jackie trembled, moaned and released the dome pendant watch from her grasp.

"Everything is fine Jackie, you're doing great. Take a deep long breath and open your eyes."

Jackie struggled to open her heavy eyelids. She blinked, glanced at her surroundings and then squeezed her eyes shut. It took thirty seconds for Jackie's eyes to remain open. "I must have gone to sleep, I had the wildest dream." She rubbed her eyes, stretched and placed her hand over her mouth as she yawned.

"What you think is a dream isn't, you visited another one of your past lives."

"I don't even believe in reincarnation."

"Okay, then are you telling me you're a history buff?"

"I don't recall. Hell, I can't even remember the day I got married, or I gave birth much less a bunch of useless facts."

"Let's discuss your memories; or, should I say your dreams?"

"Dreams, that sounds better and doesn't make me think I'm crazy."

"Jackie, your dreams reflect memories that reside deep within your subconscious. Let's do a little research to put your mind at ease and show to you that you're not going crazy. Who was President of the United States during World War Two?"

"I don't know. The only reason I know who our current President is by watching the news. Otherwise, I wouldn't know that either."

"Who led the German troops in World War Two?"

"I'm clueless." She pursed her lips and closed her eyes. *I know I know this answer, I'm a Higgins.*

"Good Jackie, you're trying to find your memories."

"Nothing comes to my mind but a little man with a small ugly mustache. Wait, he was very evil. Do you know the answer?"

171

"This isn't about my knowledge of history, it's about you and who you were in a past life."

"I'm not the crazy one, you are Dr. Grayson. Are you trying to tell me I was that little creepy man?"

"Not by what you told me during your last session. You definitely were not that little creepy man as you put it. Try to remember everything you saw and everyone you met while it is fresh on your mind. Just lay back and close your eyes and focus on your memories."

Jackie leaned against the chaise and closed her eyes. "I remember a small marble, holy shit!" She bolted upright. "That marble is just like the one I saw and held in Aunt Susie's antique store. That's strange, are the marbles connected in any way?"

"I can't answer that for you Jackie. That answer is for you and you alone. Have you ever heard of a Field Marshall by the name of Erwin Rommel?"

"Nope, never. Wait, he's the one who had the marble. He twirled it in the palm of his hand."

"Now you're connecting the dots. What do you know about Queen Elizabeth or life during the Elizabethan age?"

"Clueless, I don't recall any details."

"Yet, you recount extraordinary details of events you don't know anything about. How do you account for that?"

"I'm dreaming."

"In a way, but if you understand your past in terms of reincarnation, it becomes a maturation process. Reflect on the energy your soul provides to you and to the energy your past lives offer. There's always a lesson for you to learn or for an opportunity for you to gain insight into your current fears and phobias. That way, I can help you address them. For instance, any current fear or certain aches and pains you have now that can't be explained are often isolated during regression."

"Is that why I was drawn to that marble?" Her brow creased with worry and confusion. "Wait, my watch necklace, I was drawn to it just like Aunt Susie told me I would." She clutched the domed pendant as if it were a long-lost friend. "That's why this necklace seemed to speak out to me, it really did belong to Gertrude. I loved this necklace the moment I saw it and felt a connection to it immediately when I held it."

"It gave you meaning in some sort of significant way."

"I'd say so, I knew it once belonged to me in a different life. There's no doubt about that in my pea brain mind. I would have killed for it."

"Now you have a better understanding of how reincarnation works. Your past lives are just as real as that pendant which is a part of your past that has now crossed into the present. I believe our past life experiences make up our current personal characteristics. The older your soul, the more we mature. Some of us are old souls and have experienced reincarnation many times. I believe you're an incredibly old soul, you're in a continual cycle of rebirth."

"You sound like one of my friends, she believes in it too."

"Almost half of the world's population believes in reincarnation, who's to say which half is correct?"

"I guess that's up to each individual to decide."

"Let's suppose I'm right. Try to isolate how your past lives you have already remembered have impacted who you are today. What have you learned so far from your dreams, so to speak?"

Jackie reflectively paused as a thin-lipped grin touched her lips. "I can never stop running."

"What do you mean by that?"

"No matter what I do or what I recall, I'm always running before a horrible and tragic death. It almost seems like that's my fate."

"Is there anything else you feel you have learned?"

"I need to be in better shape in this life."

Dr. Grayson chuckled. "Have you considered that's why you became a track star starting in junior high school and you choose to run as your main way to stay in shape today?"

"Not until now. You believe this one choice in my life to run is because of my past lives?"

"We can talk more about this before your next session, that is, if you agree to another."

"I think so, I'm feeling better about all of this and need answers. You're the only one who makes any sense."

"I'll have Carla schedule you an appointment before you leave. We can start again on your next visit. For now, absorb what you remember and try to make sense of it and most of all know you're not going crazy. You must connect the dots between your past lives and your present life."

"Wait, one more question. In this last dream I know I was in Egypt in seven hundred and fifty B.C." She shivered. "Seriously, before Christ. How is that even possible?"

"Let me explain it to you this way. Under hypnosis your conscious mind is aware of the process of regression. You know what year it is, what month and your surroundings. While you're in a deep subconscious trance state, your conscious mind analyzes what you remember in your present life. As you said, the movie you see before your eyes. Your mind in a regression state maintains the awareness and knowledge of the present and puts into context with what you see in your mind's eye when you witness it, so to speak, a past life. So, if you saw the date nineteen forty-two, and you wore clothing from the forties or World War Two clothing, that is after Christ. But, suppose you saw yourself dressed in an Egyptian gown at the foot of a pyramid and you know it is nineteen forty-two. You look around and see there is no modern transportation. Your mind

174

knows the year is B.C. In your case, you knew the exact date because it was an important date for the kingdom and the Pharaoh."

"Everything sounds so unbelievably strange."

"How do you feel about it?"

"I think I'm a skeptic, but I know what I'm seeing happened without a doubt. I remember them all."

"Then, stop driving yourself crazy. Why don't you research the who, what and when from what you already know?"

"I can't remember how to read."

"What about your friend who believes in reincarnation? Ask her to help you with your research. Go to the library, get a history lesson."

$$\infty$$

Margarette entered the living room. "I tucked the boys into bed and they're asleep. They enjoyed their baths and bedtime story."

David threw his cell phone across the room. "I've called all her doctors. No one has heard from her and the police informed me they can't do anything until she has been missing for twenty-four hours. This is bullshit!"

"It's way too early to lose it now, she'll be home soon. She needs the time to think. You know it's been hard on her this last week. Maybe you shouldn't have given her that ultimatum about not going to see Dr. Grayson anymore."

"Hell no! She's never going back to that damn fraud. He's done nothing but brainwash her."

Jackie casually entered through the front door.

"See, she's home safe and sound."

David didn't know whether to maintain his anger or be thankful Jackie arrived; anger won. "Where in the hell have you been?"

"I'm glad to see you too?"

"You can't just leave this house on your own and not tell anyone where you're going."

"Who made up that rule? I'm a grown woman."

"A grown woman with a mental problem."

"That's it, David. I shouldn't have come home." Jackie stormed up the stairs and slammed her bedroom door.

Margarette took a deep breath before she spoke. "That was a little harsh."

"Harsh? No, harsh is when you have a freaking wife who doesn't know you. Harsh is when the mother of your children doesn't accept her role. Harsh is my constant life. Do you want harsh? I'll show you harsh, get out of my face!"

Margarette's eyes flushed, she barely caught her breath. Without saying a word, she left through the front door.

"I guess Jackie comes by her behavior honestly." *The apple didn't fall far from the tree.*

15. THE BLACK PLAGUE

One Week Later

J ackie drove herself a few blocks from her house to meet Beth at the local lunch spot *Le Maidliones*. She parked her car and strode briskly to the patio sitting area where Beth sat as a server placed two freshly squeezed lemonades onto the table. Beth grinned at him. "Thank you, I see my friend now. You can go ahead and put our lunch order in."

"Right away. It shouldn't take long." The waiter turned just as Jackie almost bumped into him. "Whoa! Ladies first."

"I'm sorry." Jackie shrugged and frowned. "Oops."

The waiter strode briskly toward the side door as he shook his head.

Jackie slid the black wrought-iron chair scraping it across the brick. "Thanks for agreeing to have lunch, I needed to get away." She plopped down and immediately sipped her pink lemonade. "This is refreshing. I've never had pomegranate lemonade before I don't think."

"How did you know I ordered pomegranate lemonade?"

"I don't know."

"We used to come here a lot after teacher records day and have it."

"Now that's something I don't remember, but this is refreshing."

The waiter brought Jackie and Beth a cup of soup, a half sandwich, a small salad and placed them onto the table. He quickly left before either could request anything else.

Beth placed a napkin onto her lap. "I hope you don't mind that I went ahead and ordered. We're short on time and have lots of research ahead of us."

"If you were David that would have pissed me off, but you're not, and I'm glad you did. It looks and smells delicious."

"That's a relief. I was worried a tad bit."

Jackie tasted her soup and then took a bite of her sandwich. "Very tasty, I've had this before, I think."

"Yes, you have. You're the one who got me started on this place."

"I did?"

"Very much so and you always ordered this luncheon special. It became our fix."

"Good to hear. Let's hurry and finish so we can get to the library. I'm anxious to see what we find."

"I think it's best if I drive."

"You sound like David and my mom, they don't like me driving either." Jackie's tone postured for an attack.

"I was just thinking about finding two parking places at the library."

"Sorry about that. I didn't mean to come across defensively, it's just I'm fed up with people telling me what I can and cannot do, like drive."

"Give yourself time, you're adjusting to a lot of new things. Besides, driving isn't all it's cracked up to be."

"One car it is, yours."

∞

Beth drove Jackie in her Orange Mini Cooper toward the Metairie Public Library. It was only a ten-minute drive through the suburbs. Beth powered off the music. "I hope we find something that brings you a sense of well-being."

"That's why I need your help. Remember, I can't read, but you can."

"I know, I'm here to help."

"Were you able to transcribe my regression tapes?"

"I left out the parts of Dr. Grayson putting you under and all the idle chit-chat, but I jotted down all the juicy information."

"You mean my supposed knowledge of historical facts."

"Your sessions are remarkable. While listening, I was glued to them like they were a soap opera. God, I hope they're true."

"Wait, you're the one who believes in reincarnation; so, aren't they true?"

"You got me there. It won't be long now before we isolate the history behind your so-called dreams."

"Thanks again in advance for doing this."

"What are friends for?"

The car pulled into the library's parking lot and Beth found a parking space in the front. "Those that don't look up front, don't park up front."

"Is that Buddha or Confucius?"

"Neither, the parking fairy."

"Very funny."

Jackie and Beth exited the car. Beth held a spiral notebook and a pen. "I have everything I need for our research."

"Let's make this happen."

They entered the library just as Samantha and Mrs. Forester exited.

Samantha grinned and then stepped backward as she stared at Jackie's scar. "Mrs. Hennessey, it's so good to see you."

Jackie covered her scar with her hand and looked at Samantha with bewilderment. She didn't recognize her former student.

Beth noticed Jackie's twisted forehead. "Samantha, good to see you. Mrs. Hennessey told me she couldn't wait to thank you in person for the get-well cards you made."

"Yes, Samantha, thank you very much, I loved them."

"You're welcome, Mrs. Hennessey. I love your necklace. Where did you get it? It's so pretty."

"It was a present from my Aunt Susie."

"I like it, it looks good."

"Well, thank you."

"Mrs. Hennessey when are you coming back to school? My mom said it's almost her time to come back." Beth looked puzzled after Samantha's bizarre statement.

Jackie swallowed and took a deep relaxing breath. "Soon, real soon. I look forward to meeting your mom Samantha."

"Come on Samantha." Mrs. Forester coughed as she tugged Samantha's arm. "We have more errands to run."

"She looks forward to meeting you too. She has a lot to teach you. Bye, Ms. Andreas. Bye, Mrs. Hennessey." Samantha and her foster mother left.

"She is adorable, somehow I pictured her older in my mind."

"She misses you."

"I can tell."

"She acted kind of weird though."

"Weird? Maybe she was in shock over the ugly scar across my face. I don't look the same now."

"The way you look has nothing to do with it. Her mom and dad died two years ago. She told you her mom looks forward to meeting you."

Jackie gawked toward Beth with a bewildered gaze. "It's her imagination."

"Yeah, her imagination. You ready for your history lesson?"

"More than ready."

Beth and Jackie strode to one of the computer stations and sat down. Beth opened the spiral notebook and glanced at her first handwritten note. "It's not too late to change your mind."

"You're kidding me, right? This is something I have to know. It's either learn the truth or you'll have to commit me to a psychiatric ward."

Beth typed onto the keyboard and pressed entered. "Our first stop on this tour is to the website of *AncestryHeritage.com* to search for Jonathan Longfellow."

"Thank you again, I can't do this by myself. Can you imagine either David or my mom here doing this? For that matter, we couldn't even do this at my house. They already think I'm crazy."

"I know, I'm sorry for telling them about your regression outcome."

"That's water over the transom."

"We have a hit, Jonathan Jacob Longfellow." Beth clicked onto the link to the Longfellow family tree. She scanned the names, birthdates and his relatives. "This is very interesting."

"What? What does it say?"

Beth pointed to a name on the family tree. "Look, see that name. It says Jonathan Jacob Longfellow."

"Okay, there has to be a lot of men by that name."

"Well, from what I can see, three. The first one is the most promising."

"What about it?"

"This Johnathan Longfellow died in seventeen twenty-eight and married Tohono Chee Longfellow."

"What the hell?"

"Jackie, there is no way this is a coincidence. You couldn't have guessed Tohono married a Johnathan Longfellow in a thousand years. Your odds of hitting the billion-dollar lottery or struck by lightning are smaller than this. What you saw has to be your past life as Tohono."

"Well, it looks like I could have been. Wait, in my dream Tohono and Johnathan had a son. He stood at the door of the log cabin crying. Do they?"

"As a matter of fact, they do."

Chills jetted down Jackie's spine. For a moment, pain seemed to explode in her back exactly where the arrow entered Tohono. "Don't tell me, his name is Micha Longfellow."

"You nailed it, I thought you said you couldn't read."

"I remembered Johnathan calling the child's name before Tohono died." Jackie cast her eyes downward, unable to breathe.

"This is awesome, let's search someone else."

"Search information on Queen Elizabeth the First."

"Okay, let's see what we find." Beth typed in "Queen Elizabeth I."

"What are we looking for?"

"Any information you recalled in your session to do with Queen Elizabeth."

"There wasn't much I remember other than her dress with lots of jewels. Oh, yea, that ring of hers was gorgeous."

"You mean the ring that the Earl guy, whatever his name is who gave it to her?"

"Yea, see what you can find."

"I'm scanning the articles now, give me a minute to find one that helps."

"Apparently I have an eternity if I don't find the information in this life, I'll find it in the next."

"Now you're talking."

"I meant that as a joke."

"Joke or not, I found a great article." She pointed to the screen. "Oh my God! You will not believe this."

"Tell me, don't keep me in suspense."

"That ring you described, it's pictured here, look."

Jackie studied the photograph. "That's it, I remember seeing Earl Dudley give it to her." Jackie's heart raced as small beads of sweat formed across her brow. "Oh my God, I was there. I heard her say she'd cherish that ring throughout eternity."

"You're right again, this article said she cherished that ring until the day she died."

"I don't know what to say."

"I say this is freaking awesome. Reincarnation is real, you proved it. You were Queen Elizabeth the First."

"Not so fast, I wasn't the Queen, I know that. I must have been her maidservant. She's the one I saw die after running away."

"You mean you were the thief of the crown jewels?"

"It was only one ruby, and a guard killed the maidservant because of it."

"Amazing, you remember so much detail, but you still don't remember your family or your past."

"Look up that Pharaoh and his daughter. You wrote their names down, didn't you?"

"I did, but I'm not sure if I spelled them correctly. They were weird and almost sounded like another language."

"Just try your best."

"I have a better plan. Let's look up seven hundred and fifty B.C. and see who the Pharaoh was at the time and if he had a daughter. If these people existed, their names will come up."

"Sounds like a plan." Beth typed into the search bar and hit enter.

"There you go. By what I'm reading, they all existed. Believe it or not, the spelling of their names makes sense to me now that I'm reading about them."

"So, there is a Pharaoh's daughter?"

"I'll say; and she did rise to become the Divine Adoratrice of Amun, just like you said during your regression session."

"This may sound crazy, but will you take me to your Buddhist temple? I want to talk to Buddha. Well, not Buddha directly, but I need to speak to the priest."

"He's a Buddhist monk known as a Bhikkhu. Inside the temple is usually quiet with no one speaking or asking questions, especially if the Bhikkhu is meditating or praying."

"Wow, so many rules. I would like to hear about this religion and ask about reincarnation though."

"My temple holds workshops for new believers. Why don't you start there? I'll find out when the next one is and take you. For now, I better get you home before Margarette and David send out the National Guard to look for us. A lunch date can only take so long."

"Just as long as we make this a weekly thing, lunch that is."

"Let's plan on it your royal highness."

"Stop that, don't call me by any of those names. All of this is probably coincidental."

∞

Margarette stood in the kitchen and prepared dinner for the family when David entered the back door dressed like a professional landscaper.

"It's all kinds of hot out there. It's so hot it could melt your face off. I don't know how much longer I can keep mowing my grass."

"Well, until you hire someone it's going to be a pretty long time."

"We can't afford extra expenses right now. Between Jackie's medical bills, physical therapy, medications, and the money we spent on that fraud Dr. Grayson, there's not much money left for someone to care for our yard."

"I told you I'm willing to go back to teaching. There is a teacher shortage, I won't lose my retirement."

"Out of the question, we're not that bad off. We need to follow our budget. Frankly, now that I've given Jackie an ultimatum on not seeing Dr. Grayson, that saves us two-hundred bucks a session. When she went four hours a day, twice a week, that money added up. Thank God that's over. What a nightmare."

"I'm not so sure, David."

"What do you mean?"

"I heard her talk to someone about cashing in her savings bonds. I think she has plans to use that money for something."

"How does she even know about them?"

"I think Beth reminded her."

"Great, one more problem to face. Things would have been easier if she would have died in that crash. Hell, maybe she'll crash today and die. She'd deserve that insisting she drive herself to lunch."

"You don't mean that David."

"Honestly, I think I do. Look at our lives. Don't you think it would be easier without Jackie? You can't grieve for the living."

"Hold your tongue David. How can you make such claims about the wife of your children? Much less say it to me, her mother." Margarette threw the dish towel hard onto the countertop and stormed out of the room.

David looked at his watch. *Lunch should have been over hours ago. I can't believe I let her drive.* He picked up his cell phone and dialed

Jackie. It went straight to voicemail. *Of course, she's not answering.* He dialed Beth's number.

"Hello David, how's your day?"

"Is Jackie still with you?"

"We finished lunch hours ago."

"This means she's gone missing again."

"Not exactly, I think I know where she might have gone."

∞

"All right Jackie, tell me where you are." Dr. Grayson crossed his legs.

Jackie lay in a trance on the chaise. "I'm in Strasbourg, France. It's thirteen forty-nine, the fourteenth of February."

"Tell me what you see."

"A family gathered around a dying man."

"Are you the dying man?"

"No, Thomas is the one dying. His wife and two children are gathered around his bed."

"Do you know what's wrong with him?"

"He's terribly ill. He has large black boils over his body. It's the Black Death."

"Tell me what you see, smell and hear."

∞

In the Lord's year of 1349, somewhere in the outskirts of Strasbourg, France in Alsace on the French-German border lived a Jewish family - Thomas Smythefield, age thirty-nine, Genevieve, his wife, age thirty-eight, his daughter, Jennet age fifteen, and his son Bellingham age thirteen. The family gathered in a small cold damp bedroom.

On the bed lay Thomas infected with the plague. Boils the size of plums and apples which festered or burst covered his face and body. The rotten smell of diseased flesh and death permeated through the open-air window as Genevieve, who had three boils on her face, arms and legs, placed hot rags soaked in lavender oil over her husband's boils.

186

"If this soak doesn't help, we might have to use leaches or lance them." Genevieve's grave report upset her children. *"He can't survive in his condition. His death is near."*

"Mother, we can't hide him much longer." Bellingham stood proud as he issued another warning. *"The town's leaders do not take favor with him and his business practices. They all believe the Jews have brought on this plague."*

"Don't worry my son, the church elders will take care of us as we were born Jew just as Jesus Christ is a Jew. They understand our plight and will intervene."

"No Mother, I fear there is a tide of hatred toward all Jews. The town folks hold steadfast to their mistaken belief that the Jews started the plague by poisoning the cisterns and they proclaim all Jews must die because of it. The elders of our church will not come and assist. We must flee to safety if we choose life over death."

Thomas fought to catch his breath; his words mumbled. *"You must take the children and depart from here. There is nothing more you can do for me. I am already dead. You must save yourself and our family."*

"No, Father." Jennet buried her face onto the bed as she grasped his hand. *"I will never leave you and neither will Mother nor Bellingham."*

Thomas struggled to gaze toward Bellingham. *"You're the man of the house now. Take your mother and sister and leave for safety outside this land. Travel to a land where they welcome Jews. The masses are getting close. I hear their rage forthcoming. If you do not run now, you, your mother and your sister will assuredly be burned alive. Run, run away from this black death and live; live for me, I beg thee."*

Tears streamed down Bellingham's face. *"No Father, you taught us to stand and face the truth and not to run away. I shall have to go against your request."*

Outside beneath the bedroom window hid Francis de Cundall one of the city's political leaders who eavesdropped on the conversation. He stood in rampant anger and charged to the front of the home where a large red cross marked it. *"Take them all by force."*

A fear-struck armed anti-sematic mob led by members of the butcher's and tanners' guild rammed the front door using their clubs, lances and sticks as the cities' leaders and noblemen observed.

Once they demolished the door, Francis de Cundall stormed into the home and stood at the bedroom door. "By the authority given to me by the city leaders and by the Bishop of Strasbourg, Berthold the Second, on this date of the fourteenth of February in the year of thirteen forty-nine I order you to seize them."

The mob yelled as they raised their homemade weapons and charged the family.

"Wait!" France de Cundall stood over Thomas. "You will die by fire if you do not confess your sins. We have evidence it was the Jews who poisoned the town's water supply. Now confess and be baptized a Christian or die dishonorably as a Jew."

Thomas fought his own strength. "Run, you must save yourselves."

Genevieve, Bellingham and Jennet bolted out the open-air window to escape the wrath and judgment in honor of Thomas. Genevieve glanced back long enough to see her husband who convulsed, vomited and collapsed into his death.

"Get them all." France de Cundall led the charge through the window after the Smythefield family.

The mob chased Genevieve, Bellingham and Jennet down the cobblestone streets, through alleys, and into an open field near a church. Hundreds of armed soldiers on horseback encircled them in their death trap.

From inside the church, thousands of screams in panic erupted. Those held captive within, tried by might to escape.

France de Cundall roared as if his voice needed to project to the next village. "Thousands will die at our mercy today by fire to rid our city of these vile and pestilent Jews!" His statement roused the mob as the horseman chased each Smythefield through the field.

The mob first trapped Genevieve who fought back as Bellingham and Jennet met the same fate.

France de Cundall dismounted his steed and stood bolstering his shoulders with authority. "Line the Jews up in front of me."

Several men pushed the three into a single line.

France de Cundall stepped toward Genevieve. "You don't have to die a Jew, confess yourself to God and be saved."

"I'd rather die a Jew than become one of you." She spat onto his face.

He backhanded her which left a large red whelp across her cheek. "Then you shall burn with all the lepers and Jews and rid our land from the black plague of death."

France de Cundall stepped in front of Bellingham. "Do you confess your sin before thy God and these witnesses? Will you be baptized and be freed of your wicked ways?"

Bellingham spat in Cundall's face following his mother's strength.

"Take them inside the barricade and burn them with the rest. That is the only way Strasbourg will prevail."

"No, I beg you." Jennet fell onto her knees as her tears flowed. "I must protest, we are innocent. We did not poison our neighbor's water. The only thing we're guilty of is being a Jew."

Fearful, Bellingham stepped forward. "I'll die in their place a thousand times over, let my mother and sister live for they are innocent."

"It's too late for that. You and the rest of the Jews will burn and rot in Hell."

"May the black death kill you all." Genevieve proudly held her head high. "You deserve no mercy from our God as you provide no mercy to His servants. Your evil ways will follow you throughout eternity."

"Gag them and throw them to their burning fate." France de Cundall turned his back to the latest three captives.

The captors complied with the order and bound the Smythefield family's hands behind their backs with rags they pulled from their pockets. It took three men to drag each family member to the death trap as they kicked and screamed toward the church's bolted door.

The guards who stood watch outside the church removed the chains. With extreme force they shoved Genevieve, Bellingham and Jennet through it, then secured the barricade.

France de Cundall took a deep breath. "Burn them, burn them all and the black plague with them. Fire!"

More than five hundred soldiers on horseback shot burning arrows into the church and onto the thatched roof.

Women and children screamed as the church burned and black smoke filled the sky.

Bellingham pounded his fists against the heated locked door as France de Cundall held his spine straight atop a saddled horse a hundred yards away. From the inside of the church the screams and voices erupted a sense a pride within him as he listened from afar Bellingham's last words.

"We're all innocent. You shall pay for your actions one day. There will be no forgiveness for a heathen." Bellingham's voice soon became torched within the flames and France de Cundall heard no more.

The church erupted into flames as the screams of the trapped echoed in the smoke-filled sky.

∞

Jackie sweated as if she felt the heat from the burning church. "The smell of rotten flesh is something I can't forget." She shuddered and turned her nose up.

"Jackie, you're safe; you're not in the fire."

"I know, but I see the flames all around the church and I still hear the Jews screaming."

"Jackie let's go somewhere else. Go to your safe place. Breathe and relax."

"That isn't important now."

"All right Jackie, what is important to you right now?"

"I'm afraid of David, I think he's going to kill me."

"Your life isn't predestined Jackie. I'm going to wake you. On the count of five you will awake and feel refreshed. One... Two... Three."

Dr. Grayson stood and turned off the video camera. "Four... Five. Open your eyes, you'll see everything is fine."

Jackie awakened, slowly stood and then paced the floor. "I'm no closer to answers than before." Jackie sobbed hysterically. She grabbed her head as Mrs. Grayson entered the room.

"Mrs. Hennessey, please let me help you." Mrs. Grayson extended her hand in friendship and escorted Jackie from the parlor.

Dr. Grayson stood and unloaded the videotape and placed the cassette inside his pocket just as David burst through the front door.

"Where is she? Her car is here. What have you done with her?" David frantically searched the hallway and kitchen. He returned to the parlor, noticed the video camera and stormed straight for it. He looked for the cassette tape. "Where is my wife and where are her tapes?"

"Mrs. Hennessey is in the backyard with Mrs. Grayson."

"I warned you to leave my wife alone." David's face flushed scarlet and his neck blotched red.

"She came here voluntarily, I haven't forced anything onto her. It's by her own free will that she seeks my service."

Jackie stomped into the parlor with Mrs. Grayson. "I heard you from the backyard screaming at Dr. Grayson. David, what are you doing here?"

"That's the exact question I have for you. Get your things, we're leaving."

"If I'm not ready to go, then what? What are you going to do about it?"

"Jackie, get your things and come home where you belong."

"Maybe it's best you rest." Dr. Grayson nodded at Jackie to reassure her. "This regression was intense."

"Dr. Grayson, if you ever get within ten feet of my wife, I'll have you arrested. Effective today, I'm putting a restraining order on you."

"David, that's out of the question; I want his help. He seems to be the only doctor capable of helping me. I'm a grown woman and I can make up my own mind."

"Then you better act like one before I have you committed to a psychiatric ward."

"You have no right to say such things! I refuse to have this conversation with you here. I'm heading home and maybe if you could calm your ass down, I'll talk to you." Jackie picked up her purse and stormed off toward the door.

"Jackie." Dr. Grayson stepped toward her.

Jackie's eyes filled with frustration and tears. She stopped prior to the door and turned toward Dr. Grayson.

"You forgot these." Dr. Grayson handed Jackie the tapes.

"Thank you, Dr. Grayson can I come back tomorrow?"

"That depends on what you and David work out. But, I'm always available to help you."

David tightened his fists as if he stood ready to throw a punch. "I'm warning you, for the last time; stay away from my wife. Let's go Jackie."

Jackie apologetically glanced at Dr. Grayson. To ease the tension, she agreed to leave with David.

David grabbed Jackie by the hand and pulled her toward the door. "Don't bother showing us the way out, I know the way."

The Hennessey's exited the house and David slammed the front door behind them.

Dr. and Mrs. Grayson watched from the parlor window as David yanked Jackie by the arm toward his car.

"I'm driving home, David." She jerked her arm away from him and slapped him across his chest.

"I don't want you driving, you're unstable."

"I drove here, didn't I?"

"Go ahead then, leave! Maybe you'll get in a wreck and actually die this time."

"You know what? That would be a better alternative than going home to someone who berates me, tells me they love me, and then treats me as awful as you do. I don't know what my old self saw in you, but if I could go back, I'd tell her to run and to run as fast as she could and never stop running."

"Look Jackie, I love you. I've always loved you. This, whatever this is, isn't good. I made a huge mistake by letting you come to him and I regret ever talking you into it."

"Well, once you opened Pandora's Box, it's hard to close it."

David followed Jackie to her car and attempted to open the door for her, but she kicked it.

"Don't come near me David. I want nothing to do with you!" She shoved his chest.

"For the record, I care about you." He placed his hand onto her shoulder.

She recoiled immediately. "Don't touch me! Who do you think you are coming here and threatening to throw me in a psychiatric ward like it was no big deal? None of this is okay. We're not okay. Now back off."

"We'll finish talking about this when we get home. That is if you don't act like a child and lock yourself up in your room."

"My point exactly! Get over yourself David." Her eyes filled with rage and hatred. Jackie angrily entered her car.

The instant Jackie's legs and feet touched the floorboard, David slammed the car door shut and glared at her as she sped away.

David bolted up the porch steps to the front door. He clenched his jaw and banged his fist onto it.

Mrs. Grayson answered with fierceness in her eyes. "Mr. Hennessey, things aren't always as they seem. Learn to search deep within your soul for your answers. You won't find them here." Mrs. Grayson slammed the door in his face.

David banged onto the door with his fist. "Leave my wife alone. I warn you Dr. Grayson." David stormed from the porch, got into his car, and sped away as rubber burned from his tires leaving black marks on the street.

∞

When David arrived home, Jackie locked herself into her bedroom.

David banged his fist onto the bedroom door. "Jackie, this isn't going away. We have to talk about this."

"Talk about what? You trying to control my life!"

"No Jackie, I'm trying to get our lives back."

"I don't even remember that life, this is the one we are currently stuck in. Now leave me alone. I don't want anything to do with you, ever!"

"I'm telling you this right now, you can't see Dr. Grayson again. If you do… you'll regret the consequences."

Jackie bolted to the bedroom door and opened it. She slapped David across the face. "I hate you!" She pounded her fists onto his chest. "I hate this life and everything about it."

"Stop it!" He struggled to gain control of her as he grabbed both of her wrists. "Stop it now Jackie!"

She struggled to break free as they pushed and pulled from the door to the inside of their bedroom. He shoved her onto the bed. "Is this what you want? Is this the type of man you want me to be?"

"Oh, so now you are going to resort to violence? Why not just rape me? Get the fuck out of my life. Get out!" She kicked his stomach which jolted him backward.

"If I leave, I won't come back."

"Is that a threat or a promise? I don't love you, so why should I give a damn what you do? Die for all I care."

David, shocked by Jackie's words, stood in silence and glared at his distraught wife. He regretted his behavior and choice of words. "I didn't mean that, Jackie." He shook his head and frowned. "Of course, I won't leave you. I love you too much." David bemoaned he failed to stave off his anger.

"You love the idea of me as I once was. I'm no longer that woman. The scar across my face should be proof enough. Now get out!"

The front door opened, and the laughter of the Tyler and Sebastian filled the downstairs.

David took a deep breath. "Keep your voice down, your mom just got home with the boys. We shouldn't subject them to our fighting."

She glowered at David with fire in her eyes as if they could lance through him. "Get out." Her whispered tone filled with hatred prickled David's skin as the evil tone seemed to come from a possessed spirit.

"Jackie, this ends here and now; not another word."

"Go fuck yourself." She slammed and locked the bedroom door.

David stormed downstairs with fury in his eyes. He grabbed his keys and left slamming the door behind him.

16. THE PARADE OF ELEPHANTS

The night seemed longer and miserable for Jackie as she contemplated her current life. She tossed and turned every thirty seconds unable to relax. Not because of the fight with David the night before, but because she couldn't keep her memories of her past lives from resurfacing. Eventually, the sun rose to her relief.

She tiptoed from her bedroom and checked on the boys who slept peacefully in their own rooms. *Good, safe and sound.*

Quiet as a mouse, she tiptoed downstairs, so she wouldn't wake up David who slept on the couch. When she glanced at the vacant couch, a puzzled frown graced her face. *Great, maybe he got the message I don't want him here. I don't care where he is as long as it isn't here trying to control my life.*

∞

Across town at the police station David conversed with Lieutenant Amanda Kennedy.

"Mr. Hennessey, I'm sorry but you don't have sufficient reason to have a restraining order placed against Dr. Grayson.

He's done nothing wrong, and he hasn't caused or threatened any harm to your wife."

"You're wrong, that damn black man has brainwashed her."

Lieutenant Kennedy held her tongue at the racial comment which ruffled her feathers as she didn't take kindly to slurs against her own cultural heritage. Her square jaw tightened.

"He has taken a wonderful Catholic mother of two and turned her into some Buddhist believing person who now says she remembers her past lives. If that doesn't sound like harm to you, what does?"

"Our American core values and our constitutional foundation provide everyone with religious freedom of choice, no matter their ethnic background. You can't put a restraining order on a man, excuse me, a black man, who shares his religion which is different from yours or your wife's. She has free will."

"This isn't about freedom of religion. We're getting nowhere, you're just like the rest of your kind. Is there somebody else I can speak to about this?"

"Sir, there has been no crime other than the possibility of the domestic assault you described last night when your wife pounded her fists onto your chest. Would you like to press charges?"

"This is all a joke to you, isn't it?"

"No sir, I take my job seriously. You need to take these issues up with your wife. I also suggest marriage counseling."

"We don't need marriage counseling. We need her to remember that she has a marriage and a family."

Lieutenant Kennedy stood. "Mr. Hennessey go home and be with your wife. Talk things out with her. This is not a police matter. If anything, it is your racial profiling and religious discrimination."

David stormed off. "This isn't over, I'm filing an official complaint against you."

"The complaint department is on the fifth floor. Good luck with that one."

∞

Beth's orange Mini Cooper pulled into the parking lot of the Kadampa Buddhist Temple in New Orleans East. The temple renovated from a two-story home and its copper metal roof glistened in the sun. From the gold painted siding, the ornate imported wood gold trim to the red painted wooden bridge over the pond filled with large goldfish, it reflected the Buddhist culture as if the temple were in Tibet. The signage written in a foreign language indicated the cultural environment; however, the tagline in English read, "Kadampa Meditation Center."

Beth and Jackie exited the Mini Cooper.

Jackie, awe-struck gaped at the building. "The temple is breathtaking. I'm not sure what I was expecting, but this wasn't it."

"Glad you like it."

"I'm excited about this. Thank you so much for bringing me today. It seems like it's been forever since we talked about doing this, and I had to sneak out like we were a couple of teenagers."

They progressed toward the Temple's entrance.

"I don't get it. You'd think both your mother and David would want you to discover yourself."

"David said I can't be trusted anymore. We had a huge fight again. He told me he'll watch my every move." Tears flushed as Jackie caught her breath. "He threatened me, and things got a little physical. He scares me." Jackie's hands trembled.

"That doesn't sound like the David I know."

"At least you know him. I've living with a stranger. He's saying things like he wishes I would have died in the bus wreck. I'm really scared of him. I don't even want to be near him."

"Has he hit you, as in domestic abuse? You know if he is abusing you, you must get out of there. You're welcome to come live with me. No woman should ever put up with that. For me, if a man ever lays a hand on me, I'm out and I'd press charges. Karma would be a bitch."

"It's not that, he loses his temper way too quickly. He's yelling at me, at my mother and at the boys all the time. Last night, he even punched a hole in the wall when I wouldn't open my bedroom door."

"That's a lot to take in. He better not hit you like he did the wall."

"I've already thought about that. Let's forget this and concentrate on why we're here. It's a peaceful place, I can feel it already. Thanks again for bringing me."

"My pleasure, and I have a surprise. My Bhikkhu will greet you. Look, here comes one of our monks now."

"Do I bow?"

"Yes, of course. But here is the lowdown. Don't get too close, give the monk his space and don't touch him either. When he approaches you, place your hands in a prayer position over your forehead or chest and bow a few inches in respect."

The monk, dressed in an orange saffron, stopped about two feet from Beth and Jackie. He glanced at Beth. "*Namaste.*"

Beth placed her hands in a prayer position at her forehead and bowed. "*Sukhino Bhava.*"

The monk glanced at Jackie. "*Namaste.*"

Jackie placed her hands in a prayer position at her forehead and bowed.

The monk continued his path to the side of the temple.

"Wow, that was strange. Are you sure we didn't time travel somewhere?"

"Positive, and for your enlightenment *Namaste* means I bow to the divine in you. *Sukhino Bhava* means I wish you happiness. It is said to bring well wishes."

"Alrighty then, let's get this show on the road."

"Once inside, just follow my lead."

"I plan on it, no worries there."

"Also, be mindful of the people who are meditating or in prayer, so don't speak until the appropriate time."

"How will I know when that is?"

"You'll know."

A sense of peaceful ease overtook Jackie as she strolled into the temple. She studied the open room.

Just as Beth described, about fifteen individuals in a lotus position meditated as they chanted. *"Namu Myōhō Renge Kyō."*

She glanced at Beth with questions in her eyes.

Beth leaned into Jackie; her lips next to her ear. "The chant means 'Devotion to the Mystic Law of the Lotus Sutra.' You'll learn more in the workshop."

Jackie shook her head in affirmation as Beth knelt and sat her butt onto both her back calves. Jackie followed her example.

Beth joined in as she chanted in unison with others as Jackie's eyes lingered upon the altar.

"Namu Myōhō Renge Kyō. Namu Myōhō Renge Kyō."

Upfront, a ten-foot golden statue of Buddha prolonged Jackie's gaze. The Buddha, not the baldheaded Buddha, but one with a large temple-like crown that framed the statue and reached the floor seemed worthy of the temple. On each side stood two unusual gold statues knelt in the prayer. They faced each other as if they greeted one another. Ornate candle holders with lit white candles elaborately embellished jewel incense burners that looked like something from the Ming Dynasty complimented the altar as did fresh colorful flowers.

After five minutes, the Bhikkhu who wore a dark orange saffron entered. He bowed to the assembly. *"Namaste."*

The assembled crowd responded in unison. *"Namu Myōhō Renge Kyō."*

Beth offered Jackie a quick explanation in a faint whisper. "May you find peace and happiness."

"I know, you told me that."

"We are pleased you have chosen to learn about Buddhism. Our goal is to spread peace and love." The Bhikkhu's eyes connected to those who sought answers one at a time.

Several other monks who wore a lighter color orange saffron entered and stood next to the Bhikkhu.

"We are all here for you and to answer your questions. I'll begin with an overview of what our beliefs entail. We believe we influence our world and our communities by leading positive lives with great power and by doing great works. The greatest fulfillment in life is only achieved by working for the happiness of others. We also believe each individual has the power within themselves to find happiness and to solve any problem that arises. Therefore, creating a state of life character led by compassion, wisdom and courage. By chanting *Nam Myoho Renge Kyo*, we awaken to the reality that within our life is the unlimited reserve of our courage, wisdom and compassion. We chant to the *Gohonzon*, the scroll you see engraved on the altar. *Gohonzon's* translation is a fundamental object of devotion and serves as a mirror into our own lives. It's our blueprint for how we are to live our lives and serve others for happiness. I know each of you would not have graced our temple if you weren't seeking answers. Myself and our monks will now join each visitor who seeks answers, giving you the opportunity to ask your questions."

The monks dispersed into the crowd and knelt by those who sought happiness. The Bhikkhu knelt beside Jackie and Beth. "*Namaste.*"

Jackie placed her hands in the prayer position at her forehead and bowed.

201

Beth bowed as she placed her prayer hands at her forehead. "*Sukhino Bhava.* This is the woman I told you about, Jackie Hennessey."

"Welcome to our temple. May you be blessed in finding the answers you seek and the happiness that lives within you."

"Thank you." *I feel so welcomed.*

"What is the question in which you seek the answer?"

"Honestly, it is about past lives and reincarnation."

"The answer you seek must first come from a clear awareness and understanding of death. Without this correct understanding, it would deny you to live your life without fear and without clarity of your purpose."

Unencouraged, Jackie nodded in agreement. "Fair enough, then how do I understand the nature of death?"

"Death is an issue we all face and seek to understand. Many before you have sought death and found it. You are not alone. Nichiren Daishonin once wrote, 'The life of a human being is fleeting. The exhaled breath never waits for the inhaled one.' Buddhism views life as eternal. Our lives will always continue even after death."

"Jesus Christ preached the same thing. Is this supposed to comfort me? Because I'm not." *Could all religions be nothing more than lies?*

Beth placed her hand on Jackie's shoulder. "Just hear him out."

Jackie exhaled.

The monk nodded. "Jesus preached the only way for eternal life was through him." His voice comforted Jackie. "Buddhists believe the only way to awaken to life's eternity is to emerge in the small self through self-purification with our entire being which includes a lifetime of actions, both remembered and forgotten. To live a pure life and to bring happiness to others will lead to fulfillment. To live an evil life full of lies, deceit and bringing harm upon others, you will face death with regret."

"I get it, do unto others as you would have them do unto you." *Here we go again.*

"No, treat others with respect and bring happiness to them. Ask for nothing in return, especially in the afterlife."

"Afterlife? Not eternal life?"

Beth listened and observed her friend's body language as she stared at the Bhikkhu.

"That is correct." The Bhikkhu nodded. "The period of transition from one life to another is your afterlife. At the moment of your death is what you will take with you and will continue to follow you into the afterlife. This moment has a direct influence on your rebirth."

"Do you mean reincarnation?"

"To be reincarnated is to be reborn. As a practicing Buddhist, I live every moment as though it's my last. I have no regrets to take into the afterlife."

"So, it's all about your karma?"

"Your life now as you live it comes with many responsibilities. You take your actions with you to the afterlife."

∞

David sat alone at a bar distraught in thought as he drank beer. "I'll have another." David's slurred words barely intelligible indicated he already consumed a large amount of alcohol.

The bartender removed the empty mug from in front of David. "Look, whatever it is, it won't get resolved over a drink. You tried that last night until we closed, and I had to kick you out."

"I know, I slept in my car and waited until you opened again."

"Do you want some free advice?"

"Mind your own business. Just get me a very Bloody Mary. You better make that a double."

The bartender walked off.

∞

Beth drove in silence which allowed Jackie time to gather her thoughts. Her eyes darted quickly toward Jackie, then back to the road. "So, what did you think?"

"Honestly, what I heard makes more sense than any other thing I've listened to since waking up from my damn coma."

"Glad to hear it, maybe you'll start finding some inner peace. Are you going to tell David and Margarette about it?"

"No and please keep your mouth shut about this."

"No worries. I'm sorry I messed things up telling them about your regressions with Dr. Grayson. Will you ever forgive me?"

"By you telling them I'm seeing Dr. Grayson more often than they thought, isn't the problem. I told them I remembered my past lives. They're both such stoic Catholics and they think I'm a nut job for sure. Now they want to have me committed."

"I'm terribly sorry. At the time I thought I was helping you. That backfired on both of us."

"Well, speaking of Dr. Grayson and past lives, you can make it up by taking me to him right now."

"Are you nuts? David will kill me if he found out."

"Not if you keep your mouth shut."

"That was a kick below the belt. David might kill you too."

"If my past lives are any indication for my future, he's going to kill me, anyway. It seems that's what I live for, it's my destiny. I need to find happiness and do good work. Isn't that what I just learned? Then maybe I won't endure so many violent deaths."

"You're on the right track at any rate. Do good works and find ways to make others happy."

"You can make me happy by taking me to see Dr. Grayson."

"Why now?"

"Somewhere along my timeline, I have to stop and face the music. You heard the same thing. I must understand death, to make a better future, and I can't keep on running. Only Dr. Grayson can help me realize why I can never stop running. Will you please take me?"

"You might have a point, I can only drop you off. You'll need to catch an Uber to get home. I've made other plans and can't stick around."

"I'm fine with that. Maybe you ought to try a regression session one day. No telling what you may learn about yourself. You said you have a fear of trains and railroad crossings, didn't you?"

"I've already experienced regression several times."

"You never told me that."

"It never came up."

"Spill the beans, who were you? How many lives do you know about? When did you do it?"

"Whoa! Hold on, I won't tell you mine until you're through seeing Dr. Grayson. I don't want to risk you combining my memories with yours. But I will tell you one thing, we're soul mates."

"Soul mates? Really? Like forever bonding?"

"That's one way of putting it. I know that you and I have crossed each other's paths many times in many lives. I can't explain it, maybe you could talk to Dr. Grayson about it."

"I'll consider that my good deed of the day."

∞

Next to three empty beer mugs, David's phone vibrated. He glanced at the caller I.D. and ignored it. "Another drink." His slurred words muffled by his cell phone's ring tone.

∞

The drive to Dr. Grayson's office extended longer than anticipated due to the afternoon traffic.

"Thank you for dropping me off, I need to do this. I need to understand these deaths, so I can avoid the bad karma heading my way."

"I get it, happy mind time traveling."

"What did you say?"

"Happy mind time traveling. You know, you get to travel the world and visit another era, just like a time traveler."

"That pretty much puts my life in a nutshell. Thanks for everything. You're the only one besides Dr. Grayson who understands what is going on. Have you always been my best friend?"

"In this lifetime I have. Not so much in others."

"Why haven't I seen you in my past?"

"You have, you haven't recognized my soul."

"That's a conversation for another day."

"I guess it is."

Jackie exited the car and strode quickly to the porch. She took a deep breath as she approached the front door and knocked as Beth drove away.

Mrs. Grayson opened the door flashing a curious grin. "Somehow I knew you'd be coming today, I felt it."

"Is Dr. Grayson here?"

"Yes, but he is with a client." Her tone a delicate whisper as her eyes darted to the parlor. "Why don't you come to the back and have a lemonade with me? He can see you as soon as he's finished with his current session."

"That would be wonderful."

Jackie quietly followed Mrs. Grayson down the hall. When she passed the parlor's entry, she caught a glimpse of a man in his early fifties who lay on the chaise in a deep trance.

The man took a deep breath. "I know this woman, we're related in this timeline."

"Tell me who she is?"

"She's my mother, it's Annabelle. She's just in a different body."

Jackie's eyes opened wide as her heart thumped against her ribs.

Mrs. Grayson clasped Jackie's hand. "This way."

They quietly proceeded into the backyard. "Please have a seat." Mrs. Grayson flashed a comforting grin.

Jackie glanced at the back yard and took notice of the brick patio. "This is beautiful, it has a French Quarter feel."

"That was the idea, we are in the French Quarter." Mrs. Grayson slowly sat in a chair across from Jackie. "We can talk here. I sense a great need within you to find life's answers."

"That's the understatement of the century."

"What is troubling you my dear?"

"Just about everything."

"Your thoughts mustn't trouble you, view them as a way to build your character and a way to find true happiness. Have you been meditating?"

"I try, but I can't go to that deep state like I do with Dr. Grayson."

"Finding that state takes a lifetime of practice, it doesn't happen overnight. You must be patient and persistent. Then the answers you seek will be revealed."

"Are you certain of this?"

"Let's say this isn't my first rodeo."

"Does that mean you know about your past lives?"

Mrs. Grayson nodded in affirmation.

"Will you please tell me about them?"

"I prefer not too as I feel they are very personable. In fact, I've only shared them with two other individuals."

"Seriously, only two? May I ask who?"

"My husband and his mentor, Dr. Bryan Reiss. However, I only shared with Dr. Reiss one of my many past lives."

"Why is that?"

"They're mine and mine alone. They are for my understanding. Do you share your past lives?"

"I've really only told my new best friend who was apparently my best friend before the bus wreck."

"Why do you suppose that is?"

"I'm not comfortable sharing, they're private to me."

Mrs. Grayson grinned and nodded as if to confirm her own reasons for nondisclosure. "My subconscious mind reveals many things when I meditate that I wish to remain private."

"How do you clear your mind? It seems every time I try to meditate, my mind goes berserk. I think about everything and anything. For someone with retrograde amnesia, I can never just clear my mind."

"That's because you're trying to analyze your thoughts as they happen. Give yourself the freedom to let your subconscious go anywhere without judgment on yourself or your actions."

"That makes sense, I absolutely judge myself. I'm my harshest critic."

"See? You already have discovered one answer. What else would you like to know?"

"Well, my best friend Beth, the one I mentioned earlier, told me we're soul mates, and we have crossed each other's paths many times. What does that mean?"

"Soul mates as the word indicates means that somehow both of your souls are connected. It doesn't mean that that person's soul will always be with you."

"Why is that?"

"When a soul mate keeps reoccurring in your life, there is a lesson or two you need to learn from them. Once you have learned whatever that lesson is your soul moves onward and whatever that relationship is at the time concludes naturally. They may not resurface again in your past lives or in your future ones."

"You're talking about death, aren't you?"

"Not at all, I'm talking about a relationship with another soul. There are many types of soul mate relationships."

Jackie's brow creased as she twisted her lips. "I'm confused." She exhaled exasperated.

"Just as there are many types of love, a motherly love, a sisterly love, and a love for your spouse, there are many types of soul mate relationships. Being romantically involved is one type of relationship, but your soul mate could appear in your past life as any relationship. For instance, as your son or daughter, as your neighbor, as your parent or even as your enemy."

"Now that sounds odd, you'd think the person would always be my spouse."

"You referred to Beth earlier who thinks you two are soul mates, is that correct?"

"Yes, but we aren't lovers, we're friends."

"That's my point. Her path crosses yours now because of a lesson you must learn from her."

"She has guided me in this whole past life stuff."

"You may discover Beth has always guided you. This type of soul mate is valuable throughout your lives. It's part of your spiritual journey."

"Am I understanding you correctly, Beth and I were destined to meet in this lifetime?"

"Not necessarily, it simply means she still has a lesson to teach you. Or, it could be the exact opposite, maybe it's you who must teach her the lesson."

"I doubt that very seriously. I think we were destined to be friends. Speaking of destiny, if our past lives and souls guide us in our current life, this means we have no free will to make decisions. It is what it is and what it always will be."

"Interesting choice of words. It is what it is and what it always will be."

"They're not mine. I keep hearing them in my regression sessions. If so, I'm destined for a cruel death in this lifetime."

"Jackie, that's not how it works. In this lifetime, you have free will. You can make choices. As a result, the choices you make every day changes your future. You have a destiny, but because of free choice, the outcome changes with each decision you make."

"Good afternoon ladies." Dr. Grayson strolled into the backyard.

Jackie stood at once. "Dr. Grayson, I'm glad you're here. I have to have another session."

"Aren't you afraid that David will find out?"

"I don't care. I've decided to leave him as soon as I settle the lawsuit with the trucking company and the school system and can support myself. He's a tyrant and a bully. I can't stand to be around him. My therapist spoke to me about toxic relationships and how I need to rid them from my life. David defines toxic. Never mind, do you have time for a session?"

Dr. Grayson nodded. "Come this way, it sounds as if you need to get things off your mind."

Jackie leaned down and imparted Mrs. Grayson a hug. "Thank you for explaining things, I'm finally getting clarity."

"You're welcome. Just remember to stop analyzing what you see and remember. Free your subconscious and allow the lessons you must learn to emerge. That's how you grow in this lifetime."

"Yes, Ma'am, thank you."

∞

David, drunk, sat at the bar. Higgins boldly entered, scanned the bar and eyed David. His face scowled; his jaw clenched.

The bartender sat a draft beer in front of David.

Higgins stood behind David and placed his hand on his shoulder. "Thank God you answered Anita's call. We've been looking for you all day."

"Well, you found me." He grabbed Higgins hand, squeezed it and jerked it away. His voice intensified. "Don't touch me." He reached for the mug.

Higgins intercepted, grabbed the mug and slid it six inches across the bar out of David's reach. "David, you're an irresponsible asshole. The Japanese came by looking for you today."

David grabbed the mug and slugged the beer. "Another, beer man." He slammed the mug down onto the counter.

"I lied and told them you had the flu. Damn it, you can't continue to drink your sorrows away."

The bartender sat another beer in front of David.

∞

"Everything seems smaller, or I'm larger than normal." Jackie's brow creased as her eyes darted beneath her lids.

Dr. Grayson remained silent allowing her time to analyze her memory. "Where are you, Jackie?"

"I'm with many women. We're stalking elephants, wild elephants in West Africa. No, there are young girls training to become our best warriors with spears, and to master their skills to hunt with bows and arrows."

"Warriors for what Jackie?"

"We are a nomadic tribe of women fighters. We're stronger than men, we fight like men, and we kill better than men. Today, the young warriors must prove their worth and take down the elephant as the elephant is much stronger than the beast of man."

"Tell me what you see."

∞

Sunset on a humid summer day somewhere near the West African Togan River provided the backdrop for the hunt for a tribe of women warriors who nestled on the edge of a plateau and gazed upon a parade of elephants.

Thesilia, the strongest of all and the leader sat atop her long-maned albino horse as she overlooked the others; a death-grip on her spear, and a bow and arrow strapped across her back. Her face, arms and neck filled with victory tattoos and tribal markings told of her many battles against beast and man as did the bone through her nose. Her dark coal leathery skin defined her wisdom of forty years young. She huffed air through her nose as the bone in it slightly lifted.

"On this eve, your strength and courage bring honor to the Dahomey. You hunt to eat, and you kill to survive. You fail, Benin perishes. We will be no more. Our elders are dying. We have no claim to this land if we cannot survive in it." A wailed piercing battle cry belted from Thesilia as she lifted her spear.

A myriad of women from the ages nine to thirty and outfitted with spears, bows and arrows joined the war cry as they kicked the sides of their horses. The stampede of warriors galloped through the Abomey Plateau awakening the parade of elephants.

To effectively observe the young warriors training, Thesilia stayed fixed in her position, proud as her trainees charged. Her pride soon crippled as a warrior of twelve lost her balance and fell from her horse.

"Dali!" Thesilia dug her heels into her horse's side and galloped toward Dali who quickly bolted to her feet and fearlessly ran toward the hunt as she shrieked her battle cry.

Positioned with her spear expertly aimed, Thesilia hurled it toward Dali. The spear lanced Dali through the back, her knees buckled as she collapsed.

Thesilia dismounted her horse, kicked Dali over as she jerked the spear from her torso.

Dali proudly lifted her broad jaw as she drew a deep breath. "I will not die a warrior's death, I die in dishonor."

"You die in shame. A warrior maintains the beast. If you allow the beast to control you, we all die in battle." Thesilia licked Dali's blood from the tip of the spear and smeared the rest onto her face. She gazed down at Dali with eyes as sharp as the tip of her spear. "Your soul will find no rest."

Dali's life-spirit left her body.

∞

"I can, I am." David slurred his words and quickly downed the remainder of his beer. He raised his mug. "Hey you, another."

Aggravated, Higgins jerked the mug from David's hand. "You're not getting another beer." He grabbed David by the arm and pulled him. "Come on, I'm taking you home."

"Get your hands off me, goddamn it! I'll drink if I want to and nobody can stop me." His head slammed against the bar and bounced back up.

"You've had way too much to drink, let me take you home." Higgins steadied David who almost fell from the bar stool.

"I don't have a home, it's a torture cell. You don't know what it's like living with your sister."

"I have a good idea, you know I grew up with her, right?"

"But, she's not your sister anymore. Hell, she's not a wife or a mother. You know where that leaves me?"

"Where David? Where does that leave you?"

"In a fucking mess with a wife who doesn't know who I am." Hiccups developed in succession to David's aggravation. "Can you understand that?" Hiccup.

"I won't pretend I do, but it's been hard on us too. You're not the only one in her life."

"That's my point, it's her life; not our life. Everything revolves around Jackie. Jackie this, Jackie that, Jackie, Jackie, Jackie. Fuck Jackie! I pay for that goddamn house."

"Come on, let's get you home."

"No! I'm not going anywhere!" David slammed his fist onto the bar countertop. "Just go away." He shoved Higgins and fisted his hands ready to take a punch. "Bartender, this man is harassing me."

The bartender approached Higgins and David. "Is there a problem?"

Higgins scratched his head. "I'm his brother-in-law. I'm trying to get him home."

"Leave me alone, go away." David pointed his finger toward the bartender. "You! Get me another beer."

"Sir, I can't make him go with you, for all I know you two could be enemies. I can't be responsible for that."

"So, you rather keep serving him booze and let him pass out? What kind of bartender are you?"

"Sir, please leave, you're making a scene."

"Do you think I'm making a scene? I think you got that turned around buddy."

"You can either leave, or I can have you thrown out."

David hiccupped again. "You go mister bartender, throw him out on his ass. I'd like to see that."

Higgins threw his hands into the air. "He's no longer my problem. He's all yours. Good luck with him and God forbid if he kills someone on his way home. I'll come after you. That's how my dad died, by a fucking drunk driver." Higgins stormed from the bar.

"I'll take another." David's head fell onto the bar.

17. THE SALEM WITCH

In a deep trance, Jackie's eyes darted back and forth. "This is such a strange place."

"What do you see?"

"I'm in a house, it belongs to Reverend Samuel Parris."

"Are you alone?"

"No, there's lots of people."

"Do you know them?"

"Some."

"Why is everyone there?"

∞

Hysteria on witchcraft spread quickly in Salem Village and in the nearby towns, and on May 18, 1692 the townsfolk in the county of Essex in Massachusetts packed the parlor owned by Reverend Samuel Parris prepared to witness the preliminary trial of the accused witch, Dr. Roger Toothaker.

Dr. Toothaker sat at the defense table without a lawyer accused of practicing witchcraft by Elizabeth Hubbard, Ann Putnam and Mary Walcott. The three accusers sat poised behind the defendant as they stared at Thomas Gage who sat in the witness chair ready to provide testimony.

Blythe Pudeator, twenty-six and a distant cousin by marriage to Anne Pudeator, a well-to-do septuagenarian widow, maintained her silence positioned in the back as she observed the trial. To her side sat Parris' slave Totuba, who herself had been one of the first women accused of being a witch remained motionless.

Magistrate Jonathan Corwin led the pre-examination trial. Also, in the makeshift court presided Judge Gidney, Judge John Hathorne and Judge Higginson appointed in authority by Magistrate Corwin.

Magistrate Corwin slammed his gavel. "Let the record show that on this date the accused witch Roger Toothaker of Bilrica has been brought to court for a preliminary hearing. You are in front of the Magistrates and hereby required to be bring forthwith your testimony before us and bring before Roger Toothaker of Bilrica, who stands charged with sundry acts of witchcraft by him, committed or done on the bodies of Eliz Hubert, Ann Putnam, Mary Walcott and of Salem Village or farms. It is with the law of the land whom you are well to secure in truth in order to try the accused and deliver justice by due order of our laws. Thomas Gage, you are hereby ordered to tell the truth. What information do you have that condemns a man of witchery?"

On the witness stand Thomas Gage gulped ready to declare his testimony against the accused witch. "I doeth and saith in my testimony that Dr. Toothaker and his daughter Mary Emerson, married to Joseph Emerson, practiced counter magic your honor. What I say, I say in truth to seek justice and to rid our town of witchery and the work of the Devil."

"And, you believe this to be true?" Magistrate Corwin's expression remained firm and as cold as ice.

"Yes, Magistrate, I do."

"Where were you when Dr. Toothaker informed you of his ability to perform counter magic?"

"In my house in Beverly."

"And you swear to have heard the confession of Dr. Toothaker?"

"I do, your Magistrate, on my life. Dr. Toothaker and I discoursed that sometime last spring in which he confessed that he and his daughter, Mary Emerson, practiced counter magic against witches."

The crowd erupted in chaos. Mary Walcott stood. "He's a witch, Dr. Toothaker must be hung."

"Hang him, hang him." The chant rippled throughout the room.

Magistrate Corwin slammed his gavel once again. "Quiet or thee shall be removed from this proceeding. Let Mr. Gage speak without further interruption." The Magistrate tilted his head toward Mr. Gage. "Proceed with thy testimony."

"We discoursed about John Mastons' child of Salem who fell ill and prone to unwanted fits. There was neither explanation for his unwanted fits nor for the convulsions other than the child must have come under a witch's spell. What I profess is the truth. This child shared the same infliction of another child, Phillip Whites of Beverly. After long hours of discourse, I tried to persuade Dr. Toothaker to go and see for himself the inflictions of these children."

"And, did he go? Did he go and examine the inflicted children?"

"He informed me he already had examined both and that it was in his medical opinion that the children were under the spell of an evil hand."

"You believe this to be true?"

"Yes, your Magistrate, I have no doubt. It was then that Dr. Toothaker informed me that his daughter, Mary Emerson, had killed a witch."

"Did he tell you how Mary Emerson accomplished such a feat as to kill a witch with profound powers?"

"Yes, your Magistrate. Dr. Toothaker discoursed he instructed his daughter in the means to accomplish the feat and that there was a bewitched person who professed to have complained of being afflicted by another person who was also afflicted."

"But what did he say about Mrs. Emerson and how she killed the witch?"

"I was informed by Dr. Toothaker that Mary Emerson collected the urine of the said daughter and put it into an earthen pot. Then he saith that his daughter put the earthen pot in a hot oven and stopped up said oven to keep all fumes from escaping into the room. Upon the next sunrise the witch was dead at the hands of Mary Emerson who performed the counter magic."

"And you testify that what you saith in front of this Magistrate is true and holy?"

"My statements against Dr. Toothaker are in fact truthful and holy in front of the Lord."

"Is there any other testimony you desire to bring forth to this court and to this pre-examination trial?"

"I am certain that there must be; however, these things I have truly forgotten and farther saith not."

Elizabeth Hubbard spontaneously fell to her knees and screamed as if the Devil himself possessed her. Spasms and convulsions followed.

Ann Putnam screamed violently as she tried to rip her flesh from her face. "He's a witch." Her body contorted writhing.

"Order, order!" Magistrate Corwin slammed his gavel. "I demand order or thee shall be removed from these proceedings."

The crowd silenced as several men latched onto Elizabeth and Ann and swiftly removed both from the court interrogation as they heaved the writhing girls who continued to kick and scream.

Blythe Pudeator, the young woman in the back stood. "He's lying, Thomas Gage is lying. Dr. Toothaker is not a witch, he's a healer. I've been treated by him myself and was healed of my infliction."

Magistrate Corwin's eyes lit with fire and fury. "Arrest that woman for she stands accused as being a witch. Let the court records indicate the arrest of Blythe Pudeator for witchery."

Blythe scarpered from the court as several men and the other Magistrates present bolted after her.

Magistrate Corwin slammed his gavel. "Recess!" He released his grip from the gavel and scampered after the young woman along with the hysterical crowd leaving Thomas Gage on the witness stand and Dr. Toothaker under the guard of several townsmen.

Blythe ran as fast as possible with the angry mob at her back. She darted into the woods not looking back until captured.

The angry mob jeered as three men held Blythe as one man tied her hands behind her back.

A horse-drawn wagon stopped within a foot of Blythe. The executioner stood in the back dressed in a black robe and a black cloth with holes cut around both eyes and his mouth covered his face. He raised his hand. "Silence. We must hear the witch's confession."

She fell to her knees in prayer. "Thy Lord, you knowest my heart and thoust I declare I am not of the Devil; by thy hand, I saith unto you, please forgive me and taketh me unto thy own. Our Father who art in heaven hallowed be thy name. Thy kingdom come. Thy will be done on earth as it is in heaven."

Magistrate Corwin stood over the young woman who continued to recite the Lord's Prayer. "Stand and be heard witch."

Three townsmen grabbed Blythe and forced her to stand before Magistrate Corwin.

"What have you to saith? Confess your witchery and thy shall show mercy upon your soul."

"I'd rather hang now than stand accused a witch in thy court."

"Then, it shall be commenced. She is a witch who provideth a full confession and will be hanged."

The mob jeered and chanted. "Die, witch, die."

The men tossed Blythe onto the wooden cart at the feet of the executioner. "Proceed to Gallows Hill."

As the horse-drawn cart pulled forward, the mob followed as they continued to heckle Blythe until they reached the hanging tree.

Blythe darted her eyes toward the crowd. "What I saith is thy truth. I am not a witch."

One of the Magistrate's chosen men heaved a hangman's noose over a large tree branch.

The executioner grabbed Blythe by her shoulders, jerked her to her feet and spun her to face the heckling crowd as the cart moved beneath the hangman's noose.

The hangman secured the noose around her throat.

Blythe closed her eyes. "Give us this day our daily bread and forgive us our trespasses, as we forgive those who trespass against us. Lead us not into temptation but deliver us from evil."

Magistrate Corwin took a deep breath. "Release her spirit unto His hands."

The man who held the horse's reins, clicked his tongue twice against the roof of his mouth as he cracked the leather straps onto the horse's rear. The horse neighed as the cart lunged forward pulling the witch's platform from beneath her feet.

"Amen." Blythe's body dropped snapping her neck. The young accused witch's eyes bulged, her feet jerked several times, and her body spasmed as she perished.

∞

Margarette paced in front of the formal living room couch. She looked at her watch. "It's after midnight."

A car pulled into the driveway. Jackie exited an Uber car.

Margarette looked out the window. "Thank God."

When Jackie entered the front door, Margarette stood with her arms folded across her chest. "You had me worried sick."

"I've told you before, just quit worrying about me."

"One simple phone call and my worries would stop. Would it kill you to call home just to let me know where you are and that you're safe?"

"You treat me like a sixteen-year-old with a curfew. I'm a grown woman and I don't have to account for my whereabouts."

"That has nothing to do with it, it's called common courtesy. Where have you been?"

"I refuse to answer as it will only make you angrier than you already are."

"You saw Dr. Grayson again, didn't you?"

"So, what if I did, are you going to tell David?"

Margarette took a deep breath and shook her head. "Let's sit and calmly discuss this."

"There's nothing I want to talk about, I'm going to bed."

"The boys asked about you tonight."

"If you're trying to make me feel guilty, it won't work."

"They're smarter than either of you give them credit and they know something is wrong between you and David."

"Well good for them. They won't be surprised when I tell them I'm moving out."

Margarette gasped at Jackie's words. She put her hand onto her forehead.

"Mom, did you hear what I said?"

"I heard you. You are Hell bent on destroying everything you have and, for what? Can you at least answer that?"

"Quit smothering me." Jackie stormed up the stairs.

∞

David slouched and barely held his head up when the bartender approached. "You've had enough, it's time for you to go home."

"I don't have a home, give me another."

"Sir, you've had enough. I refuse to serve you anymore; I'm calling you a cab."

"I can drive, I'll just finish this drink and go."

∞

Jackie threw her cell phone across the bedroom. It slammed against the wall, cracked open and fell to the floor into several pieces. "I don't give a shit." She grabbed her suitcase from the top of her closet, slammed it onto the bed and hastily packed her belongings. Her anger controlled her actions.

Outside the bedroom, Margarette tapped onto the door three times. "Jackie, are you all right?"

Jackie hurried to the door and leaned her head against it. "Everything's fine, just leave me alone." Tears fell steadily.

"Open the door, let's talk."

"I said leave me alone."

"Jackie, that's it, I can't do this alone. I'm calling David."

"Nobody said you had to do this in the first place. Just leave me alone, I don't need or want or need any of you in my life."

"So, you're just going to run away."

"That's what I've always done."

∞

David sat alone at the bar as he finished his beer. His cell phone and his wallet lay on the bar next to his mug.

The bartender placed a tall glass of water with a lemon slice and a cup of coffee in front of David. He picked up the other two empty mugs. "This should help to get you sober."

"This is *Nawlins*, who needs to be sober?"

David's cell phone vibrated. When he glanced at the caller I.D., Margarette's name popped up as he pushed the phone away. He downed the small amount of beer left in his mug and quickly gulped the water.

The bartender placed the bar tab onto the countertop.

David glanced at the amount, grabbed five twenty-dollar bills from his wallet and threw them onto the bar. "That should cover it." He slurred his words, grabbed his items and stumbled toward the door.

The bartender jumped over the bar and grabbed David by the arm which kept him from falling. "Why don't you let me call you a cab? You're in no condition to drive."

David slugged the bartender dropping his phone. When he bent over to pick it up, he passed out onto the floor.

∞

Jackie held her suitcase as she headed down the stairs. Margarette met her at the bottom. "Please, let's talk this out."

"There's nothing to discuss. You, David and the children are better off without me. I shouldn't have come back."

"This is your home. You belong here no matter what you may think."

"Have you even noticed what is going on or have you turned a blind eye? You're the mother to my kids. They're afraid of me and my scarred-up face. You're more of a wife to David than I care to be or want to be. The only thing missing between you two is sex. You shop, you prepare the meals, you clean, you bathe the boys and you put them to bed."

"Jackie, you're being unreasonable."

"Unreasonable? Let me continue with what's unreasonable. You cook our meals, you clean David's house, you greet him at the door when he comes home from work, you do everything. It's you, you, you. You do everything. I've got to find my independence; can't you understand that?"

"This will take time Jackie, lots of time."

"You don't get it; this life isn't mine. No matter how much time I may have, I don't want to be a part of it. I hate it here. I'm not happy. Before I can consider being a wife, a mother or even a daughter, I have to know who I am and right now I don't know who that person is."

"Jackie, listen to me. We'll make this work, you'll find happiness again."

"I won't find it here in this house. Don't you understand anything I have said? I have to leave, or David will kill me. He'll kill me like all the rest of them did. It's only a matter of time. I've seen it with my own eyes, I can never stop running."

"Jackie Adel, you're not making any sense."

"Nothing in my life makes sense, don't you get it?"

"You need to stay, it's one o'clock in the morning. You're upset. Where will you go?"

"It doesn't matter because anywhere away from this house would be better than remaining here."

"We don't know where David is; so, you're just going to pack up and leave your kids and home? Has everything you've struggled with over the last year meant anything to you?"

"You really don't get it, this life it isn't mine. I don't remember a damn thing about it. This is your life."

"You'll never remember it if you run. Where will you go?"

Jackie dropped her suitcase and sobbed.

Margarette wrapped her arms around her as Jackie buried her face into her shoulder. "Jackie, running away from your struggles isn't the answer. Facing them head-on is what makes you stronger." She grasped Jackie's hand. "Let's sit and talk this through."

Jackie nodded and wiped her tears.

They sat next to each other on the couch in the formal living room. Margarette put her arm around Jackie's shoulder and gently pulled her close. "Come on, snuggle in. It looks like you need a good cry to let everything out."

"My life is a mess, was it always this way?"

"Not by any means. You're a strong woman, a fabulous mother and you have more determination and guts than any person I know."

"Why did God do this to me?"

"You've got it all wrong, God doesn't do anything to us. We have free will. Sometimes life will give you lemons. As Aunt Susie always says, when life gives you lemons, make lemonade."

"I like lemonade."

"Honey, you're getting stronger every day. You still need time to adjust and more time to heal. You got this, I promise."

"Do you really think so?"

"Not only do I think so, I believe it. The worst part is behind you. Things will get better, you'll see."

Jackie inhaled and exhaled as if to balance her inner soul. "You might have a valid point. God knows my life can't get any worse than it already is."

"Now that's my girl, keep your chin up."

"I'll just keep praying for patience."

"Oh, don't do that, it could be a dangerous thing."

"I don't understand, I thought you could pray for just about anything and God will answer your prayers."

"That's the problem when you pray for patience. God will deliver and test you in unexpected ways all in the name of patience. You just think you need patience, see what happens when you pray for it. Trust me, you don't want to go there because it comes with growing pains."

"Then what exactly should I be praying for if not patience?"

"I think pray for trust and understanding during a difficult patch in your life. Those two things are the building blocks for patience."

"I might be in a lot of trouble because the last couple of days I've been praying for patience at every turn. Do you think God heard me?"

"He heard you, you can take that to the bank. Now you'll have to sit back and wait to see how He answers."

The phone on the kitchen wall rang. They gazed at each other puzzled. Margarette patted Jackie's thigh. "I don't know who that is, but at this time of night it has to be important. I'll get it."

"Mom, I have a funny feeling about this."

18. NEVER STOP RUNNING

David, drunk and with a throbbing headache sat on the bench in a jail cell with his head in his hands while three inmates glared. Four others slept wherever they could on the other benches or in the corners of the cell.

"You smell like a brewery." An elderly alcoholic cellmate wobbled toward David. "Let me sniff you."

David rose and stumbled to the other side and leaned against the cinder block wall; his head wobbled.

"What ya in for?" The alcoholic staggered toward him.

"None of your business."

"Look, us drunks need to stick together."

"I'm not a drunk." His words slurred staccato; and his body swayed.

"Right, that's why you're still drunk and your ass is in jail. You're not a drunk. I'm not either." He guttered a huge belch and farted.

The other inmates snickered.

An officer approached the cell. "Mr. Hennessey, your bail has been posted. You're free to leave."

"Thank God."

The alcoholic with his back against the wall slid down and sat. "God got nothing to do with it. That would be the Devil."

∞

The police officer behind the counter handed Margarette the receipt for the bail she paid for David at 7:08 a.m. and then handed her a large brown envelope. "These are the items he had when he was booked. See to it he makes his court date."

"I will sir, thank you."

The officer glared at her.

Margarette placed the envelope in her oversized purse. "I suppose you do this a lot."

"Too much, but it beats attending funerals when a drunk driver kills someone. It's always cheaper to call Uber."

"Excuse me, my son-in-law didn't drink and drive."

"Take that up with him, I'm not his judge, jury or his mother. I'm just doing my job."

A loud buzzer sounded; the door clanked opened.

David stumbled as he entered and sighed as he gazed toward Margarette. "Mom, thank you for bailing me out."

"Let's go David, I'm not talking about this here." She stormed toward the exit as he stumbled after her. *Jackie should have never prayed for patience. God help us all.*

∞

Jackie sat on the edge of the bed, her breath quick. The front door creaked as it opened. *The drunk is home.*

"We're home." Margarette threw her purse onto the couch and stormed into the living room.

Jackie fell to her knees and pounded her fist onto the floor.

Margarette sat in the rocking chair while she watched David who stumbled toward the couch. He plopped onto his back slamming his body against it. His feet touched the floor as he attempted to focus his eyes to stop the spinning sensation and nausea which overwhelmed him.

With fire in her eyes, Margarette tossed a magazine toward David's head to get his attention. "I'm not going to pretend that any of this is all right, I am furious with you."

His body jerked as he rolled over and spewed vomit onto the oriental rug.

"If you think I'm cleaning that mess up, you have another thing coming. How dare you do this to your family?"

Upstairs, Sebastian opened his eyes. He sat up, grabbed his blanket and climbed out of bed. "Grandma, I'm up."

Margarette stood over David scowling. "You fool, what kind of example are you setting for your sons?"

"Grandma!"

"I'm coming, sweetheart." She stood, slapped David's back and quickly strode toward the foyer. Margarette tripped on a toy truck in the formal living room and landed on her back.

Sebastian stood at the top of the stairs. "Grandma, I'm up."

"I'm coming." She grabbed the toy and struggled in sharp pain to stand. She stepped toward the stairs as her face grimaced. The pain took her breath away before she stepped forward again.

Sebastian stepped down the first stair, wobbled and took another.

"Wait! I'll help you." She took several quick breaths in the hope they would ease her pain.

Sebastian slipped, rolled head over heels down the stairs hitting his head several times before he landed at the base. He lay motionless.

Margarette screamed as she struggled to reach him and then knelt beside him. "Sebastian! Help me, Sebastian is hurt."

A pool of blood formed around his head.

Panic and pain filled Margarette's voice. "Jackie, call nine, one, one." Her heart raced. "Jackie!"

Jackie bolted from her bedroom, raced down the stairs, knelt, and examined Sebastian. "Mom, he's not moving."

"Jackie, call nine one, one. Hurry!" Margarette grabbed Sebastian's blanket and pressed it against his head wound as she forgot about her own pain. "Now Jackie, time is important."

Jackie sprinted toward the kitchen, grabbed the receiver and frantically dialed. She paced as her heart raced. She glared at David. "Get up you bastard, we have to take Sebastian to the emergency room."

David barely opened his eyes.

Tears streamed as Jackie waited on 9-1-1 to answer. "My son fell down the stairs. Blood is everywhere. He's not moving... Yes, that's my address... How long?" Jackie slammed the receiver into its cradle and stormed toward David. She slapped him across his face and punched his chest. "I hate you, I hate you."

David pushed back. "Go away." His brutish tone enraged Jackie further as she punched him.

Margarette continued to press Sebastian's wound. "How long until the ambulance arrives?" Her chest constricted as Jackie's head trauma flashed before her eyes.

Jackie punched David's chest again in a fit of rage. "You're a drunken bastard."

"Hit me again and I'll kill you. Now go away."

"Sebastian could die, get up and help save your son."

"I don't care."

She slapped him with enough force his head jostled. He kicked up at her, but she feinted and jumped out of the way.

David rolled onto the floor and landed into his vomit on his back. He opened his eyes to a spinning room.

Jackie glared at him as if fire shot from her eyes. She spat on him. "I hope you die, you're a worthless piece of shit." She stepped backward, shook her head and hurled a kick which connected solidly into his ribcage.

He grunted and remained motionless in his vomit.

"Stop it Jackie, Sebastian needs you." Margarette continued to press Sebastian's head wound to stop the bleeding.

Jackie ran to Sebastian and dropped to her knees; her face contorted. "Why God are you doing this to me? He's just a baby. I've changed my mind, I don't wan't patience."

∞

Three hours later, Jackie stood at the side of Sebastian's hospital bed. His head wrapped with gauze and I.V. fluids pushed into his veins as he slept.

The monitor beeped rhythmically and created an uneasy sensation in Jackie as she fought to keep her own fear of confinement in a hospital hidden. A swirl of nervous knots formed inside her stomach. The smell in the room reminded her of the sterility odor while hospitalized for her own recovery.

She tried to erase the memory of the constant sounds in the hall, the frequent announcements and calls for the doctors, the coded alerts, and the myriad of squeaky carts pushed down the hall. It all came back to her from her confinement and reverberated in her mind.

"Dr. Evangelista report to emergency triage, room three."

The last blare over the intercom sent chills up Jackie's spine. Her throat contracted. She knew what that meant--someone else with a traumatic brain injury. *Is it a child or an adult, this time?*

Jackie teary-eyed stared at Sebastian who lay motionless. She rubbed his arm and hand. "Baby, I'm so sorry. Mommy should have been there for you." Guilt encapsulated her thoughts and her heart.

Her fingertips traveled gently down his arm to his hand. Her queasiness increased. *Is this how my mom felt when I was in a coma?* She whimpered, kissed his hand and whispered through her tears. "I should've been there for you. As your mother I'm supposed to protect you and keep you safe. It's too late for that now. I promise I'll be a better mother." She coughed and choked on her tears. "I love you." She kissed Sebastian's bandaged head as another tear burned down her cheek.

Sebastian's head moved against the bed. He whimpered from the pain.

"Sebastian? I'm here. I'll never leave you. I promise."

A knock on the door disturbed her inner confession. "Come in." Jackie dried her eyes using the starched bed sheet.

Samantha and Mrs. Forester entered the room.

"Mrs. Hennessey, I brought you some flowers." Samantha smiled.

An apologetic expression crisscrossed Mrs. Forester's face. "She insisted."

"I made your son a get-well card." Samantha handed the flowers and the card to Jackie.

"Thank you, Samantha, they're beautiful." She sniffed the flowers. A slight grin flashed across Jackie's lips.

"I'm glad they made you smile, Mrs. Hennessey. My mom always smiled too when she smelled flowers. She told me to tell you that when your heart is happy you will have a happy soul."

Jackie's forehead wrinkled. *What does she mean by that?*

Mrs. Forester coughed up blood into her hand.

Jackie retrieved a tissue and handed it to her. "Are you all right?"

"Trying to be I suppose, I have cancer."

Jackie caught off guard by the statement glanced at Samantha genuinely concerned. She took a quick breath. "How long?"

"I've known about six months, it's terminal."

Beth, who listened at the door, entered. "How's Sebastian?"

"There isn't much change. We're still waiting on the MRI results."

"Good morning Samantha and Mrs. Forester."

Mrs. Forester coughed up more blood.

"I'm sorry Mrs. Forester." Although Beth's tone a solemn whisper, it reflected an urgent worry. "I overheard you when I entered. If there's anything I can do, please don't hesitate to ask."

"There's nothing anyone can do, it's all a part of God's plan. I'm ready to go be with the Lord. My concern is finding another home for Samantha."

Samantha's eyes swelled; her voice trembled. "Everyone around me always dies." She buried her face into her foster mother's side.

"Now, now sweetheart. Everything will be fine. Come on, it's time for us to say goodbye."

Samantha took a deep breath and wiped her tears. "Yes, Ma'am. Goodbye Mrs. Hennessey, I hope your son gets better soon. Bye Ms. Andreas."

Jackie grinned the best she could muster at the moment. "Take care of your foster mom."

"I am. It's like my mom says, we're only on this earth for a short time. We better make the best of it because you don't want to come back as a fly."

"Enough of that Samantha." Mrs. Forester gazed at Jackie. "I'll be praying for you and your family."

Samantha touched Jackie's arm. "Mrs. Hennessey, Sebastian will get better. My mom just told me."

Mrs. Forester cleared her throat. "You'll have to excuse her. She talks to herself as if talking to her mother. It's been hard on her since her parents died. Let's go child." She took Samantha by the hand and pulled her out the door.

The door closed.

Beth averted Jackie's gaze. "That poor girl, she can't get a break in life."

"I'll say. It breaks my heart learning her background. I lost my dad in a car wreck when I was six. At least I still had my mother."

"Did you just remember that?"

"Not exactly, I saw my birthday during a regression session."

"Well, the last thing Samantha needs is for her foster mother to die and get bounced around inside the foster system again. It hurts my inner soul."

"Mine too. Do me a favor and watch out for her. She's special in some weird way."

"I will do what I can for her. Look, I came by to offer support. If you need anything at all, you know my number."

"Thanks, right now I need a miracle. Are you in the miracle business?"

Margarette held Tyler's hand as she entered the room "Good afternoon everyone."

Jackie and Beth nodded.

Jackie inhaled to gain courage. "Tyler go sit on the couch and color. Let Grandma and Mommy talk."

Beth grasped Tyler's hand. "Come on over here." She escorted him to the loveseat by the window.

Tyler quickly jumped onto the loveseat, removed his small backpack, retrieved his colors and a coloring book.

Beth sat beside him and watched him color.

"Jackie, how's he doing?" Margarette rubbed Sebastian's arm.

"No change." She sniffed.

"I wish I could say today was a wonderful day, but I can't."

Jackie nodded in agreement, her face full of sadness and on the verge of tears.

"I have to agree, it's an awful day." Beth handed Tyler a green crayon.

Margarette inhaled. "Look you two, there is to be no pity party in here. We have to be strong and positive for Sebastian."

"You're right, Mom. It's just so difficult."

"We've been through something worse than this. The Hennessey family are fighters. They don't give up. Now, put your big girl panties on and don't lose faith. God will never give you anything you can't handle, remember that."

"I'm not so sure if I like your God. I prayed for patience and now look what happened. I wish you would have warned me sooner."

Beth pursed her lips. "I think it has more to do with karma than God."

Margarette gave Jackie and Beth a cold stare as silence penetrated the room.

Beth broke the tension and spoke after the awkward moment. "I have more errands to run." She made her way to the door. "Jackie, remember what I said, you know my number. Use it any time of the day or night if you need me."

"Thanks Beth, it's good to know you have my back."

"Please call me the moment he wakes up."

"I will."

"I'm on my way to the temple, we'll pray for a speedy recovery." Beth walked to the door, waved at Jackie and left.

Margarette kissed Sebastian on the hand. She touched his cheek with the back of her hand. "He feels a little feverish. When was the last time the nurse checked his vitals?"

"About twenty minutes ago."

"What's the latest update from his doctor?" Margarette took a deep breath.

"Dr. Viale says she'll keep him in an induced coma for now. They have to watch for any swelling around his brain." Jackie fought to hold back her tears, she didn't want to sob in front of Tyler.

"Grandma is Bubba going to remember me when he wakes up?"

"Of course, he will."

"Mommy didn't."

Jackie rolled her eyes and sighed.

"It's not the same, he'll be fine." Margarette sat next to Tyler. "Everything will be back to normal when Sebastian wakes up. For now, just color a pretty picture for your brother."

"Okay, I'll color this one for Bubba."

"You do that, he's going to love it." Jackie trembled. *Please God, let him wake up and remember his family. I'll do anything for you if you just do this one thing for me. I'm begging you.*

"He's such a good boy." Margarette's words failed to comfort Jackie.

"Yes, he is." Jackie clenched her fists. "Did you revive David?" Her tone hateful and filled with disdain captured the same feeling Margarette felt but couldn't express.

"He's on his way. He has one massive headache and sore ribs. You almost broke them when you kicked him."

"I wish I had, he deserved it. I blame that drunken bastard for everything."

"That's not fair Jackie. No one is at fault here." *Except for me.*

"That's what you think. He blames me for everything, he's a tyrant. I can't stand to be in the same room with him."

"Mommy, are you and Daddy getting a divorce?"

"Not now Tyler." Jackie instantly regretted her scolding words. "We have to worry about your brother."

Tyler in a fit of anger broke his crayon in half and hurled it onto the ground. "This isn't fair, Mommy this is all your fault."

He flung his coloring book across the room which hit Jackie's legs.

Jackie's face flushed. "Tyler, stop! This isn't the time or place. You're acting like a brat. Another word out of you and I'll... I'll..."

"...Enough Jackie." Margarette immediately hugged Tyler. "Tyler is affected by this too, we're all a little stressed."

"Tyler pick up your things and go stand in the corner." Jackie's reproach set ill-willed with Margarette.

"Jackie, you need to think about what you're doing and your tone with Tyler. He's only a child and is hurt by this too."

With clenched fists, Jackie crossed her arms over her chest.

The usually well put together David entered the hospital room extremely unkempt. Although he had a clean shirt and pants, he still smelled like a brewery from the night before. His hangover added to his crappy appearance and mood.

Jackie glared at him with disgust her lips twisted in scorn. "You know this is all your fault. You're a drunken bastard, Mom should have left you in jail."

"Jackie, not now." David's eyes filled with rebuke. He crossed his arms in defiance. "You're out of line talking like that in front of our sons."

Jackie stepped closer to David. "You have no right to tell me I'm out of line." Her tone low and fierce seethed in anger. "You're the one that spent the night in jail and couldn't get up to help me while our son bled lying motionless on the floor. You have any idea how much of a failure you are?"

"Failure? I have done everything possible to hold this family together one day at a time. You're the one that distanced yourself from us."

"All right, you two." Margarette stepped between them as if she wore a referee's black and white striped uniform in a boxing rink. "You both need to stop this. Do you think this is what they need to hear or see from the two of you?"

A brief silence prevailed as David and Jackie glowered at each other with pursed lips and tightened jaws.

"Children need love." Margarette's sage advice failed to bring the harmony needed in the room.

"I tried to do my part." David conscientiously took a chance to throw shade toward Jackie. "Unfortunately, I haven't had any help with all of her bullshit regression sessions."

"That's not fair." Margarette stepped closer to David as if to block him from reaching Jackie.

"Fair, who said anything in life is fair?" Jackie pushed Margarette toward the wall.

David lowered his chin and glowered toward Jackie. "Just close your trap. You're making things worse than they already are; so just shut up!" His tone abrasive riled Jackie's anger to another level.

Jackie stormed toward David and shoved his shoulders with both hands. "I can't stand the sight of you." Her eyes glittered with anger. "You disgust me." She pounded his chest.

David slapped her across the face. "Shut up before I shut you up."

Jackie touched her scorching whelped face. "Meaning? You're going to hit me again?" She furrowed her brow. "You won't get the chance." A rush of heat transported throughout Jackie's body as she bolted from the room.

Margarette gobsmacked tilted her head toward the door. "Go after her."

"Jackie, wait! I'm sorry." David bolted from the room.

Tyler kicked the loveseat repeatedly. "I hate my mommy. She should have died."

Jackie sprinted down the hall. Her temperature rose as her heart filled with fear. She raced to the elevator and pressed the button continually. A punching bag would have been a better choice as she used significant force powered by adrenaline as she repeatedly pressed the elevator's down button. She glanced over her shoulder. "Come on open."

David bolted around the corner. "Jackie, stop!"

She glanced to her left toward the stairwell exit. Her face crinkled in panic as she ran for the emergency exit door.

David, closing in on her position slipped and landed on his butt. His old high school football knee injury resurfaced and throbbed which momentarily slowed his progression.

Jackie pushed the exit door open, entered the stairwell and escaped down the stairs two and three at a time.

David bounced up and pursued her.

Memories of Jackie's past lives flashed before her eyes as she disappeared down the stairs to the first floor. *It's happening, it's happening now.* Her heart pounded against her ribcage as she remembered Gertrude running from the sinister man. She increased her pace and pushed the door which led to the covered parking garage. *Tohono ran too.*

David took long strides down the stairs to catch her. "Jackie, please stop!" The exit door slammed shut. He pushed the handle and blasted into the covered parking garage. He quickly scanned the parking structure and caught a glimpse of Jackie at the east ramp. "Jackie! We have to talk. Stop!" He continued his chase closing in on her.

Jackie dashed out of the concrete structure as she remembered Adel fleeing the Nazi Field Commander. Once onto the grassy area in the back, she ran toward a dozen construction workers who worked to repair a broken water valve.

Eight feet from the construction workers, Jackie glanced over her shoulder. "Help! He's trying to kill me!" She tripped over a two inch by six-foot rusty pipe and fell as she remembered the quarrymen chase, the burning church and Blythe's hanging. She fearfully looked toward David. He stood within three feet of her.

The lead construction worker's eyes widened. "Miss, is everything all right?"

I was an Amazon warrior, don't let the beast control you or we all die.

David's face wore a formidable look of rage. "Jackie, I only want to talk to you." He put his hands above his head, clasped his fingers together and rested them onto his scalp to show the construction workers he intended to bring no harm to her. "Just talk to me, I'm sorry for everything." He turned in circles grasping his hair with both hands.

"You threatened to kill me."

David took one step toward her. "I just want to talk."

Jackie rolled, grabbed the pipe, stood and postured herself in a defensive stance. "Leave me alone, I'm done with you." *I need the strength of the royal guardsman. That's my only chance to live.*

David stepped forward. "I only want to talk, put the pipe down. I'm not going to hurt you."

Jackie's throat closed in fear as David encroached. She held the pipe like a golf club. *Use it like the knight against the wizard.* Gripping the pipe like a sword, she swung it upward and smashed David with enough force to his lower jaw to knock out several of his front teeth.

Blood oozed from David's mouth. He wiped the blood from his lip and spit out a tooth. He lunged toward her. "You bitch."

With all her might, she swung the pipe channeling the strength of Sir Oriholt and hit David across his right temple.

He fell as blood oozed from his cracked skull.

Jackie released the pipe and scarpered away. *I can never stop running.*

19. THE WHEEL OF FORTUNE

Three Weeks Later – Hennessey Home

On the left of the Hennessey fireplace mantle, the family portrait replaced by an eight by ten inch framed portrait of David created the mournful tone for the family. Next to it a matte gray-stone colored brass urn etched with an American flag and a proud eagle held the cremated remains of the husband and father who once lived a white picket fence life. On the right, a bouquet of yellow and white daisies in the crystal vase graced the mantle in a mournful tone.

On each side of the fireplace stood two funeral wreaths. White carnations and red roses covered the first wreath shaped like a cross. A cascade of white and yellow roses formed the second wreath. A blue silk ribbon with the word "Daddy" embossed in gold lay across it.

Margarette, somber, sat on the couch between Tyler and Sebastian. Blood seeped through the gauze wrapped around Sebastian's head wound. She read the last sentence of the book

Till We Meet Again: A Children's Book about Death and Grieving by Julie Muller and closed it.

"When will Mommy be home?" Tyler pouted his lips.

"I'm not sure."

Tyler's eyes flushed. "Did Mommy kill Daddy?"

"No, it was an accident."

"Then why is Mommy in jail?"

"That's a good question, let's not worry about that. You boys ready for lunch? We can go to the park afterward. We all could use a change in scenery."

"No thank you. I'm going to play in my room."

The doorbell rang. Margarette placed the book on the side table and stood. "That must be Auntie Beth, she said she'd stop by today."

Tyler leapt from the sofa. "I don't want her to come here anymore."

"Why not?"

"She brings bad luck. Mommy was with her when she had her wreck. She's going to take Mommy away." Tyler sobbed as he bolted up the stairs and into his room.

Why, God, are you testing me like this? I'm not the one who prayed for patience.

The doorbell rang again. "I'm coming, just a moment." She strode to the front door, opened it to Beth who held Samantha's hand.

"Well, this is a surprise, come on in. I was about to make lunch for the boys. You two hungry?"

"We already ate." Beth patted Samantha's back. "But, thanks anyway. May we come in?"

"Certainly." Margarette gestured for them to enter.

When Beth reached Sebastian, she leaned down and kissed him on the cheek. "Glad to see you're feeling better."

"I got a boo-boo."

Samantha knelt beside Sebastian. "Does it still hurt?"

"Yes." Sebastian pouted his cherub lips.

"I'm sorry." Samantha handed him a small stuffed animal. "I brought this for you."

Sebastian grabbed the toy and pulled it tight to his chest.

"Beth, please sit, while I make us a glass of tea."

"No thank you, we can't stay long. We only wanted to stop by to bring Jackie a card Samantha made."

Samantha stood and handed Margarette the card. "Please tell her I miss her."

"I will sweetie, I know it will make her happy." Margarette forced a fake-as-they-come smile to appease Samantha.

"I'm happy too." Samantha flashed a huge grin. "Ms. Beth is my new foster mom."

"Well that is something to be happy about." Margarette stared puzzled toward Beth. "How?"

"The day I left the hospital I went to the temple and mediated. That's when it hit me, I wanted Samantha. She deserves better than being bumped around and getting lost in the foster care system. For now, I'm fostering her, but I have full intentions to adopt."

"Yep." Samantha's sappy-sweet smile broadened. "I'm finally going to get my forever home, just like my mom said I would."

"That's wonderful sweetheart."

"Where's Tyler? I want to play with him."

Margarette lifted one brow. "He's in his room."

Beth placed her hand onto Samantha's shoulder. "Why don't you go say hello to him." Samantha skipped away and up the stairs.

"Margarette, I know things are difficult for you. They have to be. It can't be easy for you trying to pick up the pieces for the boys since David passed and well with Jackie's current situation, you don't know how long it will be until she's released."

"I love my grandsons and I'll raise them alone if I must. Before you know it, Jackie will be home where she belongs. I have to believe in Jackie's future vindication and that they will drop all charges. Damn it, it was self-defense."

"Please know I'm here for you anytime you need me. I can help you with the boys."

Margarette reflected. "Don't you think you've done enough?" Her harsh tone sliced the air. "If you hadn't encouraged her to continue to see Dr. Grayson, none of this would have happened."

Beth flabbergasted by Margarette's hurtful remark gasped. "I'm sorry. I think we should go. Samantha! Please come back down, we're leaving."

With eyes filled with anger, Margarette paused to regain control of her emotions.

Samantha skipped into the living room. "Are you okay? You look upset?"

Margarette exhaled. "I'm fine, nothing you should be concerned about."

"My mom said when we face our true selves, we find freedom." Samantha tilted her head as if someone spoke to her. "But, first, we have to forgive others and forgive ourselves."

Margarette forced a grin. *Out of the mouths of babes.* She absorbed the unwarranted guilt not able to prevent Sebastian's fall. "Samantha, when did your mother tell you this?"

"Last night."

"Samantha, when last night?" Beth's expression turned to concern.

"She told me this would be her last visit because I'm with you. She's going into another body."

∞

Jackie wore orange prison fatigues and shackles around her ankles and arms as she shuffled down the hall escorted by a guard toward the visitor area in the New Orleans County Jail. *I've made a fine mess of things. God can't save me now.* She entered the visitation booth separated by a glass panel and plopped onto the aluminum rusty chair.

Dr. Grayson sat across on the other side of the panel and waited patiently for her to adjust her position as he retrieved the phone receiver.

Jackie picked up the other. "Thank you for coming to see me Dr. Grayson. I wish this was under better circumstances."

"Me too, Jackie. Your mother said you had something particularly important to discuss with me."

"Yes, I do. Do you believe in fate or destiny, Dr. Grayson?"

"I don't understand."

"Mrs. Grayson said our destiny may be set, but because we have free will, that course can change. I've been thinking about this for three weeks, not much else to do in jail."

"Go on."

"I'm trying to figure out if it was my fate or my destiny that I killed David."

"Jackie don't say that. What you did was in self-defense."

"Not according to the prosecutors. They have me on tape whacking David with a pipe."

"You were scared he was going to kill you."

"Try telling that to the witnesses. During my bail hearing, witnesses said David never threatened me and he was only trying to talk to me. I'm never getting out of here. I can hear it now. The prosecutor is going to have a heyday questioning me."

"What do you mean by that?"

"My attorney advised me to plea insanity and explain to the court I reacted the way I did because of my past lives and that I believed my life was in danger. Even he thinks I'm a nut job."

"This is something that has to be determined in a court of law. But, if you're asking me if finding yourself running for your life was fate or destiny, I think you have to understand the difference between them."

"I think I do. Fate is what life gives you no matter what decisions you make. Destiny happens because of the decisions you make."

"Let me explain the difference, a little history so to speak."

"Go on."

"Early in Christianity the concept of a wheel of fortune bound a person throughout their life. Sometimes, when the wheel spun, it took that person on a high road where good things happened. Then other times, the wheel turned taking a person on a low road and dreadful things happened."

"What does this have to do with fate or destiny?"

"Well, with fate, people viewed the wheel pessimistically. It didn't matter if the wheel was high or low. There wouldn't be anything a person could do about it. It was their fate as if written in stone. When death came knocking on their door, an individual viewed it fatalistically with apathetic dread. The flip-side to this was destiny. If a person chose destiny over fate to believe in, no matter where the wheel landed or the number of spins, a person would always try to influence his place in life with each rotation. To do this, a person sought a better way of life through education, by making good decisions and doing charitable deeds. When things didn't go as planned, a person never doubted the veracity of the wheel. Pending death was never viewed as gloom, it was considered the last spin on the wheel."

"So, now you're telling me I have to choose whether I believe in fate or destiny?"

"Jackie, I sense there's something you're trying to tell me and you're beating around the bush so to speak. What do you have to tell me that was so important you requested my visit?"

"I've had nothing but time to think about everything. Most importantly my life and my past lives. You told me I could learn from my past lives and bring a resolution to my problems I have in my current life, right?"

"That's correct. Often deep feelings of mistrust, phobias and unexplainable pains have their origins in a past life. To recognize those helps you confront them and to overcome your fears in your current life."

"That's what I thought. You know my fear, right?"

"You believe because you have always seen your death in your past, and you were always running right before you died, you think that's how you're going to die in this lifetime."

"The fear I would never be able to stop running was my fate, but it wasn't my destiny."

"Are you referencing how you died in your past lives?"

"No, Dr. Grayson, I finally understand my fate. I analyzed my regressions from the wrong angle."

"What do you mean?"

"Karma, Dr. Grayson. This is my karma."

"I don't understand, how is this your karma?"

"Dr. Grayson, I was never the victim, I've always been the executioner."

The End.

NEVER STOP RUNNING

BOOKS IN KSK SAGA
BY DR. MELISSA CAUDLE

The Keystroke Killer: Part I – Transcendence

The Keystroke Killer: Part II – Reborn

The Keystroke Killer: Part III – Preeminence

The Keystroke Killer: Part IV – Opacity

The Keystroke Killer: Part V – The Fourth Dimension

The Keystroke Killer: Part VI – New Realm

DR. MELISSA CAUDLE

AN EXCERPT FROM THE KEYSTSROKE KILLER

New Orleans – 2058 - MATTHEW RAYMOND, a private investigator, locked into a maze of deceit and deception uncovers the truth of Project Transcendence.

For Matthew Raymond, his job as a private investigator is personal. Extremely personal. After the disturbing 2053 murder of his sister  Livia, Matthew left in a rage searches for her killer and answers to the mysterious questions that lurked around her death. Now years later, Matthew realizes his problems just went from bad to worse as he discovers himself immersed in a city where the wealthy and corrupt politicians rule. With his sister's murder still his focus, he finds himself in a cunning game of cat-and-mouse when he stumbles across The Keystroke Killer and uncovers a secret device capable of sending people to the fourth dimension without a trace. Project Transcendence becomes Matthew's new fixation. Searching the Deep South for answers, he uncovers family secrets, lies, corruption and a world on the brink of destruction. Can Matthew survive and save the world from the threat? Will he untangle the mystery of Livia's death? Find out in this powerful story, *The Keystroke Killer*.

THE KEYSTROKE KILLER: TRANSCENDENCE

Excerpt from Chapter 3

There's No Place Like Home

Matthew rose and kicked the chair beside him. "Damn it." *Why didn't I listen to her?*

The desk clerk slid open the frosted window divider. "Detective Raymond." She waited for a response. "Detective Raymond."

Matthew's eyes flushed. *If I'd only gotten there in time.*

"Detective Raymond!"

"I'm not a detective, I'm a private investigator." He approached the door that led to a hall.

"Good luck in there."

A loud hum released the locked door. He stepped through the uninviting invitation.

In the middle of the hall stood two additional armed guards. The area consisted of several recessed secured eight by ten-inch lockers, a checkpoint station and an ironclad entry door that included an eye recognition keypad developed by Dimension Global. The door, dark gray metal six inches thick and eight feet tall, and how it sounded as it locked behind him made the biggest impression on Matthew over the last four years.

A loud buzzer, a clang and a big bang echoed throughout the hall. Going out didn't sound as menacing. As he approached the guarded area, his heart raced, his temperature rose and the tension throughout his entire body increased. He soon would sit across from the monster who killed his sister.

"Mr. Raymond, Check your weapon here." The husky guard remained alert as Matthew gently removed his gun from the holster.

"I know the drill." He handed it to him. "I don't like being unarmed."

The second guard pierced his eyes. "You don't have a choice if you want to visit Milo. Or, you could stop your yearly visitations."

"Not a chance. That shithead knows what happened to my sister. If it's the last thing I do, I'll beat the truth out of him."

"Don't you mean get the truth out of him?"

"Yea, that's what I meant. The bastard murdered my sister."

"Your sister was a victim of the Co-Ed serial killer? I thought you were the U.S. Marshall who captured him?"

"I should have killed him on the spot."

"Meaning, you could have?"

"Can I get on with this or am I the one being interrogated?"

The guard stepped to the retinal scan. The red light zipped across his eye and turned green. Click. The locker opened, and the guard secured Matthew's weapon.

Clang. The door slid into the recess of the wall giving way to the rancid urine smell and smeared dried fecal matter on the walls. The guards led Matthew down the unwelcoming hall. A faint whisper of burnt flesh permeated from the left, the odor of carbolic soap from the staff restroom on the right and the stench of unwashed clothes from the air vents filled the air.

Matthew looked at the visitor's restroom door. "I need to go in."

"Make it quick. Visiting hours are almost over."

***

The restroom door creaked as it shut behind him. Someone took a dump in the toilet and left it unflushed.

In the far corner by the janitor's closet, a rusty tin bucket served as the final resting place to an enormous and decomposed rat which reeked of rotting decay stifling Matthew.

"Disgusting people." *Did they leave their manners and dignity outside the gate?* He shuffled to the sink and scrutinized his reflection wrinkled by torment. A tear fell from his left bloodshot eye as he thought of the exact moment Milo slaughtered his sister.

***

250

Milo clutched Livia's hair as he dragged her into the Army green public restroom at Kenner City Park. The pervasive odor of urine filled the air.

Matthew in hot pursuit retrieved his magnum and sprinted toward them. He raced into the bathroom high on angered emotion out of breath.

Milo held a machete against Livia's throat as he grinned sinisterly. "You made it in time to watch your sister die."

"Let go of her."

"If I let her go, you will kill me." Milo taunted him as he pressed the knife harder against Livia's throat. "And, if I don't let go, you will kill me. Either way, you lose."

"Let go now!" Matthew's muscles contracted knowing the monster before him would take her life.

"What will big brother do? Save baby sis, or capture a serial killer?" His ice-cold stare of gunmetal gray prevailed.

"Both. I'll do both. Put the fucking knife down and we all can walk away."

"Giving up your vow to serve and protect?" Milo taunted to get a rise out of Matthew. "You'd let me walk, if I let her go? I think not. I must protest."

"I'll kill you. Put down the knife and let her go."

"Too bad." Milo slit Livia's throat and shoved her to the ground. "You're too late, hesitation kills."

Matthew lunged to save Livia. He knelt over her and tried to stop the sprouting blood from her neck with his hands pressed hard against the wound. "Livia." Her eyes rolled back; she took her last breath.

Milo snickered as he watched the loving embrace between a brother and a very bloody sister.

"You're a butcher. You'll pay for this!" Matthew lunged toward Milo and struck the cumbersome machete from his grip. He heaved him against the cracked roach infested sink. Milo's cheek connected to it and split open. Blood smeared onto the sink and dripped down Milo's face. Matthew grabbed Milo by the shoulders

and heaved his head against the mirror which shattered into several pieces and crashed into the pool of Livia's blood.

Milo snatched a sharp mirror fragment, charged Matthew, stabbed him and sliced his left shoulder.

Matthew glowered at him, bent to deliver a reverse round kick, but slipped on Livia's blood falling backwards onto his butt.

Milo laughed as he held back his mental powers to provoke Matthew. "I'm just getting started."

Matthew bolted up quick onto his feet and delivered a round kick. His foot connected solidly into Milo's ribcage cracking several ribs.

Airborne, Milo slammed against the wall. He grunted, took a deep breath and charged Matthew.

Matthew outmaneuvered the serial killer. He dodged him, clutched Milo's shoulders and used the momentum to propel him head first slamming him against the wall.

Bloody, Milo zigzagged toward Matthew.

Matthew rushed him, grabbed his shoulders and butted his head against his forehead.

The room spun as Milo staggered toward his opponent. His eyes rolled into the back of his head collapsing next to Livia.

Matthew kicked Milo's ribs. He yanked his handcuffs from the pouch so hard it busted his lip.

Milo groaned and barely opened one eye, more of a wink.

A drop of blood fell from Matthew's nose onto the back of Milo's bald tattooed head. Matthew dropped to his knees and handcuffed him. "I have you now, you son of a bitch. You will rot in Hell for what you have done."

Matthew knelt by his sister, checked her pulse and closed her eyes brushing his fingers across them. He stood and kicked Milo's face.

Police sirens blared as seconds ticked away.

Matthew glimpsed his bloody reflection in the mirror. He ambled to the sink and washed his face.

A light blue electrical power surge, originating at the overhead light fixture, radiated downwards onto the mirror which captured his attention. The blue light pulsated, zipped through the running water, across the metal pipes and onto the floor to Livia's blood. Livia shimmered a faint blue as the surge entombed her. She became transparent and vanished along with her crimson blood.

Matthew became faint as he felt Livia's life leave her body. "No!"

S.W.A.T. burst into the restroom pointing their rifles toward Matthew. Matthew raised his hands above his head. A red laser dot centered on his forehead. Without lowering his hands, he pointed at the unconscious and bloody Milo. "That's the Co-Ed serial killer. Notify my father, Squad Commander of the New Orleans Police Intelligence Unit, Matthew Raymond."

***

Matthew exited the bathroom. The guard escorted him to the interview room at the end of the dreary hall. "You have ten minutes. Anything before that, knock on the door and I'll let you out."

The nine by nine-foot room had a two-way mirror on the north wall. By mandate, Warden Stronghold and several guards watched the conversation between the rugged investigator and the ice-cold serial killer. The camera mounted high in the corner of the room reflected onto a bare bulb hung from the fourteen-foot ceiling.

Milo shackled at his feet and chained at his wrists sat on a metal stool behind a metal table. Both secured to the floor by bolts. A single wooden chair on the opposite side of the table near the door entrance awaited the interrogator.

When Matthew entered, Milo's hands pulled tight against the round metal restraint. He jerked the chains sneering at Matthew. "These necessary? I thought by now you and I understood each other."

Matthew didn't fall for the bait unaffected by Milo's threatening gesture or posturing and calmly sat. "Had, is the operative word. Why should I trust you without them?"

"You're not dead, are you?" *I could kill you with one thought.*

"The chains stay."

"Then, I don't talk." *He's an idiot.*

A standoff ensued as neither the interrogator nor the killer wanted to retreat. Matthew maintained the upper hand confronting Milo. He sat stiffly. Milo followed suit. Neither man wanted to blink first as they glowered into each other's eyes. The silence roared until Matthew made the first move as he tussled his fingers through his scruffy uncombed hair. "Let me remind you the position you're in. I put you here. I can keep you here."

The table vibrated as Milo scowled back unnerved. He responded to Matthew's emphatic statements by sneering more amused than intimidated. "That's supposed to make me talk?" Milo jerked toward the resolute Matthew. Only the chains that bound Milo prevented him from reaching his visitor.

Matthew didn't flinch. Not one recoil gave Milo the result he hoped.

"Oooo! I'm really scared now. Big brother needs protection by the chains that bind me. You're afraid to unchain me. Rightly so."

Matthew reached into his back pocket, grabbed a folded envelope and pretended to hand it to the chained prisoner.

Milo gritted his teeth, grunted and growled.

Matthew pretended not to notice as he dangled the envelope back and forth in front of Milo one inch out of his reach. "Open it."

"Not today." Milo desired to keep the upper hand.

"You scared of what you'll see?"

"Nothing in your show and tell game scares me." Milo extended his left middle finger and wiggled it.

A sneer crossed Matthew's lips; he didn't take the jeering bait as he placed the envelope onto the table out of Milo's reach. He flexed his fingers, folded his hands and slowly placed them on the table. Matthew sat upright. "What I can show you should scare the piss out of you. It's from Nathan Hammer."

"You piqued my curiosity." Milo tried to slam his bound hands onto the table.

A lump formed in Matthew's throat as he secured the envelope between his thumb and index finger and lowered it one inch from Milo's shackled hands. "I'm not interested in what does or doesn't pique your interest." Matthew provoked Milo by fanning the envelope.

Unnerved, Milo deepened his cold stone stare, remained motionless fighting the urge to use his telepathic ability to suck air from Matthew's lungs.

The chair scrapped across the floor as Matthew rose. "Maybe next time you'll show me respect and play my show and tell game as you emphatically called it." He strode to the door.

Milo sneered as he chomped his teeth to taunt him.

Matthew used his knuckles and tapped on the door protruding his middle finger. "Up yours."

Tap. Tap. Tap.

Unamused and unaffected by Matthew's blatant gesture, Milo leered toward Matthew. "Watch your back. That's, if you can."

"Meaning?"

"You couldn't watch your sister's. Now could you?"

Matthew turned toward Milo as his eyes trickled the calculated insolence of his stare. "You're not allowed to talk about my sister." He spewed spit with each angered word.

"You should have seen her face when I slit her throat." Milo gloated him further. "Oh, excuse me. You did." His tone in Joker fashion more befitting a character in *Batman* seemed to bounce in the room against the walls. "Such a thing of beauty to feel as her body jerked going limp before her last breath. Big brother couldn't save little sister." Milo smirked and tilted his head to the side. "I remember her sweet perfume and the silkiness of her hair." A grin of wry amusement dashed across his lips.

Matthew bolted toward Milo, grabbed the villain's head and slammed it against the table. Blood oozed from Milo's nose. He pressed Milo's bloody face relentlessly on the table as if he had the strength of a Western lowland gorilla from the jungles of Africa. "You son of a bitch!"

Milo strained to avert Matthew's glare. His yellow stained teeth bloody.

"Where did my sister go?"

Milo's blank stare enraged an already violent Matthew.

"How did you make her vanish?" Matthew slammed Milo's head against the table over and over.

"Lost control big brother? I think so."

"You son of a bitch."

"That's the only name you have left in your arsenal? Low on vocabulary for a Tulane graduate."

Matthew slammed Milo's head three more times against the already bloody surface. "How's this for vocabulary? You're demonic."

Three guards rushed into the room and restrained Matthew. To break free, Matthew thrashed in their arms to escape from the three-man hold.

Milo licked the blood from his lips and sat up. "Tastes like your sister's."

A.D.A.M.

By Dr. Melissa Caudle

A scientist. An alien lifeform. A secret base.
Consequences for mankind.

Meet Dr. Sandra Eve Bradford, an astrobiological researcher in charge of the A.D.A.M. Extraction Team who discovered a microbe which thrives off of arsenic on the bottom of Mono Lake in California. General Anbar, Chief in Charge of the U.S. National Defense, orders his team to confiscate the samples and her research.

Dr. Bradford enlists her fellow researchers, Dr. Gregory Peterson, and her undergraduate assistant, Jessica Parker, to retrieve a new sample setting of a series of events and consequences.

In a government research facility, the microbe transformed into something alien. Once it becomes apparent to General Anbar the life form presents a national security risk, he orders his men to kidnap Dr. Bradford and holds her captive in an underground facility to continue her research.

The life form over a seven day stretch, morphs into a humanlike life form aging every moment toward death. His journey makes him question- What is life? What is love? What is hate? And, is there a God? This a story of possibilities and raises the questions - Are we alone in the universe? What else could be out there?

A.D.A.M.
Excerpt

CHAPTER TWO – TRUTH

Dr. Bradford drove her hunter green Fiat on Interstate 10 from New Orleans towards Slidell.

Jessica twisted her long brunette hair into a bun and secured it with a pink scrunchy. "I'm hungry. I'm not waiting any longer to eat." She dug through a white fast-food paper sack that rested in her lap, retrieved a breakfast sandwich and unwrapped it. The odor permeated through the car. Jessica curled her nose. "The eggs smell rotten."

"Get over it. Nothing has smelled good to you since you took in that mouthful of salty water at Mono Lake."

Jessica gagged, crumpled her breakfast sandwich back into the wrapper and threw it back into the paper bag. "You can eat yours if you want, I'll wait for lunch."

Dr. Bradford darted her eyes over at Jessica. "Give me mine."

Jessica dug through the bag and retrieved another wrapped breakfast sandwich and handed it over.

Dr. Bradford unwrapped it, took one bite and spit it immediately back into the wrapper.

"Told you, but, no! You didn't believe me."

"Please be quiet, let me think."

Silence between them ensued as they crossed the bridge over Lake Pontchartrain.

Jessica leaned toward the dash to stretch her back. "Are you sure it's safe to go to the lab?"

"They can't kill me in public; so, I believe it's safe."

"It makes me nervous. Let's listen to Stephen Stone Diamond. He's talking about extraterrestrials today."

"That's what we need, an alien conspiracy."

"I thought that's what we're in now." Jessica pressed the radio's knob. "It's not working."

"That's the best news I've had all day."

Jessica grabbed her phone and opened her blog radio app.

". . . Not just life here on earth, but also extraterrestrial life." Stephen Stone Diamond's deep and golden voice enhanced the mysterious topic. "It is unknown if there is any connection to the mysterious deaths of Dr. Gregory Peterson and the late husband of Dr. Sandra Bradford, Dr. Jeffrey Peck, who were both members of N.A.E.T. For those of you who don't know what N.A.E.T. is, I will gladly inform my listeners. It is a branch of NASA and stands for National Astrobiological Extraction Team. Coincidently, the research team led by Dr. Sandra Bradford. Phone lines are open."

Dr. Bradford slammed her fist onto the dashboard. "Damn! It's out on Blog radio."

"I'm Stephen Stone Diamond. I'll be right back to take your calls."

Dr. Bradford clenched her jaw. "Turn it off. I don't care to listen."

Jessica grabbed her earbuds. "That's exciting. E. T. phone home. I got to call in."

"Like hell you will."

Jessica secured her earbuds, dialed the blog radio number and waited. "I'm on hold."

"Jessica. Hang up. You can't bring attention to yourself or to me. Now hang up."

"So why are you doing a press conference?"

"The public needs to know the truth about my research. If the public gets wind of what I've discovered, they'll demand the truth."

"Well, in my opinion that is exactly what Stephen Stone Diamond will do."

"Jessica!"

NASA Astrobiology Institute between the Louisiana and Mississippi border not only provided jobs but also fundamental research. From the spacecraft and booster shuttle rocket the entry to the multi-functional compound reflected the nation's attitude about space exploration. Everyone wore either an official NASA or N.A.E.T. employee badge representing they worked either as an independent scientist on the National Astrobiological Extraction Team or a part of NASA. Visitors must sign in and wear visitor badges on their lapels too.

Dr. Bradford rushed toward the three story "Carl Sagan Astrobiology Lab" which housed the N.A.E.T. lab. Behind her, Jessica, Rebecca Newcombe and George, a cameraman quickly followed.

Without provocation, Dr. Bradford collided into Dr. Phyllis Gordon, a forty-four American scientist, and Dr. Edward Stolz, a fifty-two German scientist. Rebecca motioned for George to roll the camera.

Dr. Gordon's eyes pierced toward Dr. Bradford's. "You've gathered quite a following since our discovery."

"I'd have to agree."

"Too bad our samples were confiscated."

"This isn't the time nor the place to discuss this." Dr. Bradford strode briskly toward the N.A.E.T. research building.

The entourage followed as Rebecca motioned for George to continue to roll the camera. "What was all that about?" She caught up to Dr. Bradford.

"Common professional jealousy. That's all there is to it."

Jessica frowned. "I think not. It's about..."

"...Loose lips sink ships." Dr. Bradford motioned using her fingers as if locking a key for Jessica to close her mouth.

Jessica confirmed when she moved her fingers across her lips as if zipping a zip-lock baggy.

Rebecca glowered toward George. "Cut the camera. Damn it!"

The entourage barged into the N.A.E.T. building.

The morning sun reflected off the five test tubes of murky water which rested on one of the lab's counters. A microscopic particle floated inside one test tube and for a nanosecond glowed neon yellow.

Moments later, the entourage entered Dr. Bradford's lab. Jessica flipped on the lights as she wrinkled her nose and smelled the faint musky and sulfur smell. "I'll never forget this smell."

The well-equipped lab included beakers, flasks, a Liebig condenser, and graduated cylinders showed the lab's importance. Most prominent, a silver and white 60X-2599X-2 binocular turret professional biological microscope proved essential in isolating micro-organisms. In the corner an assortment of lab experiments and three twenty-five-gallon tanks filled from the murky waters retrieved from several lakes labeled Lake Pontchartrain, Grand Isle and Honey Island Swamp filled the area. On the wall above the door a twelve-inch round battery-operated clock and a sign - "A.D.A.M. Extraction Team" marked the entrance to the lab. Each white cabinet had stainless steel handles which enhanced the sterile environment.

Rebecca tapped George onto his shoulder. "Be sure to capture everything in the lab. I want lots of B-Roll."

Dr. Bradford and Jessica dressed into their white lab coats, proceeded to the sink and washed their hands.

Jessica prepped a microscope and a sterile slide. "I'll make sure everything is ready Dr. B."

"Perfect Jessica. Just follow protocol. We have to get this correct." Dr. Bradford stepped to a locked cabinet, retrieved a bottle of arsenic and an eye dropper and placed the items next to the microscope onto the lab counter. "Rebecca, it won't take much longer to set up."

"That's good to know. I don't have much longer."

Dr. Bradford retrieved the test tube which contained the particle. She extracted a sample as Jessica handed her the glass microscope slide. Dr. Bradford placed three drops of the murky liquid onto the sterile slide.

Jessica lifted her brow with excitement. "Isn't this amazing?"

Rebecca's frown deepened. "That's it, a test tube full of murky water and three drops on a slide."

Dr. Bradford defended her actions. "It's evidence that challenges the way we think and view life as we know it."

Jessica handed another test tube to Dr. Bradford. She filled the tube using the water sample and handed the vial back to her. "Jessica, mark this sample A."

"Yes, Ma'am." Jessica looked at Rebecca. "It's in there. I've seen it."

Again, Dr. Bradford's posture became defensive. "You can't see it without the aid of a microscope." She filled the second vial and handed it to Jessica.

"Sample B." Jessica nodded with pride.

Dr. Bradford confirmed with a nod. "Remember, at its current state it is a microbe." She placed the prepared slide beneath the microscope as everyone observed and focused the microscope.

"I'll prepare the boiling water." Jessica predicted what Dr. Bradford would want as it had become standard procedure in the lab. She briskly strode across the room, filled a tea kettle and set it onto the single electrical coil burner. She walked away, but quickly returned to turn the knob to the on position.

As Dr. Bradford viewed the microbe under the powerful microscope, it vibrated and morphed into Dr. Bradford's eye. She lifted from the microscope, blinked and rubbed her eyes.

Jessica noticed. "Something wrong Dr. B?"

"Nothing, an eyelash was in my eye." Dr. Bradford peered through the microscope and adjusted the focus again.

Rebecca's patience grew thin. "How did you obtain these samples? I thought the government confiscated them."

Dr. Bradford exhaled. "A few more seconds... There you are, look." Dr. Bradford stepped to the side as Rebecca stepped to the microscope. She glanced at Dr. Bradford before she lowered to view the microbe.

Dr. Bradford rubbed her neck. "Jessica, hand me my notebook please."

Jessica strode to Dr. Bradford's desk, retrieved a brown leather journal and strutted to Dr. Bradford and handed it over.

The tea kettle whistled. Jessica at once prepped a beaker of hot boiling water and brought it to Dr. Bradford.

Dr. Bradford handed her journal back to Jessica and then placed five drops of arsenic into the beaker.

Rebecca peered through the microscope. "Honestly, I see nothing."

Dr. Bradford exhaled in disappointment. "My best hypothesis is the microbe transitions as fast as I isolate it. I'll isolate it again for you."

The two women exchanged places. Dr. Bradford once again adjusted the microscope settings.

"You never answered my question. How did you obtain these samples?"

"Let's suffice it to say I was on the extraction team and managed to keep a sample for further study."

"You stole it?"

Jessica came to Dr. Bradford's defense. "We didn't steal it. We went..."

Dr. Bradford lifted from the microscope long enough to glare toward Jessica and twisted her fingers as if locking a door.

Jessica put her hand over her mouth as she lifted her brows.

Rebecca annoyed at the silent gesture, huffed. "You agreed you would tell me everything." She gazed harshly at Dr. Bradford.

"I promised you an exclusive interview for a no question asked policy. When the time is right, we'll reveal our evidence and our source as to how we obtained another sample."

"I'll get another Emmy."

"I'll surely get my doctorate."

Dr. Bradford gave Jessica another cold glance.

"Well, I will. Won't I?"

The lab became uncomfortably silent as Dr. Bradford continued to isolate the microbe.

Rebecca tapped her foot. "Anytime would be ideal. I have a deadline for tonight's news."

"Patience, I almost have the microbe isolated."

"Yes, Dr. B always tells me that patience is a virtue."

"We go live at six. After the murder of your husband and Dr. Peterson, the world is waiting with bated-breath to hear from the now infamous Dr. Sandra Bradford."

A reflective sadness came over Dr. Bradford; but she regained her professional composure. "You sound skeptical, Rebecca."

"Wouldn't you be? You claim to have evidence of an alien life form."

"Don't forget about me. I've seen it. Be sure to add that to your story. You know how to spell my name, right?"

Rebecca rolled her eyes. "This sounds ripe for a sci-fi murder mystery for *The Twilight Zone* and not the headline news story I wanted to break."

"I've isolated it, be quick this time." Dr. Bradford backed away from the microscope.

Rebecca quickly assumed her position and peered it as she squinted her left eye. "Like before, nothing."

"Maybe you don't know what you're looking for."

"Insults I don't need and won't tolerate."

"I didn't mean it to demean you. I apologize if I came across that way."

"Let's talk about the murders of your associates."

"I can't speak to the murders. I can only comment about the great men who were taken from this world. I was shocked to learn my husband was involved in a head on collision and it was an accident. The investigators ruled there was no foul play involved. Frankly, I'm horrified Dr. Peterson was gunned down while on a boating vacation on the same lake where we made our discovery."

Jessica bit her lower lip and paced. *I don't like the way this is going.*

"Doesn't this frighten you?" Rebecca swallowed and leered toward Dr. Bradford with unashamed confidence.

"Of course, I am as anyone in my situation would be. You never know who your enemy is even if they stood in front of you as a friend. It's a cut-throat industry when claiming a scientific discovery."

"Especially one that's as big as this." Jessica beamed with delight.

A quiet knock on the lab's door caught everyone's attention.

Dr. Bradford looked at the samples and over toward the door as Jessica jumped and dropped Dr. Bradford's journal as a wallet size photograph of an infant tumbled from it and onto the floor.

FBI Agent Morrison, a handsome African American male, late forties, and Agent Turner an African American female in her late thirties brashly entered.

Jessica's eyes widened as her trembling hands went straight toward the ceiling. "Whoa, gun!"

Agent Morrison flashed his shield. "Miss, you can put your hands down. We're here to speak to Dr. Bradford. I'm FBI Special Agent Morrison and this is my partner Special Agent Turner."

Jessica slowly placed her hands to her thighs as she glanced at the journal and the photograph. She retrieved the journal and placed the photograph back inside the journal.

Dr. Bradford stepped forward. "I'm Dr. Bradford. How may I be of assistance?"

Agent Turner stepped forward. "Not in the presence of others. What we have to say is confidential. Everyone needs to leave but Dr. Bradford."

Agent Morrison put his hand in front of his face and grabbed George's camera with the other. "Stop filming. You're in that directive too."

George jerked his camera out of Agent's Morrison's hands and stepped backward to put distance between them.

Jessica stomped her foot. "You're telling me, you barge into our lab and ask us to leave."

"We're not asking." His stare as cold as ice seemed menacing.

"But, I'm her graduate assistant."

"I have Freedom of the Press on my side." Rebecca stood steadfast.

Dr. Bradford raised her hand chest high. "Wait, anything I have to say, they can hear."

Agent Turner stepped closer toward Dr. Bradford. "In that case you leave us no choice but to take you to FBI headquarters. Please Dr. Bradford, retrieve your belongings and come with us. It will be easier for all involved."

A silent standoff prevailed.

"I'll consent, but I want it documented that I am cooperating." Dr. Bradford gathered her belongings and headed for the door.

Rebecca motioned for the George to follow. He pursued the agents and Dr. Bradford as they exited from the lab.

"Wait! Dr. Bradford, your journal." Jessica handed over the journal.

Dr. Bradford hesitated. "You keep it. Jessica, lock down the lab. Use protocol FRIC."

"FRIC?" Agent Turner's brow creased. "And, that is code for what?"

"Factual Research Investigative Control."

Jessica smirked in agreement. "Lock up the science experiment to avoid contamination. FRIC that!"

Agent Morrison looked at Dr. Bradford. "Come with us please."

NEVER STOP RUNNING

The two agents escorted Dr. Bradford from the lab as Rebecca, George and Jessica chased after them. The door shut behind them.

In a few seconds, Jessica re-entered the lab and secured the samples. The murky water in one of the five tubes glowed neon yellow as the water vibrated around it.

She retrieved her cell phone and dialed.

ABOUT THE AUTHOR

"If reincarnation is real, in my next life I want to come back as Stephen Hawking." **Dr. Melissa Caudle**

 Dr. Melissa Caudle, AKA Dr. Mel, is an American author of more than a dozen books, both fiction and non-fiction and numerous articles in magazines as a freelance writer. She is also the Senior Editor at Absolute Author Publishing House and has helped hundreds of authors reach their publishing dreams. She is best known for the novel *The Keystroke Killer: Transcendence* and *A.D.A.M.*

Another best seller for Dr. Mel is her book series for screenwriters. The series includes quick guidebooks for screenwriters on how to develop and use a beat sheet, write a logline, synopsis and create a one pager for screenplays. She also has published two books for filmmakers and reality show creators to raise funds for their projects.

As an artist, Dr. Mel illustrated six adult coloring books in her series *Abstract Faces* which include several her favorite art creations. She describes her style of art as a mixture between Picasso and Salvador Dali. She uses professional markers, acrylic paints and water colors. Take a look for yourself below. Dr. Mel also sells original art pieces on her website.

Another side to Dr. Mel is her love for music. At the age of eight, she began taking viola lessons and played in her school's orchestra. Soon after, she learned the cello and the violin. As an adult, she taught herself to play the piano. Her love for music inspired her to compose songs. She has five albums under the name *Mystic Towers* and has composed original scores for independent films and dozens of book trailers.

In the summer of 2017, Dr. Mel met Liz Ashe Havrilla, author of *One Step at a Time*. After hearing her story of surviving Hurricane Katrina in 2005, she helped Liz by editing her book and writing the introduction. "It is a special book with power to heal with God's grace."

Because of *One Step at a Time*, Dr. Mel is writing the companion book, *The Golden Needle and Thread*, a devotional for healing which will be published in the summer of 2019. Both books are based from real-life experiences and show the power of faith and hope. One Step at a time is available on Amazon.com.

Dr. Mel's hobbies include drawing, composing music, and collecting marbles, both antique and contemporary. Her original art and her marble collection of more than 30,000 are on display at Family Tree Antiques & Treasures in Bay St. Louis, MS. And, yes, this is the antique store that Jackie and Margarette visited in *Never Stop Running*. You can have that experience too. If you travel to the area, be sure to stop and visit.

NEVER STOP RUNNING

Dr. Mel lives in New Orleans, LA with her husband and two cats. She is the mother of three daughters and has seven grandsons and one granddaughter. When she is not writing or drawing, she loves to go to the New Orleans Saints games, ballroom dance, swim, camping and spend time with her family. Her goal is to keep living life to the fullest and cherish every moment.

For more information check out Caudle's website at www.drmelcaudle.com and subscribe to her blog at www.drmelcaudle.blogspot.com. Also, follow her on her social media sites.

https://twitter.com/#! /DrMelcaudle

https://www.facebook.com/DrMelCaudle

https://www.facebook.com/The Keystroke Killer Fan Site

linkedin.com/in/dr-mel-caudle-650a4036

If you are interested in having Dr. Melissa Caudle serve as your editor, contact her at drmelcaudle@gmail.com or visit www.absoluteauthor.com.

ADULT COLORING BOOKS

BY DR. MELISSA CAUDLE

One of my hobbies, other than writing, is drawing abstract faces in a Picasso kind of way. I put together my favorites in a series of Adult Coloring Books. You can buy them on Amazon, Barnes and Noble, and on my website: www.drmelcaudle.com, and other online retailers. I also have my art for sale on my website and at The Family Tree Antiques & Treasures in Bay St. Louis, MS.

BOOKS ON FILM AND SCREENWRITING
WWW.DRMELCAUDLE.COM

Made in United States
Troutdale, OR
01/12/2024

16909128R00170